A DANGEROUS WOMAN

The phone rang and Seth Coit went inside the Oak Street Bed and Breakfast he managed for his mother, Jill Boggs, to answer it. He recognized her voice immediately.

"Hey, baby," Jill said. "It's over . . . and it's messy."

Seth recoiled as the words penetrated, a surge of panic rising up from his stomach and spreading through his whole body. This time she wasn't lying.

"Don't talk to me like that over the phone!" he shouted.

"It's over," she repeated, and hung up.

It was about 4 P.M. on Thursday, October 21.

Twenty-three hours later, Gerry Boggs, Jill's ninth husband, was found in his kitchen lying facedown in a pool of his own blood, tortured and shot to death by Jill and her lover, Michael Backus.

CHARMED TO DEATH
STEPHEN SINGULAR

PINNACLE BOOKS
KENSINGTON PUBLISHING CORP.

To Joyce,
who made it all possible

PINNACLE BOOKS are published by
Kensington Publishing Corp.
850 Third Avenue
New York, NY 10022

Pinnacle and the P logo Reg. U.S. Pat. & TM Off.

First Pinnacle Books Printing: October, 1995

Printed in the United States of America

Part One

The Curse

One

Steamboat Springs, Colorado, sits on a flat patch of high country known as the Yampa Valley. At 6,750 feet above sea level, the valley holds clusters of aspen, squares of farmland, and the Yampa River, which flows through the heart of Steamboat. The town has more than a hundred mineral springs, rising up from below the earth's surface and carrying a sharp sulfuric odor. People relax in the warm pools and feel better; some even feel healed. Old-timers still drink from the springs, referring to its waters as "iron water lemonade." They claim that the water, which contains bicarbonates and lithium, can cure everything from skin disorders to manic-depressive illness.

On all sides of the valley, the Rocky Mountains rise into the clouds and disappear. The peaks have given Steamboat a worldwide reputation as a ski resort, bringing in tourists from all over America, Europe, the Far East, and Australia. Skiers return here year after year, testing their skills on the slopes and adding to the legend of a famous local curse.

Long before white settlers moved into the Yampa Valley in the 1870s, it was inhabited by Ute Indians, who revered its richness, beauty, and diversity. These Native Americans believed the mineral springs were sacred—the Great Spirit lived beneath them, and after the tribe had fought a harsh battle, they visited the waters, breathed in the vapors, and performed rituals in order to regain their strength. They also used the bubbling springs as oracles, listening to the murmurs for revelations of the future.

To the Utes, the valley represented endless bounty. In the summertime, it had vegetation to feed their horses, a source of water that never ran dry, wildflowers of every color, and a startlingly beautiful blue sky. It had deer and elk and bear. It had berries and trout. In autumn, the aspen turned golden and their leaves rippled in the chilly wind, shimmering in the clear, cold, hard-edged Colorado sunlight. From a distance they evoked visions of pockets of fire.

The Utes were so drawn to this landscape that they placed on it a curse meant to last forever. They declared that everyone passing through the Yampa Valley would fall so deeply in love with these surroundings that he or she would feel compelled to return again and again.

By 5 P.M. on October 22, 1993, Doug Boggs felt locked in the power of a curse, but it was not the one the Utes had had in mind. He was having the worst day of his life, and the irony was that it should have been one of the best. Thirty hours earlier, his daughter, Carlynn, had gone into labor in San Francisco, about to give birth to his first grandchild. For months, Doug and his wife, Jan, had been joyously awaiting this event—yet now, while they were on the very threshold of grandparenthood, Carlynn's condition had become guarded and her parents were filled with worry and fear. The young woman's blood pressure had fallen, she was rapidly losing strength, and her doctors had become so concerned that they'd warned her husband, Craig Tanner, that both mother and baby were in critical condition. Either of them, they'd told the expectant father, could die in the delivery room.

Tanner had called the Boggses at their home in Steamboat Springs, telling them just how grave the situation was. Early that Thursday evening, Doug and Jan had waited by their phone, anxious beyond words, terribly afraid of what they might hear next. They'd smoked and paced, trying to reassure one another that everything would be fine, then smoked and paced some more. They'd called Doug's father and step-mother, Harold and Sylvia Boggs, now in their eighties and also living in Steamboat, passing along messages from San Francisco. They'd called Doug's younger brother, Gerry, another resident of the small mountain town, but he hadn't answered the phone.

By 5:30 P.M., as the tension was becoming unbearable, Tanner finally called back to say that all was well. The baby, a granddaughter named Bryce, had been delivered safely, and while Carlynn was very weak, she was going to be all right. Doug and Jan were grandparents at last. Harold and Sylvia now had a great-granddaughter. The Boggs family gave a huge sigh of relief and a prayer of thanks before exploding into tears and congratulations.

Doug called his brother again, but he was unable to leave a message for Gerry conveying the great news because Gerry's answering machine had been turned off. Doug was disappointed, but not entirely surprised; Gerry had received harassing calls lately, and sometimes he disconnected the recording device. At 8:30 that evening, Harold and Sylvia suggested that they all drive up to Gerry's to tell him about the baby and take him some supper. The younger brother was 52 years old and lived alone, and Sylvia still worried about him getting enough to eat. Doug didn't think much of this idea. Gerry was a grown man and perfectly capable of feeding himself, he explained to the elderly couple, and besides, he didn't want his parents driving around town after dark or fretting about such things.

The Boggses did not visit Gerry on Thursday evening. They went to bed that night enormously grateful that the worries of today were behind them and they had a new life to celebrate.

At 7:30 the next morning, Doug arrived at work as usual, unlocking the doors of the hardware store that he owned with his brother. At 10 A.M., he called Gerry again to tell him of the birth and to remind him of the meeting they'd scheduled that afternoon with a local architect. Receiving no answer this time, Doug decided that his brother must have left town for a couple of days. Who could have blamed him? He'd been under tremendous pressure recently, with a nasty lawsuit pending and a trial scheduled to start in just five days. Throughout the past summer and into the fall, Gerry had been living with unrelieved stress. Everyone around him had noticed it and had given him a wide berth.

"He hasn't been worth a damn around the store lately," Doug had told several customers, after they'd noticed that his brother didn't seem to be himself. "We've got to get all this behind us so he can get back to normal."

Gerry had been making small mistakes in his bookkeeping at work, something he'd never done in the past. He was forgetting things or misplacing them. He was distracted, unable to focus on much of anything except the upcoming trial, which centered on a longstanding, complicated dispute over the ownership of a bed-and-breakfast establishment just a block off Main Street.

Gerry was always on the phone with his lawyer, Vance Halvorson, who had an office on the main street of Steamboat Springs and would be representing him at the proceeding next week. He and Vance spoke constantly about the strategies and fireworks they might expect to see in the courtroom. If Gerry wasn't talking to Vance, he was probably faxing something to Judy Prier-Lewis, a close friend and private investigator who lived in Denver and had been collecting legal ammunition for him during the past two years. And if he wasn't talking to Vance or to Judy, he had probably jumped into his Jeep and driven down to Denver, three hours to the southeast, where he'd be studying the charts that had been created by a graphic designer for use at the trial.

"The hardware business is in the background for Gerry now," Doug had been telling people in Steamboat. "We understand that, and we haven't been pushing him at all when it comes to work."

Gerry was no doubt in Denver, Doug surmised that Friday morning, when his brother again failed to answer the phone.

Then it occurred to Doug that Gerry might have

11

gone elk hunting with Thane Gilliland, his closest friend for several decades. In late October, when the snow began falling and the trees had shed most of their leaves, Gerry and Thane could be found tromping over the foothills around Steamboat, carrying rifles and looking for game. They liked spending time with one another, talking candidly about their lives. Elk hunting was an excellent way to relax, but Gerry was known as anything but an accomplished marksman.

"He wasn't a good hunter," Doug says, "but he really liked being out-of-doors. He enjoyed sitting on a rock, taking in the sunshine and letting other people flush out the game. Gerry was more likely to pull out a book and start reading than he was to shoot a deer or an elk. I don't think he ever killed anything."

At 1:30 P.M., Doug went by himself to the meeting at the architect's office. Then he picked up his mail and decided to drive out to Gerry's house, which sat atop a hill overlooking the Yampa Valley. It was a balmy day, warm for late October, and as Doug wended his way up to his brother's home, the view beyond his windshield was clear for miles, fields rolling in the distance and mountains climbing behind them.

It was 3:30 when he pulled into Gerry's driveway. Doug turned off the engine but did not immediately get out, surprised to see half of the double garage door open and his brother's Jeep parked in its usual spot; he must not have been out of town after all. Doug stepped out of his Ford Bronco and walked into the garage, a feeling of alarm rising up from his stomach and into his chest.

Gerry often carried a black satchel full of papers

or tape recordings. Doug saw the satchel and some tapes scattered on the hood of Gerry's Isuzu, which was parked next to the Jeep. The feeling had climbed into Doug's throat.

He went around to the front of the house and tried to open the door, but it was locked. He walked around to the back door, but it, too, was locked. He approached a third door, one that led into Gerry's kitchen. When Doug pushed against it, he met resistance. He pushed again, with more effort this time, and the door gave a little. He pushed harder, gradually moving something that appeared to be lying on the kitchen floor, propped up against the door.

Doug forced his way into the kitchen but stopped as soon as he'd crossed the threshold.

His brother lay on his side, blood pooling around his balding head. His face was deeply bruised, his brow held a wide, ugly gash, and his chest was punctured by bulletholes. Blood had been splattered on the floor and the walls. Gerry was rigid and his skin looked pale and cold, as if he'd been in this position for some time.

The bitch, Doug told himself, as he stared down at his brother.

"The bitch killed him," he whispered, unable to take his eyes from Gerry or move away from the door.

Then he ran to the phone in the kitchen. He dialed 911—screaming into the receiver and telling the operator what he'd just discovered. When she tried to calm him down and ask him some questions, he continued shouting wildly, repeating what he'd said while standing over Gerry's body.

"She killed him!" he said. "The bitch killed my brother!"

Two

Doug walked out onto the wooden deck behind Gerry's home, sat down, and waited for the police to arrive. In too much shock to cry, and too enraged to do anything but stare out across the valley, he asked himself a series of questions that had no answers. Why hadn't he seen this tragedy coming and done something to prevent it? Why hadn't he driven up here sooner, after realizing that Gerry's phone machine had been turned off? Why hadn't he said yes last night, when his parents had suggested visiting his brother and bringing him something to eat? Why had he waited until this afternoon—more than a full day since he'd last seen Gerry—before getting in his car and taking action?

Minutes later, Officer Kevin Parker pulled up in front of the house, soon followed by Officers Jerry Stabile and Robert Del Valle and Detective Richard Crotz. When Doug began telling them about the embittered lawsuit Gerry had been involved in and about who had murdered his brother, the men seemed noncommittal, nonresponsive, and almost uninterested in what he was saying. As they walked into the house and looked at the crime scene, the officers were not at all sure that a homicide had taken place here. A superficial inspection of the body and the kitchen indicated that it could have been a suicide. And if it *was* a murder, the officers had been taught that the natural suspect in this case, as in every other similar one, was the next of kin.

As Doug kept talking to the men, he felt himself growing more and more agitated. He explained to them that they needed to find the killer—*now*—or she would flee both Steamboat Springs and Colorado.

Politely but firmly, Officer Del Valle interrupted Doug and asked him to step inside one of the police vehicles.

"Why?" Boggs said, astonished at the request.

Del Valle is a solidly built, swarthy-complected man. He has a deep voice, and when he is working, he looks fundamentally tough and very serious.

"We need to go downtown to the station," he said. "I have to ask you some questions."

The words struck Doug like a blow to the face. He suddenly lost control and began yelling at the officers, telling them that they were wasting valuable time speaking to him while a murderer was getting farther away with each passing minute.

Del Valle patiently repeated what he'd said earlier: they needed to go downtown to the station.

"Can I at least call my wife before we leave?" Doug asked him.

The answer was no.

"What about my lawyer?"

Del Valle shook his head.

Boggs got in the car and rode down the hill, seething. Finding his younger brother beaten and shot to death on his kitchen floor had been grim enough—an image that would haunt him for the rest of his life. Knowing exactly who had done this to Gerry and why she'd done it was grimmer still. But being considered a suspect in the death of your best friend and only sibling—this was beyond grim.

This was outrageous.

Some people have a recurring nightmare in which they're forced to strip naked before a group of total strangers or before someone they know, but not intimately. Sometimes, they have to do this in a classroom or an office or some other familiar setting. After shedding their clothes in public, they are left feeling utterly vulnerable and degraded, violated on some basic level. But at least they can wake with the knowledge that it was all just a dream, something that floated up from the unconscious and faded as soon as they opened their eyes.

For Doug Boggs, being nude before a group of strangers would have been thoroughly humiliating. But having to do this in front of a police officer—someone he'd regularly greeted on the streets of Steamboat Springs—would be an even greater humiliation. And this would not take place in the shadows of the dream world, but in the real world.

For the past half century, Steamboat had been Doug's home, the place he'd made his living, a place he felt comfortable in. Over the decades, his family had earned admiration and respect in the town, and Doug was used to a certain kind of treatment. As a former county commissioner and part owner of a successful business on Main Street, he was one of the more prominent citizens in the mountain community. His father, Harold, had founded the store 54 years earlier, back in 1939, and Boggs Hardware was more than just a place to buy screws and bolts. It stood for more than a well-stocked inventory and reasonable prices.

Firm and square-looking, made of pale red brick, and with the family name chiseled into its facade, the store represented something of a tradition in the town, a set of values, even a way of life. When you wanted friendliness, personal service, integrity, and a sense of old-fashioned decency, you went to Doug or Gerry Boggs, or to the store's other longtime employee and part owner, Bob McCullough.

"If you need something and we don't have it on the shelves," McCullough once said, summing up the philosophy at Boggs Hardware, "we'll order it. And if we can't order it, we'll make it for you."

In his mid-fifties, Doug had spent his life keeping his family's name and his store's reputation at the highest level. He believed that these things, at least within the borders of Steamboat Springs, were unassailable. But when he arrived at the police station shortly after 4 P.M. that Friday afternoon, he realized that both his name and his reputation could be shredded in less than half an hour—by officers who were relative newcomers in town.

The police ushered him into a small room and asked him about his relationship with his brother. Had their partnership been marked by any conflict lately? Were they quarreling over who should control the store, now that their father was too old to run the business? Did they fight about money?

Doug felt helpless, and helplessly enraged. He

asked some questions of his own. Didn't these people understand that he'd just lost one of his most heartfelt connections in life? Couldn't they see that he was the last person on earth who'd have harmed Gerry? Didn't they realize that his brother had been engaged in a hateful legal battle, and that if they'd simply look in that direction, they'd soon learn everything they needed to know about the murder?

After blowing up at the officers again, Doug apologized, saying that he realized they had to do their job and eliminate him as a suspect before they could pursue other leads. He felt so shaken, he told them, and so distraught, that he was having trouble following their questions, let alone answering them.

"Can I please call my wife," he said, "and tell her what's happened to my brother?"

The answer was the same as before: no.

Then he continued trying to answer their inquiries, but a few minutes later, when the police left him alone in the interrogation room, he sneaked out, found a telephone, and called his wife. Jan was attending a class at her real estate office.

"Gerry's dead," he told her, "and they're holding me at the police station. You've got to get down here."

Jan began screaming. She ran outside, got in her car, and fired the engine. Sitting behind the wheel, she started howling, crying, wild sounds of pain and grief rushing up from her throat. She tried to drive, but for several moments she'd almost forgotten how, so she parked and then tried again.

Aiming the vehicle in the general direction of downtown and wiping at her eyes, she began to drive. After several moments she realized she didn't really know where the Steamboat Springs Police Station was. She'd never been there before and had to stop and ask for directions.

Before the police resumed interviewing Doug, he also called Vance Halvorson, the lawyer who was to have represented Gerry at his upcoming trial. Both Jan and Vance were soon at the station, and both attempted to explain to the officers that there was a terrible misunderstanding here. Doug would never hurt his brother; they needed to let him go and get someone else in custody. The police were unmoved.

When they asked Jan where she'd been the day before and what she'd been doing, this attractive woman with salt-and-pepper hair and some fire in her manner shot back, "I was waiting for my daughter to give birth."

When they tried to ask her another question, she said, "You are questioning the wrong woman."

Halvorson interrupted to tell the police that if Gerry's opponent in the lawsuit was desperate enough to have killed him just five or six days before the trial was scheduled to begin, then she might stop at nothing. The attorney said that he had in his possession five boxes of written material that were going to be used against her in court—five boxes of enormously damaging evidence that had been gathered by him, Gerry Boggs, and private investigators during the past two years. These boxes were kept in his office, but they now had to be removed, the lawyer insisted, or they could be stolen. They had to be put under police protection and hidden away somewhere, or this woman would come after them.

The officers skeptically listened to Halvorson, but at least they were paying attention to him. He was, after all, a well-known attorney in town, and if the police weren't ready to believe everything he was saying or to turn their investigation in another direction just yet, they were far more open to his suggestions than to anything Doug—the dead man's brother—had to say.

While Halvorson and the officers kept talking, Doug was escorted to another room, where a forensic technician took his fingerprints and examined his hands and arms for traces of gunshot residue. None was found. A policeman then drove the suspect to Steamboat's Routt Memorial Hospital, where a nurse was ordered to pluck some hairs from Doug's head and place them in small plastic bags. Word of Gerry Boggs's death had already spread through the town of 7,000 and to the hospital. The nurse who was taking hairs from Doug Boggs did not know him personally, but she was being watched closely by a police officer and she had reason to believe that she was in the presence of a murderer. She was very, very nervous and plucked awkwardly at the man's scalp. She had considerable difficulty yanking out a couple of hairs.

Then she was ordered to draw blood from Doug's arm and put it in a small capped medical vial—another standard procedure after a homicide suspect has been taken into custody. The Routt County District Attorney's Office and its prosecutors might need this blood later on for DNA tests, which could reveal that an individual's blood matched that found at the crime scene. Because of her unsteady hand, the nurse had even more trouble getting blood from Doug's arm than she'd had removing the hairs from his head.

She kept missing his vein. This process took longer than usual and was much more painful for Doug.

The policeman then drove Doug to his home just outside Steamboat Springs, accompanied him into his bedroom, and told him to spread out a white sheet on the floor. He then told Doug to stand in the middle of the sheet and undress slowly, removing one piece of clothing at a time and laying each one on the sheet. Doug began with his right shoe, and as it came off and was laid down, the young officer picked it up and placed it in a brown paper bag. He did the same with the left shoe, with Doug's socks, and with every other item of clothing.

As the suspect stripped, the policeman overcame his own self-consciousness and embarrassment, staring at Doug, scrutinizing his body for wounds or signs of a struggle or anything else that might look suspicious. He watched closely as Doug's belt came off, his shirt, his pants, and then his underwear, until he was standing naked in front of the officer. Doug's skin revealed no wounds or other markings, no cuts from fingernails, no blows from fists, no punctures or scrapes along the flesh.

Boggs is a handsome man with short gray hair and bright blue eyes. Something about the shape of his head and the way his hair falls across his brow conjures up the image of a Roman senator. His body is not large, but it looks volatile. He has a naturally explosive streak and the kind of intensely focused energy that would give pause to anyone about to challenge him.

For the past few hours, Doug had been trying his best to contain himself, but now, at 8:30 P.M., he was ready to explode. The police officer in his bedroom knew this. He also knew that Doug had been fully cooperative and appeared to be hiding nothing. He told Doug he was free to get dressed and he was being released from custody, at least for now. He also informed him that the vehicle he'd driven to Gerry's that afternoon was going to be hauled off by the police, impounded, and inspected by the Colorado Bureau of Investigation. The CBI would hold the Bronco for the next five days.

As soon as he was dressed, Doug jumped into another family vehicle and drove back into town and straight to the police station. He found a couple of detectives working on the case and told them who had murdered his brother.

Three

At 3:30 on Friday afternoon, October 22, 1993, just as Doug Boggs was entering his brother's home in Steamboat Springs, Sue Heiser was giving a manicure to a new customer in her beauty shop in Greeley, Colorado. The woman having her nails done, Jill Coit, was chatting up a storm. There was nothing unusual about that. She loved to talk, she was good at it, she spoke fast and freely—punctuating her speech with smiles and giggles—and her words still carried traces of Dixie.

Jill was from Louisiana. She liked telling people that she was born and bred a Southern woman, and that her father was a gentleman and a tugboat pilot who'd raised her to be a lady. She'd been a model and a beauty queen, she often said, before becoming a wife and a mother. She was the type of woman, she let you know quickly, who wanted to be treated with decency and respect, if not outright chivalry. She didn't believe in sleeping with a man unless she was married to him. Other, more modern women might not agree with her, but that was just the way, she liked to say, that her father had raised her.

Most of what Jill said was accompanied by a

friendly, disarming grin. When she talked, her eyes conveyed a mixture of delight and mischief and a calculating intelligence. She always seemed to be thinking. Some people found her charming. Others thought she was a little too forward, at least around strangers.

She no longer possessed the face or the figure of her youth, when she'd caused a lot of men to turn around and take another look. Years ago, she'd borne some resemblance to the pop star Cher, with her wide, innocent eyes, her long, straight, dark hair, and her exotic appearance. She claimed to be part American Indian, from Louisiana's Houma tribe, but she could just as easily have been taken for Hispanic, Italian, or perhaps—because of her sloe eyes—Eurasian.

"She is," one of her early admirers once said, "just a damn beautiful woman."

Jill was heavier now, but her hair was still dark and she'd retained her peaches-and-cream complexion. She was buxom, lively, and unpredictable, and she enjoyed being the center of attention, just as she was this afternoon while she was having her nails done. She talked, and Sue listened. Jill's eyes were usually full of light, but on occasion they could suddenly turn flat and dark. When this happened, her face became very hard, and people who'd never seen it before were shocked by the transformation.

All in all, Jill had become rather matronly looking. At a glance, you'd have taken her for a high school-teacher from a Midwestern town. She still had a flash of style and more than a touch of vanity, but she was not someone who'd immediately catch your eye. And she did not look remotely like the sort of person who'd say things or tell stories that could make you gasp.

As Sue Heiser worked meticulously on Jill's left hand, the customer began talking about the bed and breakfast she owned and operated in Steamboat Springs. She'd had it for several years now, she said, and it had been a real dump when she'd purchased it. Back then, it was called Rainbow Cottages—a terrible name—but she'd changed it to the "Oak Street Bed and Breakfast" and renovated all the rooms. Now it was quite attractive and business was picking up.

"Do you know any good lawyers in Greeley?" she said, changing the subject.

"Well," the manicurist replied, while buffing the woman's nails, "I'd have to think about that for a minute. Why do you need a lawyer?"

"I have to go to court next week. I'm being sued for slander."

"Slander? What did you do?"

Jill looked up at her and smiled. "I said some revealing things about my ex-husband. He's a very prominent man in Steamboat. We were only married for a few months, before I got the marriage annulled."

"Why did you get it annulled?"

"I found out that he was a homosexual."

"No!"

Jill removed her hand and held up her fingers, admiring Heiser's work. Jill was highly critical of her appearance and had a great appreciation for anyone who could make things look more beautiful than they were.

"I began telling people some of his secrets," she

said, "and now I'm being dragged into court for speaking the truth. Can you believe that?"

"How did you find out he was a homosexual?"

"You just know things like that, honey. You can just tell. You know what I mean?"

"I think so," the woman said.

"You know those things when you're in bed with someone. They come out in the dark."

Heiser nodded.

"He had lovers, gay lovers that lived outside of Steamboat, and I let people know that."

"Really?"

"He's a very respectable citizen in that town and he didn't want anyone to know about his sex life. He kept it hidden for a long time, but he couldn't do that forever. Now I'm being punished for speaking out."

"He's suing you?"

"Right."

"That's too bad."

"For exposing him."

Sue finished with Jill's left hand and now turned her attention to the right one. If nothing else, she found the woman in her chair entertaining. You never knew who might walk in the door and want her nails done.

"You do need a lawyer," Heiser said.

"Do you have any recommendations?"

"I know an attorney here named Bob Ray."

"Does he do criminal work?"

"I'm not sure about that."

"What's his number?"

Heiser put down her tools, found the number, and gave it to her patron.

"As soon as I'm finished," Sue said, "you can call him from here."

Jill shook her head, saying that wouldn't be necessary.

Part Two

The Soul Of Steamboat Springs

Four

Gerry Boggs's hometown was isolated up in the high country, but snowfall had kept it from being a true provincial backwater. Without abundant snow, there would be no glamour in the village, and without glamour, very few people would come to visit— let alone return again and again. Without all the visitors, Gerry Boggs would most likely still be breathing the fresh mountain air today.

In the middle decades of the twentieth century, Steamboat became nationally known as "Ski Town, USA." In 1947, the village had 1,700 people and claimed 1,685 skiers. It was featured in early promotional films about skiing, and it offered skiing lessons to every child within the city limits—free of charge. Because of this emphasis on healthy outdoor activities, and because everyone was expected to participate, the community took on a certain atmosphere. In the 1962 book *Ski Town, USA,* John Rolfe Burroughs wrote that Steamboat Springs "has been remarkably free of the feuds and schisms which only too often characterize small town life."

In 1989, the huge Japanese corporation Kamori Kanko went to Colorado and purchased the Steamboat ski area for over $100 million. The business is still run by locals, but the sale underscored the feeling that the town was no longer just another quaint village in the Rocky Mountains. It was now part of a huge foreign conglomerate, overseen by people and forces on the other side of the globe.

Steamboat has a love-hate relationship with its tourists. The busier the town grows, the more complicated the relationship becomes. Feelings run deep.

"People like the dollars the ski industry brings in," says a longtime resident, "but not all the other things that come with it. They don't like the crowding or the skyrocketing price of real estate. Workers here can't afford a place to live. We now have people tucked away in garages or attics or trailer parks or anywhere else they can find a room. Some of these spaces are illegal to rent, because of zoning restrictions, but the owners don't care about that. Let's squeeze just one more buck out of our home.

"The locals used to know everyone in town, but not anymore. They don't like living next to strangers. They don't like the rise in petty crime. Now they have to lock their car doors and the doors of their homes when they go out. They don't like the earthmoving equipment that's tearing up the hills outside of town so that developers can construct some more cheap, tacky-looking housing.

"They don't like Texans moving here and throwing around their influence and money. They don't like people coming in from California and building their Malibu fantasy homes in our countryside. These monstrosities belong by the ocean, for God's sake, not in a mountain landscape. We're getting a lot of architectural wetdreams around here, and some people are growing sick of it. What about the ground squirrels and nesting birds that are replaced by these huge new homes? Who's looking out for them?

"Some locals don't like all the cutesy little boutiques that have sprung up on Main Street lately, where you can buy expensive Western clothing or carvings of bears or works of art featuring cowboys and Indians. The shops have ruined the frontier charm that was once a part of Steamboat. Now we have some goddamn vendors standing on our street corners selling espresso and cappuccino."

These days one sees bumper stickers in town that read, "Stop the Brutal Marketing of Steamboat Springs."

The town has 7,000 full-time residents, but it feels both larger and smaller than that. It retains the quirkiness, the crankiness, the pride, and the provinciality of a rural burg. It has its own gothic attitudes. Speak to the locals, and you hear things like:

"You're pretty safe walking our streets late at night or going to the 7-Eleven store, but it's a different story if you mess around on your spouse. That sort of thing can get you killed."

Or: "Steamboat kids used to like to skateboard down Rabbit Ears Pass—that big, steep hill just east of town. They'd do this late at night, in the moonlight, but one night a trucker came along, ran over a kid, and took off his head. They stopped skateboarding after that."

When ten or fifteen thousand skiers from all over the world descend on the village in late December and January, the place takes on a cosmopolitan flair. Women from New York and Los Angeles wear mink coats into the local cafés and eat lunch next to beefy-armed, mud-encrusted ranchers. People with European accents sit alongside Americans who have never learned how to speak proper English. Buff-looking skiers don tight, shiny designer suits and augment them with glitzy chains, belts, or other gold and silver jewelry, while some of the ranch hands who wander into town wear soiled cowboy hats and smell like . . . ranches.

The region's latest proposed development, seven miles south of Steamboat and known as Catamount, would add 3,750 condo units and 1,000 hotel rooms to the area. Most local residents have gone along with the idea of building Catamount: it's good for business, and what's good for business is ultimately good for everyone. But not everyone feels that way.

Mark St.-Pierre, an intense and articulate man who operates the Amer-Indian Art Gallery on Main Street, has more complicated feelings about Steamboat's recent history. He's lived in the town for the past decade.

"I've opposed some of the more reckless projects they keep coming up with," he says, "but they just keep building more condos and more homes that look and feel insubstantial and ugly. One good mudslide, and these houses are literally going downhill. In private, a lot of people will tell you that they don't like what is going on in this town, but they won't speak out in public. If you criticize it too loudly, some people say, 'Look, you've moved here from someplace else and now you want to close the gate behind you. That isn't fair.' I don't want to shut the gate. I just want to preserve some of the town's quality of life. When you create certain conditions, the money people and the sharks arrive. You can't keep them away.

"Steamboat is torn between its rural ancestry and the forces of change and growth. It's a spiritual struggle. The town's soul is being wrestled for here and now. It's old versus new; progress versus natural beauty; tradition versus glamour; it's the good people versus the sharks. You can feel all this being played out underneath our daily lives."

35

Five

Jill Coit and her husband, Carl Steely, felt the pull of the ancient Ute curse the first time they entered the Yampa Valley in the late 1980s, when they visited Steamboat Springs for a winter vacation. Steely, a teacher and administrator at the Culver Academy, a boy's prep school in Culver, Indiana, was an avid skier who could instantly appreciate Steamboat's champagne powder. He loved gliding over these slopes and vowed to come back to the resort whenever he could. In 1989, after he and Jill had returned home from Colorado, they concluded that Steamboat had so much charm and offered so many opportunities that they wanted to live there year-round. Steely would be retiring in a few years, and he'd been looking for a change of scenery. In Steamboat Springs, he'd finally found exactly what he'd been searching for.

Early in 1990, he and Jill went back to Steamboat for the spring skiing. While there, they made a bold decision. He would return to Culver to finish out the school year and she would stay in Steamboat and buy the Oak Street Bed and Breakfast, which stood just a block north of Main Street and a block and a half from Boggs Hardware. Then he would join her in Colorado for the summer.

The couple already owned a bed and breakfast in Culver and had lately become intrigued with this Steamboat Bed & Breakfast. Real estate values in the village were climbing monthly; if they didn't do something soon, they reasoned, they might not be able to afford the small business, now priced at just under a quarter of a million dollars.

The Oak Street Bed and Breakfast consisted of a freestanding home and nine small, low-ceilinged cottages that formed an L-shape around the house. From the outside, the connected cottages resembled an army barracks. Inside, they were surprisingly attractive—after Jill had come in and refurbished them with colorful quilts and comforters, wooden dressers, glass-covered cabinets, and subdued, tasteful wallpaper. The rooms contained old-fashioned lamps and tables and small paintings of country scenes, and one cottage held a photograph of Jill herself dressed up like a nineteenth-century Southern belle. She wore a huge hat and a long mauve Victorian dress with a reddish cummerbund. Ringlets fell over her shoulders, and she carried a small black purse and a parasol. She looked young and coquettish, like someone in an antebellum romance novel. At first glance, the photo seemed to be an actual image from the early days of photography, not a woman striking a pose more than a century later.

While remodeling the bed and breakfast, Jill inevitably needed a number of supplies, which sent her in search of a hardware store. In the past few years, a Wal-Mart had opened up in Steamboat and was competing with the Boggs establishment on Main

Street. The Wal-Mart had many home accessories and very reasonable prices, but there were some things it couldn't offer a customer—at least, not when compared to the older hardware business. The Boggs store not only had good inventory, it had atmosphere and a feeling that it was connected to the town's past. The place felt homey and even historical.

Wandering through the aisles of merchandise, you noticed a Western art gallery over in one corner, a pawnshop near a small flight of stairs, and a collection of antiques that included hand-crank telephones and tack from horses that had been dead for generations. You noticed ancient ski poles and snowshoes, grandfather clocks, a huge bellows for starting a fire, sleighbells, and red flannel longjohns.

You were reminded of an old-time general store where you could not only find just about anything you wanted, you could also sit down for a while and talk about the weather or the headlines or what your neighbors were up to.

Yet it would be wrong to suggest that the store evoked only the past. The latest ski gear was also here, and some of the winter patrons looked as if they'd been dressed by fashion designers. Boggs Hardware was a potpourri reflecting the essence of Steamboat itself: it was both rural and worldly at the same time.

Six

When the 1990 school year ended in June, Carl
Steely packed his bags and went west to rejoin his
wife. For months he'd been looking forward to returning to Steamboat, being with Jill, and seeing how
she'd fixed up the bed and breakfast. Carl couldn't
wait to spend his mornings and evenings in the high
country, and Steamboat was as appealing in the
warm months as it was in the winter. The area offered dude ranches and horseback rides, great trails
for hiking, shooting waterfalls, streams full of trout,
golf courses, and scenery that humbled the eyes.

At the Culver Academy in Indiana, Carl had taught
astronomy. If ever there was a place that gave you
a clear view of the heavens at night, with countless
stars shimmering against the black sky, that place
was Steamboat Springs.

During the past several months, Carl and Jill had
been communicating regularly by phone. She called
him from the bed and breakfast and said that everything was fine; the business was going to be a great
success, and the town was a wonderful spot to live.
Hearing this, Carl grew even more excited and eager

for the next chapter in his marriage to this enterprising woman.

Years earlier, he'd been married to someone else. He'd fathered four children with his first wife, who'd been an alcoholic and had eventually died from the disease in 1985. His divorce from this woman had, as Carl once put it, left him feeling "very vulnerable." Since 1949, he'd been a deeply religious man and had even done some lay preaching. His faith in God and his participation, first in the Baptist Church and then in the Methodist Church, had carried him through his worst times. If he ever got married again, he promised himself after the divorce, it would be to someone who shared his values and beliefs.

In the early 1980s, Jill Coit was a State Farm Insurance agent in North Manchester, Indiana, and two of her three sons, William and Andrew, were attending the Culver Academy. While visiting her boys at school, she met Carl, and he was quickly captivated by her. She was outgoing, upbeat, and dynamic. She was assertive and flirtatious. She told him that he needed to get out of the house and have more fun, and that she could show him the way. And more important, from his perspective, they had the Christian faith in common. She went to his church and respectfully listened to the sermons. She learned the words to the hymns the congregation was singing and stood up and sang them loudly herself. She memorized the biblical verses that were important to his denomination. When Carl decided that he wanted to spend his life with this woman, it wasn't just because he was attracted to her. It was also because he admired her character.

In January of 1983, they were married in Indiana,

but that December they flew to Haiti and got a divorce. When Jill asked him for the divorce, she said that it was purely for financial reasons: she wanted to file a single person's income tax return that year and could not do so if she and Carl were married. He understood this perfectly and granted her the divorce, and nothing changed between them. They continued living together, and in time they remarried. Going to the altar became something of a ritual for them.

"We were married three or four times in front of a minister," Steely says. "Jill really liked for us to stand up and repeat our vows. I liked this, too. It reaffirmed our love for one another. On some of our trips west, we stopped in Reno and Las Vegas. She liked to go to those wedding chapels they have in Nevada, look around, and talk about getting married in them. She was the kind of woman who just really liked getting married."

If Carl found his wife to be eccentric, he'd long ago accepted her for what she was: a chatty, high-energy woman. When she told him that she'd once dressed up like a man and attended an all-male paramilitary survivalist training school in Georgia, he heard these words without giving them too much thought. When she bragged about learning terrorist skills at the school, or about her ability to shoot firearms, he didn't pay that much attention. When she said she carried a loaded gun in her purse, he doubted if it was the truth. Jill was a storyteller and a good one. She came from the South, which had produced a long and distinguished line of yarn-spinners, and she was just following in their footsteps.

She talked more than anyone he'd ever met, and

he was certain that some of what she said was pure exaggeration. But that was part of her charm, and, as Carl liked to say, that was what made her the life of almost every party they'd ever attended. He knew she was a character, but she was also fun and unpredictable, so he'd married her—at least twice.

Over the years, she had done a couple of things that had given Carl pause, but he hadn't said too much about them at the time. While working as a State Farm agent, she'd reported that a male attacker had broken into her office one evening and savagely beaten her. She'd filed a claim on this beating, saying that the incident had left her partially disabled, and she'd gone on to collect handsomely from her employer. Carl himself knew that the injuries she'd shown her doctors and the State Farm people had actually come as the result of a ladder falling on her head.

"I once tried to talk her out of filing this claim," he says, "but she told me that everyone is either crooked or stupid. I said, 'Well, I guess that makes me stupid.'

"Then she said, 'Do you know what you need? Someone who lives in the real world.' "

On another occasion, she told the insurance company that one of her diamond rings, valued at $20,000, had been stolen. She collected on this claim, too.

"She wore that ring after she got the money," Steely says, "but only when we went out of state and she didn't think any insurance people would see it."

Carl was also not entirely comfortable with Jill's interaction with her parents, Juanita and Henry Billiot, who'd once lived in the South before moving to Indiana. In Steely's eyes, the Billiots went along much too easily with everything their daughter said and did.

"Jill had them wrapped around her finger," he says. "They never challenged her on anything and they stuck by her no matter what. She told me some terrible stories about the awful things—abusive things—her parents had done to her when she was young, but I didn't rely on any of them being true."

Carl was aware that his wife had a volatile relationship with her younger brother, Marc, but it took a few years for Steely to realize just how volatile it was. Jill complained bitterly to him about how her parents liked their son better than they liked their daughter, and about how they'd shown favoritism to Marc throughout their lives. One time, when Jill believed that her brother was saying bad things about her to some people in Los Angeles, she floated the idea of going to California and breaking Marc's legs.

"I thought it was a joke," Steely says, "but she was serious."

Despite all this, he remained enamored of Jill and her view of matrimony.

"She always told me," he says, "that married people should be totally honest and open with one another. I agreed with her. That's how marriage should be. She'd say, 'We should always speak the truth to each other and trust each other implicitly.' Her values were so high. For years we were inseparable. We traveled everywhere together and we never had an argument. We went to Europe, to Australia, to New Zealand. She was a great companion for me."

Jill often told Carl that he was a schoolteacher, an

academic, and he really didn't know much about handling money. He would be a lot better off letting his wife do this for him, because she was a woman of the world, who was very good at paying bills and managing bank accounts.

"After a while," Steely says, "I told her she was right. I thought she was better at those things than I was."

As time went on, two curious things happened to Carl and left him puzzled, but he eventually shrugged them off. On one occasion, he was riding his bicycle in Culver when the garbageman, who was a friend of his wife's, nearly ran him over, knocking him off the bike and giving him a scare. It was purely an accident, the teacher told himself, and no one was really to blame. On another occasion, he'd passed out in front of his class at the academy and had been unconscious for several seconds, but he hadn't thought too much about that, either. These events had nothing to do with his marriage to Jill Coit. He and Jill loved each other dearly, as they kept saying to each other when they repeated their wedding vows.

Steely was in his early sixties and bore some resemblance to Spencer Tracy. He was barrel-chested and broad-shouldered and looked very solid and fit. He had short white cropped hair and determined eyes. Sometimes, his mouth curled into a kind of smile, as if he found the world an amusing place.

In the summer of 1990, when he went to Steamboat Springs to rejoin his wife, his smile quickly disappeared. He had a long talk with Jill and learned several shocking things. The first was that he no longer controlled any of his bank accounts. They were now in his wife's name and had been transferred out to Colorado; the money was legally hers. The bed and breakfast that the couple owned in Culver was also exclusively in Jill's name. And while Carl was partially responsible for the $200,000 debt that he and Jill had on the Oak Street Bed and Breakfast in Steamboat, his name was not on the title to this business, either. He'd stashed some gold coins back on his property in Indiana, but she'd dug them up and stolen them, too.

"The way my lawyer explained the situation to me," Steely says, "is that I had all of the indebtedness, but none of my old assets. She'd taken everything."

Carl was stunned, yet he still had some forgiveness and some Christian charity for the woman he'd married. Soon after discovering what his wife had done, the two of them were having dinner at a restaurant when he told Jill that at least they could be thankful for their faith, because it would help them get through this horribly difficult period and decide what to do next.

"She looked right at me," he recalls, "and she said, 'That's just bullshit.' I looked back at her and said, 'Thank you for showing me your true colors.' This was a very serious blow to my value system. Until this happened, I really thought that she loved me."

He left Steamboat, went home to Culver, and called his attorney. That summer he filed for divorce. When he refused to take any more of Jill's phone calls, she tried reaching his children, but he told them not to talk to her. Carl vowed never to go back to the mountain town, but like so many others, in time, he would return for the skiing.

Seven

In the late 1950s, Gerry Boggs had begun attending the University of Colorado at Boulder, taking a political science degree in 1964. Then he'd flown off to Vietnam, where he'd earned a Bronze Star for outstanding service in military intelligence for the U.S. Army.

"My dad and I," says Doug Boggs, "sent him a pistol in Vietnam. We couldn't ship the gun through the mail all at once, so we sent it a piece at a time. After a while, he had the whole firearm and he kept it with him over there for protection."

Gerry served two tours of duty and spent part of that time interrogating Vietcong prisoners of war. He saw things that he'd never imagined seeing and felt things that were fundamentally disturbing.

"Something happened to Gerry in Vietnam," his brother says. "Being over there was a real shock to him, and when he came back, he was different."

"He never wanted to talk about the war," Jan Boggs says. "He just kept it to himself."

Before going to Vietnam, Gerry had seriously considered the notion of entering the diplomatic corps and living abroad, but after returning to the United States from Southeast Asia, he went back to Steamboat and began working for his father, just as his brother had done.

Once, in the 1970s, he decided to try something new and took a job in the computer business, but before long he was back doing the books for Boggs Hardware, keeping his own schedule, and basically working for himself. He much preferred his independence and being his own boss. It was a good situation for him, and he knew it.

Gerry Boggs had almost everything a man could want. Approaching his fiftieth birthday in 1990, the tall, bespectacled hardware store owner had financial security, a number of good friends, an impressive two-story home at the edge of town, and several interesting hobbies. He liked scuba diving in the Caribbean and studying anthropology. He liked reading about ancient archaeological ruins. He enjoyed photography and had volunteered at Denver's Museum of Natural History when touring exhibits had come through the city. He could speak and write Russian.

"He knew more about the history of the Third Reich and about Australian frogs than anyone you ever met," says Judy Prier-Lewis, a private investigator from Denver and one of Boggs's closest friends. "When someone would come up with a scientific question—for example, how do sound waves travel through water?—I was always amazed that Gerry could rip into a lengthy explanation of this. He would go on and on, but the amazing part is that he was right."

Gerry read books that most folks in Steamboat Springs had never heard of. One of his passions was arguing about religion. He'd long ago given up the Christian beliefs of his youth, and many people thought that he did not believe in God.

"After his death," Doug says, "I found two Bibles in his home. I could tell from the pages that he'd been reading them, and that really surprised me. It was like he knew something was coming."

Gerry also relished arguing politics. According to those who'd debated with him in local taverns about Republicans versus Democrats, or capitalism versus socialism, he never lost one of these arguments, or at least he never admitted he did. Calling him a conservative, some of his political opponents said, did not go far enough. "Libertarian" was probably more accurate.

"Gerry's politics," says Bob McCullough, "were somewhat to the right of Attila the Hun's."

With his high forehead, his thick eyeglasses, his delicate features and sensitive face, his desire to argue, and his preoccupied manner, Gerry Boggs created the impression of a man who was always contemplating something. Naturally, he offended certain folks. He was pondering a big idea when he could have been doing something important. When people came into the hardware store looking for a part to repair a broken appliance, Gerry might be fiddling with his computer, lost in cyberspace. At that moment, customers didn't want to talk about the fine points of America's economic policy—they wanted their washer fixed.

Despite all that, most Steamboat residents had nothing but good things to say about Gerry Boggs: he was kind, patient, gentle, and trustworthy. He had an excellent sense of humor. He quietly did good deeds, asking for nothing in return. He was terrific with kids, very unselfish, and if the right woman had come along earlier in his life, he'd have made a great father.

He badly wanted a child. Being around kids brought out something in him—a lightness and playfulness—that otherwise was not there. You don't debate religion or politics with children. You don't try to defeat them in intellectual arguments. You don't attempt to convince them that your view of life is the best one. You just talk in a higher tone of voice, act silly, tickle them, laugh a lot, and roll around on the floor. When you do these things, kids naturally think you're great and want to be around you all the time.

Some men are so serious that you'd never believe they'd instantly be drawn to children and loosen up in their presence, giggling and dropping three or four decades in age in ten seconds. Gerry was one of them. He was so enamored of babies that he once asked Bob McCullough if he could be present when Bob's wife, Cathy, gave birth to their first child. (Bob politely said no.)

Years before, Gerry had fallen in love with a woman from Florida who had gone to Steamboat on vacation. Their attachment was serious, but they had one problem neither of them could solve. Joyce wanted to live in Florida—she had a child there, from an earlier marriage—but Gerry wasn't quite ready to move away from his birthplace and start his life over. Steamboat was his home; his roots were there; it was almost the only thing he'd ever known. He was comfortable in Steamboat, and yet . . .

"That woman," says Cathy McCullough, "was his true love."

"He had some regrets about Joyce," says Gerry's longtime friend Judy Prier-Lewis. "For quite a while he felt torn about her. He felt responsible to his family in Steamboat. He felt responsible for the hardware store. In my opinion, it was Gerry who kept the business going. He kept people happy. He talked about Joyce for years after they parted, and I think he felt that he might have been as content in Florida as he was in Colorado. He really loved this woman, but it just didn't work out."

"He didn't want to uproot Joyce's son from Florida and move him to Steamboat," says Thane Gilliland, Gerry's oldest friend outside of his family. "He worried about that. And he didn't know if he could make a living if he left his hometown. He analyzed all this very deeply and decided not to be with Joyce. Had he gone to Florida, he'd been working in a bookstore now and he'd be happy."

Gerry first noticed Jill Coit when she came into his store, looking for some materials for her bed and breakfast. Word had spread around town that a woman—a single woman from an Eastern state—had recently purchased the bed and breakfast and was remodeling it from top to bottom. She planned to reopen the business very soon. The new owner, according to virtually everyone who saw or spoke to her, was a whirlwind of activity. She was shopping from one end of Steamboat to the other, she was driving up and down Main Street in her 1957 Thunderbird, she was making big plans for her business, and she talked so fast that all many people could do was listen.

Her bubbly personality was hard to ignore and she gave off something that, rightly or wrongly, has been called "female energy." When she entered a room, she tended to become the focal point, saying hello and smiling at everyone, chatting in a breezy Southern accent, telling people of her latest ventures, and giving the general impression that something was now happening here because she had arrived.

"I thought," says Bob McCullough, "that she was just an eccentric aging woman. You see them all the time in Steamboat. They come here when they're around 50, but they dress with some flash and they act about half their age. Jill was lively and she knew how to get your attention."

She grabbed Gerry's attention in Boggs Hardware. One afternoon, in the early fall of 1990, he spotted her in the City Market parking lot at the eastern edge of town. She was standing near her mint-condition T-bird. He approached and asked her about the car.

If Jill's body had filled out and her face had lost its youthful allure, she had other qualities that are more subtle and harder to explain. She instantly gave you (if you happened to be a man) the impression that she was happy to see you, that she liked men better than women, that she wanted to have a conversation with you and tell you some important things about herself, and that she would be delighted to see you again. She was what some people call a man's woman.

Around males, she was lighter on her feet, her face easily crinkled into a smile, her hands moved quickly through the air in front of her, and she hinted that she didn't look nearly as good as she could, once her hair was fixed up and she'd put on some makeup and changed her clothes. She managed to let you know, without saying a word about it, that she could be a lot of fun. Men liked hearing those kinds of things, especially men who were no longer young.

On the other hand, there are people who strongly believe that she wasn't truly a man's woman at all.

"She hated men," says Judy Prier-Lewis. "She really hated them and just used them to cover her or to help her make her next move."

Gerry Boggs wasn't thinking about any of these things on that afternoon when he and Jill saw one another in the City Market parking lot. He just looked at her and felt the woman's powerful presence. When he admired her car, she said thank you in her time-honored Southern way and gave him a kind of curtsy, something she often did when first meeting a man.

When he asked her out to dinner, she didn't hesitate before saying yes, that would be delightful. She was good at saying yes and at conveying the same answer with her eyes and body. She knew how to make everything about her say yes, and sometimes, yes is the most wonderful sound in the world.

"I think," says Judy Prier-Lewis, "that men in general are very gullible and stupid about women. They don't stop to think about what's in a woman's past or what she's really after. Is it love or money or what? A woman shows up and they have great fun and great sex and they start traveling together. Gerry didn't have that much going on in Steamboat until Jill arrived."

Eight

Gerry and Jill were soon a new item in town, the source of many congratulations on Main Street and in Boggs Hardware. Customers came into the store, shook Gerry's hand, clapped him on the back, and said that he'd never looked better or happier; some people even claimed that he appeared younger. There were folks in Steamboat who'd thought Gerry was too old and too sedate for this sort of thing, but most others were thrilled for him and wanted to know all about Jill. Where had she come from? How had they met? Was she now a permanent resident in Steamboat? Were the couple merely having an affair, or could this turn into something serious? What did the future hold for these two middle-aged lovers?

Late-blooming romance stirs enormous gossip in a small town.

Not everyone was taken with the affair. When married people in Steamboat discussed the subject, the husbands usually felt better about it than their wives did. It was a good thing, the men said, for Gerry to go out and kick up his heels, after all those years of sitting home by himself and reading strange books, but the wives weren't so sure.

"Women just know certain things," said one local female observer, "especially when it comes to other women. We feel them."

"I was never comfortable around Jill," says Cathy McCullough. "I always look at people's eyes when I meet them, but hers were not warm. She tried to be your friend too fast, rather than letting it develop naturally. One time Jill went to New Orleans and she bought our daughter, Colleen, a whole wardrobe and lavished it on her when she came back to Steamboat. To this day, Colleen hasn't worn any of those clothes."

It wasn't Jill's tight-fitting garments that put the women off, or her fast-looking T-bird, or her coy Southern drawl, or her ability to dominate a room full of people, or even the fact that she talked so much and flirted with most of the men she encountered. Something else about her was disturbing, the women said, something that was harder to pin down, just a feeling she carried around with her, or something she gave off when you were in her presence.

After a while, most of the women decided to put their doubts aside and hope for the best. If this relationship pleased Gerry, that was all that mattered. He needed more joy in his life.

Not all of the women changed their minds.

"When they first started dating," says Jan Boggs, "I was at a luncheon and we were all talking about Gerry and Jill. We were so happy for him. There was a woman present from Texas, and she didn't seem so thrilled about this. She said, 'Does anyone really know anything about the woman who's running the Oak Street Bed and Breakfast?' She said this as if she knew things about Jill that Gerry ought to be aware of.

"We all just looked at her and then someone shut her up by saying that she shouldn't talk about Jill unless she could back up what she was saying. But I thought about what she'd said. I went home and told Doug that maybe we should have Jill checked out. But at that time, Gerry was so happy that we decided not to pursue it."

By early 1991, the love affair, despite more than a little friction, was still alive. Jill spent several nights a week at Gerry's home and sometimes they talked about living together, but they also quarreled intensely.

"They would fight and break up," says Jan, "and we would all think the relationship was over. Then they would get back together again. In January of '91, they made plans to go to San Francisco to visit our daughter, Carlynn. At the last moment, Jill told Gerry she was staying home and he told her he was going anyway—by himself. When he got ready to leave, he found out that his airline ticket and his hotel room in San Francisco had both been canceled. Jill had done this without telling him anything about it. She had a travel agent's license, which she'd used to cancel these reservations. This made Gerry incredibly angry and cost him a lot of money.

"We thought that would be the end of their relationship, and for a while, it looked like it was. During that period, Jill would call us, very upset, and say that she loved Gerry so much and didn't want to lose him. The next thing we knew, they were going out again."

Something held them together.

"The first night I ever met Jill," says Thane Gilliland, "I told my wife that things were real wrong here. Jill talked about studying psychology and about having college degrees from San Francisco State and she just didn't seem like that kind of person. I'm a physician's assistant and I know something about psychology and something about medicine. She wasn't sophisticated enough and you could tell that by the way she talked. I thought she was a liar, but I decided to let it ride.

"Gerry was drawn to her because he'd never had a woman dote on him before. Not the way she did. She would sit on his lap in public and tell him that he was the greatest lover in the world. He hadn't had a lot of girlfriends. He was very intelligent, but he hadn't had that much experience with women. He was also as horny as a duck.

"Suddenly into his life comes this woman who takes him home at lunch, screws his brains out, and tells him what a wonderful man he is. The best. She stroked him and flattered him and it worked. She knew exactly where he was vulnerable."

In March of 1991, Jill informed Gerry that she was pregnant. His first reaction was amazement; he'd believed that Jill was too old to bear children. Then he was genuinely delighted—he'd always wanted to be a father. Then he felt an overwhelming sense of responsibility. And then, when all those things had subsided long enough for him to think about what Jill had just told him, he was very pleased with the prospect of settling down with a wife and child.

"Jill once explained to me," says Jan Boggs, "that she'd become pregnant with Gerry's child before this, but she'd aborted it. She also said that she'd told Gerry she would have this child aborted, too, if he didn't marry her."

The couple had soon set a wedding date.

When the shock of becoming a father had begun to wear off, Gerry realized that he now had everything he'd ever hoped for: a woman who loved him, and a baby on the way. His big, usually empty house was about to be turned into an intimate home. He was finally going to be something more than the "favorite uncle" of kids around Steamboat or the godfather of Bob McCullough's child. Now he would be someone other than the man his friends or relatives called just before Christmas, when they wanted him to drive over and assemble the toys they were giving to their children.

At last he would have a baby of his own, a new life to care for, and a child to watch grow up as he grew old. He was not a man given to great expressions of emotion, but in the first weeks of receiving the news, he could barely contain himself. He told family members, acquaintances, and customers who came into the store. The very definition of the proud, expectant father, he even bragged a little about his future. Jill's pregnancy was a dream come true—one that he'd long ago stopped believing he would ever be a part of.

His brother watched him and was more cautiously optimistic, hoping that Gerry had finally found what he was looking for.

"I was very lucky," Doug Boggs once said, "because when I was young, I met the right woman and she changed my life. She did so many things for me. She taught me how to dress, she showed me social skills, she taught me so many things that Gerry and I just never learned when we were growing up. He always needed a woman to do the same things for him, but he was never that lucky. He would meet a woman, have an affair, and then things would go to hell."

In preparation for the baby's arrival, Gerry immediately began remodeling his home. He hired carpenters and spent $20,000 creating a nursery, decorating it with stuffed animals, a crib, wall hangings, toys, and dolls. He spent another $500 on children's videos, a carseat, and baby clothes. He indulged himself on his first love, buying numerous baby books and reading extensively on being a first-time father. He sought advice from other men who had gone through what he was about to experience. He was 50 years old and he knew next to nothing about parenthood, but he was willing to learn and he was about to have a new, unimaginable adventure.

At times, he was filled with doubt. Was all this happening too late? Would he have enough patience and stamina to be a father and a husband, after all those years of being by himself? Would he want to run away some days and duck the responsibilities that came with having a child?

If Gerry had many questions about his ability to manage a new life at 50, he also believed the one thing about himself that was crucial for anyone taking the step into parenthood, especially anyone who was middle-aged: he was ready. He'd already done the other things in his life that he'd wanted to do. He'd taken the time to explore his inner world and his outer hobbies. He'd sown a few wild oats and spent decades alone. In truth, he'd often grown weary of that lifestyle. He wanted change now and more involvement with others.

On April 4, 1991, he and Jill were married in Steamboat by a justice of the peace. The brief ceremony took place downtown at the courthouse. Only two of his relatives—Jan and Doug—were present, and none of Jill's three grown sons was there.

Her oldest boy, Seth, in his mid-twenties, had recently moved to Steamboat and was helping his mother run the bed and breakfast. He lived at the bed and breakfast with a young woman named Julie English, and the couple were well-liked in town. People said that Seth Coit was hardworking and friendly and had good manners. He said hello to strangers and he cooked delicious breakfasts and fine loaves of bread over on Oak Street.

"He was always very nice and polite to me," says Doug Boggs, who frequently talked with Seth when he came into the hardware store. "He called me 'Mr. Boggs,' and kids just don't do that anymore. I was impressed with him."

Jill's middle child, Andrew, worked for the Denver Police Department, analyzing crime statistics, while her youngest son, William, lived in Manhattan Beach, California. He was employed by a construction company.

None of Gerry's friends was invited to the wedding.

"At that time," says Judy Prier-Lewis, "my husband and I were living up in Jackson Hole, Wyoming. I hadn't met Jill yet, but I knew he'd been seeing her. Gerry called me one night and told me that I'd better sit down. I didn't immediately reach for a chair. He said that he was getting married to Jill the next morning and she was going to have his baby. Then I sat down. After telling me the news, Gerry laughed and I laughed. There was a pause and then I said, in a teasing sort of way, 'Have you lost your mind?' We laughed again.

"He would never have married her if this pregnancy issue hadn't come up. But once it surfaced, he was hooked. He took the idea of being a husband and a father very seriously. That's why I liked him so much, because he was such a thoughtful and sincere man. Gerry was very respectful around women, low-key and considerate, not a chauvinist at all."

"After Jill and Gerry were married," says Jan Boggs, "we had a party for them at our home. Seth came to it. I like Seth, but I've always felt sorry for him, because he was so attached to his mother. He followed her everywhere, and now he was in Steamboat Springs and working at her business.

"At the party, he was standing in front of us, looking very nervous, and his feet were moving up and down—just jumping up and down. I kept watching them and they looked very odd. I thought to myself, What the hell is this? What's wrong with him? Now, years later, I realize that he must have gone through so much with his mother that he was just having a very hard time watching her get married—again. Some people have said that Seth is retarded, but I don't think he is. He's just a little slower than normal. He's just a simple-minded person, and nothing at all like his mother."

"A few months after the wedding," says Judy Prier-Lewis, "Gerry and Jill came to visit my husband and me, after we'd moved back to Denver. This must have been in August of '91, and that's when I first met her. From day one, I was stunned by their marriage. Jill never stopped talking. Never. Gerry would try to talk and she would interrupt him. He would try again and she would talk over him. He and I would be having a conversation and she would jump in and offer opinions about things that had occurred five years before she met Gerry. She talked constantly, trying to act like a social butterfly, telling me that I could borrow her furs if I wanted to or that she would help me in other ways. She never shut up.

"That first night when they came to visit, after we'd eaten dinner with them, I looked at my husband and said, 'What has Boggs done?' But then we figured he was our friend and we would respect his choices. The thing about Jill was that she tried so hard to impress you and to be a part of things. Much harder than other people did. She badly wanted to fit in."

Not long after his wedding, Gerry went with some friends on a diving trip to Belize, an excursion he'd been planning for months. Jill was annoyed with her husband because she hadn't been invited and told everyone about her feelings. Gerry tried to placate her by pointing out that she wasn't a diver and had no intention of taking up the sport, but she remained upset. He was going away to have fun and she had to stay home.

While Gerry was enjoying himself in the Caribbean, Jill called Cathy McCullough one morning and began shouting into the phone.

"She said that Gerry's home was totally flooded," Cathy recalls. "She asked me to come up there and bring a fan, in order to dry things out. When I arrived at his house, I had no idea what I was walking into. There was water everywhere—all over the floor and the carpet and on many of his possessions. She had a rough-looking crew of men helping her out, and they'd torn the kitchen cabinets off the walls, carried them outside, and put them on the lawn. It was a mess. She claimed that a water supply line had accidentally broken upstairs and flooded the whole house.

"This was no accident, believe me. Her husband was in Belize, she was angry, and everyone believed that she was responsible for the flood. Gerry's books were soaked, and so were his computer printouts. I knew how much these things meant to him, but when I asked Jill if she thought we could salvage them, she shrugged and said, 'Oh, just throw them over in the corner.' They meant nothing to her. Gerry's home was drowned and she later collected the insurance from this 'disaster.' "

Nine

Some of the Boggses could not have been more pleased after learning about Jill's pregnancy. When Gerry's parents, Harold and Sylvia, had first met his wife, they hadn't been particularly taken with her. She was too loud for their taste, and a bit pushy. At times she dressed aggressively, and she wasn't the sort of woman they'd ever imagined Gerry would take to the altar. But now their opinion of her began to change. They were downright joyful at the prospect of Jill giving birth, because they'd waited a very long time for another blood grandchild to be born into the family.

Back in the early 1960s, Doug and Jan had had a son, Van Douglas, but he'd died in his second year and was buried on a hillside cemetery at the edge of Steamboat Springs. The couple had later adopted two children, but for decades following the death of Van Douglas, it had looked as if the bloodline for this branch of the Boggses' family tree had come to an end. Now, when everyone least expected it, Gerry had fathered a child and the line would go on. For Harold and Sylvia, who were well into their eighties, this brought a sense of comfort and completion to their old age.

After announcing her pregnancy, Jill regularly visited her mother-in-law in Steamboat. She told Sylvia about how much weight she was gaining; about her morning sickness, which she said was particularly bad this time; about how her breasts were becoming larger; and about how exciting it was to have a new life stirring inside her. She liked showing off her stomach, raising her blouse and patting it in front of people. She liked discussing the details of pregnancy. She complained about how much her back hurt when she was carrying a child and told everyone that she carried her babies very "high," meaning that they grew under her rib cage, instead of out in front of her, and for this reason she didn't look as pregnant as most other women did.

When Jill visited Sylvia, they now had something to talk about and something to look forward to together. The younger woman asked the older one if she would mind letting out three of her skirts; Sylvia said she'd be glad to do that for her. Jill asked her to sew some baby clothes and a receiving blanket; Sylvia enthusiastically took up needle and thread. Jill said that her pediatrician had already determined that the child was a boy and she intended to name it Harold, in honor of the Boggs patriarch. The grandmother couldn't have been more pleased.

Following the news of Jill's pregnancy, she and Gerry visited his friend, Thane, who lived in a suburb of Denver. Thane gave the expectant couple a crib, some infant clothes, and other baby accessories that he'd once purchased for his own daughter, Jenna, who'd died at age 4. Because of his job as a physician's assistant, Thane took a special interest in Jill's pregnancy. He voiced some concerns to the expectant mother, because of her age. To his surprise, she took this very badly. When he suggested that she see an obstetrician specializing in high-risk pregnancies, she became so upset that Gerry had to take her outside and calm her down.

On another occasion, when the couple was staying at Thane's, Jill told her host that she'd recently undergone an abdominal pelvic ultrasound examination at a pediatric clinic in Greeley. The exam, she said, had conclusively revealed that her baby was a girl. When she returned to Steamboat and told Sylvia Boggs that her grandchild would be female instead of male, Sylvia was disappointed. Jill cheered her up by saying that she was young enough to have another baby, a boy next time, and she would name this child Harold.

In Steamboat Springs, when Jill ran into Pamela Sue Nettleton, a registered nurse in the town, she told her that she'd been taking drugs in order to increase her fertility; now she was carrying multiple fetuses and one might be in the process of miscarrying. Pamela insisted that she get immediate medical help, but Jill told her not to worry, she was handling this problem through a midwife in Greeley.

She told Georgia Taylor, an acquaintance of Jill's and a local insurance adjustor, that she was against getting an amniocentesis test, which determines the gender of a fetus, because she'd reacted badly to this exam in the past. She told another Steamboat physician, Dr. Donald Tomlin, that although she was pregnant and experiencing some difficulties, she didn't want any more tests run on her because she felt they could harm the infant. When her path crossed that of dentist Richard Boyes, she asked him about taking care of her child's teeth in the future.

While Jill talked about her pregnancy with virtually everyone she saw, Gerry continued reading books about parenthood. He was becoming something of an expert, at least on the academic side of child-rearing. The toys and other things he'd been purchasing for the baby had lately been piling up under his desk at the hardware store, and his co-workers and customers couldn't help noticing them. When people asked him what he still needed to buy, he said he'd like to have a stroller to use while jogging around Steamboat with the infant.

A number of people were struck by the change that had come over Gerry. Cathy McCullough, the wife of Doug and Gerry's business partner, observed it and was delighted.

"I was so happy for him that he was finally going to be a father," says Cathy, the mother of a boy and a girl. "Unlike a lot of adults, he was genuinely interested in kids. He listened to children when they talked—really listened to them. He thought about what they were saying. He loved playing with them. Because he was a bachelor, you didn't expect this of him. You thought that he might be bothered by kids, the way some men are, but he was just the opposite. He was tolerant and patient. He doted on them. And he loved giving them gifts. Bob and I almost felt that the gifts he gave our kids were extravagant, but that's what Gerry wanted to do."

People were also observing Jill more closely, now that she was carrying a child. Some of them were surprised by what they saw.

In the summer of 1991, Doug noticed his brother's wife one evening at a gathering in Steamboat Springs. Doug (and others) were often struck by how different Jill looked each time they ran into her. First she grew her hair long. Then she cut most of it off. Then she dyed it darker, and then she became a blonde. Then she overhauled her wardrobe. She was always changing, yet the most intriguing thing about her these days was that she always seemed to be the same weight.

On this particular evening, after Doug noticed that she was wearing a very tight blouse, he went up to her and said that she didn't appear to have gained an ounce since she'd become pregnant. Jill immediately left the gathering, but she soon returned wearing loose-fitting, maternity clothes.

By mid-1991, Vance Halvorson had been the Boggs family attorney for nearly twenty years. He handled both personal matters and the legal affairs for the hardware store. Like Doug Boggs, he also saw Jill that summer and thought not only that she seemed too old to be pregnant, but that she didn't seem to be putting on any weight. It was Vance's impression that when she talked about how big her stomach was growing, she stuck it out in front of her to make the point. And when she said the fetus was kicking and then asked people to feel her stomach, most of them reported no kicks at all.

After Gerry and Jill were married, Halvorson changed Gerry's will so that his wife and child would now be his beneficiaries, in the event of his death. He set up a trust fund for the woman and the baby. And Jill wanted Gerry to sign what amounted to a bogus deed of trust worth $100,000 on the bed and breakfast, so that if she ever encountered any financial difficulties in the future, it would look as if she had very few assets and owed people a great deal of money. Her husband didn't think much of this plan, at least at the start.

"Gerry gave in to her a lot," says Judy Prier-Lewis. "He did this so she wouldn't throw fits. She would just hammer on him about something until he agreed to do it. He didn't want to put his name on the deed of trust to her business, but she thought this would offer her more protection for her assets. When Gerry resisted doing this, she would say to him, 'You don't care about me! You don't care about our child or its future! You don't care about anyone but yourself!' Eventually, he went along with her and put his name on the deed. That's when all the trouble started."

"Gerry and Jill came to visit me around August of '91," Thane Gilliland says. "This was months after she said she was pregnant. She hadn't gained any weight and she was wearing tight halter tops—not the kind of clothes a pregnant woman wears. I took her aside one day and said, 'You're fucking with my best friend.' I told her that I was watching her closely.

"I was very candid with Jill and we never, ever got along after that."

Part Three

The Call

Ten

In mid-November of '91, Jan and Doug Boggs received a phone call from an acquaintance who told them about an event that had taken place in Houston, Texas, nearly two decades earlier. The caller said that in late March of 1972, a man named William Coit had been found shot to death in his residence and the crime was never solved. The prime suspect in the case was the woman he'd recently been married to—she'd filed for divorce three weeks before the murder—the same woman who was the mother of his two children. This suspect had never been arrested or charged with anything connected to the killing. Since the early 1970s, she'd remained free, and her name, at least some of the time, was Jill Coit. The caller also said that Jill was still married to another man named Carl Steely, from Culver, Indiana.

Jan and Doug were confronted with a terrible dilemma. If the caller was telling the truth, when and how should they convey this information to Gerry, who was eagerly awaiting the birth of his first child?

The couple already had a number of worries and questions regarding Gerry's wife. For one thing, they were concerned that she was trying to divide the

Boggs family—a family that had never been known to have internal strife. Jill had gone to Doug and Jan's son, Greg, and told him that his parents did not treat him very well or have his best interests in mind. She'd gone to Sylvia Boggs and told the elderly woman that Jan was a failure as a daughter-in-law and that Doug was an ungrateful son. She'd gone to her husband and told Gerry that his brother and his wife were meddlers who could not be trusted, especially when it came to business matters. And she'd gone to Doug and Jan and told them that the child she was now carrying—the only blood grandchild of the Boggs family—was more important than the two children the couple had adopted.

"As a family," says Doug, "we were beginning to get divided."

Jill talked constantly about things that were becoming very uncomfortable within the Boggses' inner circle.

"She kept asking me," says Jan, "to feel her stomach. When I would do that, I could tell there was no child in there. She once said to me, 'I'm eight months pregnant.' And I said back, 'If you're eight months pregnant, then I'm twenty-four months pregnant.' She didn't like that at all."

"We just thought," says Doug, "that at some point she would start telling people that the baby had miscarried."

Beyond the pregnancy issue itself, something about Jill was very disruptive. People felt this when they were around her. It made everyone nervous.

"She was a nymphomaniac who just loved sex," says Doug. "She had to have it, she let you know that, and she used it to get everything she wanted.

74

That was how she pulled men in, and that's how she got to my brother."

Throughout his adult life, Gerry Boggs had been known as a meticulous man who paid attention to details. For many years, he'd also been a rather sickly looking man, with a thin, drawn face and a body that was in need of muscle and bulk. In his younger days, he drank and smoked freely, but when he entered middle age, he decided to start taking better care of himself. He read books on nutrition and exercise. He studied ways to make himself stronger and more vital. He put himself on an exercise program and a diet that caused him to gain weight in some good places and to feel healthier than he had in years. He was so thoughtful in his approach to building up his body that each day he wrote down what he'd eaten and what form of exercise he'd done, making a detailed catalog of his self-improvement.

Gerry had always lived within his means, and at age 50 he owed nothing to anyone. As the bookkeeper of a thriving business, he didn't find personal debt any more acceptable than running the hardware store in the red. But ever since his brother had met Jill, Doug Boggs had noticed, Gerry was incurring significant credit card debt for the first time in his life, because his wife was always charging things to his accounts. This alarmed Doug, but he didn't want to say too much about it to his business partner. Their relationship had always been on an even keel, and he wanted to keep it that way.

"People have a hard time believing that Gerry and I never fought with one another," says Doug, "even though we were brothers and partners at the hardware store. Bankers who dealt with us were always surprised at how well we got along. So were customers. Gerry and I never fought as kids, and we never fought as adults. We didn't have any problems between us—until Jill showed up."

Doug had never seen anyone pay bills the way his brother's wife did. She carried around Steamboat a bag of uncut diamonds and handed them out as installments on her debts or as gifts to people she liked. Jill never looked happier than when she was reaching into the bag and bestowing a treat on someone who was currently in her favor.

In the months after Gerry's wedding, his wife did not stop at saying inflammatory things to one set of Boggs family members about another set of family members. That was disturbing enough, but she did something else that Doug was not willing to overlook: she began investigating the ownership of the hardware store.

"First she got Gerry to change his will and then set up a trust fund for her," says Thane Gilliland. "Her next step was for him to change his corporate arrangement with the store. She wanted to crucify Boggs Hardware."

This proved to be more complicated and difficult than she'd anticipated.

"My father was a very smart businessman," says Doug. "When he sold my brother and me controlling interest in the store in 1976, he set it up in such a way that neither of us could sell it out from under the other one and make a killing. He arranged it so that if one of us tried to do that, the other could come back and make an offer for the store at what is called 'book value'—which is just the value of the assets and the inventory—and the other person would have to accept that offer. This was designed to prevent any conflict or other problems, and it worked out very well.

"In August of 1991, I was in the store one day and saw Gerry and Jill looking at our company books. I said to them, 'What the hell is going on here?' Jill realized, after looking at the way the ownership was structured, that Gerry would have a lot of trouble making big money by selling the business. When she saw this, she backed off."

After receiving the call about Jill's past, Doug and Jan thought about it for a couple of days and decided not to tell Gerry anything at the moment, but to pursue an alternative plan. They asked his two best friends to look into his wife's background. Judy Prier-Lewis was a private detective in Denver and Thane Gilliland was knowledgeable about medical issues, including pregnancy.

Doug contacted Judy and requested that she try to learn something about Jill's past, as well as her present. In particular, was Jill studying for a postgraduate degree in psychology at the University of Northern Colorado in Greeley, as she'd been telling Gerry for months? Doug asked Thane to find out if Jill had been visiting a woman's clinic in Greeley for pregnancy exams, another thing she'd told Gerry she'd been doing since the previous summer. Doug also phoned his lawyer, Vance Halvorson, and asked him to see if he could chase down the rumor that Gerry's wife was still married to a man in Indiana.

"When I called Judy," Doug says, "she was very excited about conducting this investigation. She immediately went to Greeley and discovered that Jill did not even have any degree in psychology. Thane made a few calls and learned that she'd never been to this women's clinic. Then Judy told me that she'd done some checking and discovered that Jill had three social security cards and four birth certificates. Nobody even knew how old she was.

"I went back to the store and told Gerry about some of this. He didn't like what I had to say and he didn't agree with it. We began arguing for the first time in thirty years. I asked him if he'd ever gone to this women's clinic in Greeley with Jill and he said no. I said, 'Then how do you know she's pregnant?' He got mad, and I said, 'Gerry, she comes into the store wearing tight tights and no one in Steamboat thinks she's pregnant.' These words really hurt him."

"She was very clever," says Jan, "because she'd already told Gerry a few things about her past. She would mix a little bit of truth in with her lies so that when we would approach Gerry and try to tell him something, he would say, 'Oh, I know about that. It's not important.' "

"When I went to my brother," says Doug, "and told him that William Coit had been murdered in Houston in the early 1970s, he didn't believe me. He said that the man had died of a heart attack."

"When we told him," says Jan, "that Jill had been married a number of times, he said that he'd talked about that with her and she'd only been married twice before."

Eleven

After decades of close observation, Doug understood one thing about his brother very well. Gerry's grasp of everything was much better when it was put in writing and placed in front of him in black and white. Words on paper were in some ways more real to him than most other things in life. With that in mind, Doug asked Judy Prier-Lewis to jot down some of the facts she'd lately been turning up on Jill Coit. The private investigator complied with this suggestion and then sent the results to Steamboat Springs. One of the items on the list was something that Vance Halvorson had also helped uncover. After contacting a lawyer in Indiana, Halvorson had learned that Jill was still married to Carl Steely, which made her guilty of bigamy.

"On previous occasions," Doug says, "when I'd tried to tell my brother some things about his wife's past, he would deny them, then go home and tell Jill what I'd said. You can imagine her reaction. He'd come to work the next day and argue about this with me. I would say to him, 'Gerry, she's not pregnant.'

And he would say, 'Yes, she is, and I still want a jogging stroller for Christmas.'

"This went on for a while, and then one evening, I took the writing that Judy had put together and set it in front of Gerry. I said to him, 'I'm your brother and I love you very much, but I want you to read this carefully.' The next morning, when I got to work, both Gerry and Jill were at the store, sitting in his office. As I walked into his office, Jill was coming out. She paused, looked at me, and said, 'It's been nice to know you.' I said, 'What?' She said again, 'It's been nice to know you,' and she just kept walking past me. She knew we were onto her.

"I went into Gerry's office. I'd never seen him look this way. He was just devastated that his wife was married to another man and hadn't even told him about this. But it wasn't what this meant for his marriage that really got to him. He was worried about what it meant for their child. He wanted that baby more than anything. His whole life was going to revolve around the child. He wanted to travel with it, take it everywhere, give it books, and teach it things. He just couldn't believe that Jill hadn't been honest with him."

After Gerry learned that she was still married to Carl Steely, the couple decided, in late November of '91, to get an annulment. But they kept living together and continued their preparations for the arrival of the child.

"When Jill first started saying she was pregnant," Jan says, "Gerry believed that the child would be here for Christmas. All he wanted that year was to walk into our home with the baby in his arms. That was his dream. He wanted to be something more than 'Uncle Gerry' to other people's children.

"But by Christmastime there was no baby, he and Jill were fighting badly with one another, and things really started to fall apart. The holidays made it even more painful for him. In our home, we had a number of presents for Gerry and Jill sitting under the tree— mostly baby things that other people had given us. On Christmas day, Gerry came to our house by himself, and before he arrived, I pulled all of the baby presents out from under the tree so he wouldn't have to look at them. It was just awful."

In late December, the couple split up and Jill left Steamboat, apparently headed for Texas.

"For weeks and months after that Christmas," Jan says, "people would come into the store or see Gerry on the street and ask him how the baby was and when it had been born. He didn't know what to say. He was so embarrassed. This is a small town, and people gossip. He'd never been involved in anything like this before. None of us had been. It killed him to have to say there was no baby."

By January of 1992, Gerry had fallen into a deep depression. He was hurt, angry, and confused. He wasn't sure where Jill was living, and he wasn't yet ready to concede that he'd not fathered a child with her. For a man who had always been in control of himself and his life, he suddenly felt lost.

His brother had never seen him in such a dark mood. Neither had Thane Gilliland, nor had Gerry's other friends. He felt demoralized, because a baby had not arrived—at least, not in Steamboat Springs—

and because he'd been humiliated in his hometown. Gerry was losing something that he'd managed to hold onto for fifty years, despite the fact that he'd served two tours of duty in Vietnam and seen the horrors of war first-hand. What Southeast Asia had not been able to do to him his involvement with Jill Coit had. His innocence and his sense of the basic goodness of other human beings was slowly being eroded.

"He was profoundly disturbed by what had happened," says Thane Gilliland. "He had so much intellectual pride, and when he felt that his intellect was being sabotaged by this woman, he could not deal with it."

Throughout his life, Gerry had been trusting of people, even of strangers. It had never before occurred to him that anyone, let alone the woman who was his wife, would lie to him about something as fundamental and precious as a baby growing in her stomach. That level of deviousness was beyond not just his experience, but his imagination.

He was confronting something new and wild and strange. Jill didn't have just one or two aliases, Judy Prier-Lewis was learning, but eight or ten, and perhaps even more. She didn't have two previous marriages, as she'd told Gerry, but four or five or six. She didn't have one identity, but a dozen.

Gerry couldn't concentrate on his work at the hardware store and he didn't feel like going scuba diving or pursuing any of the other hobbies that had occupied him for years. Even reading was difficult now. Worst of all was having someone near you tamper with your mind and your heart. His friends told him that he needed to get angry, to become enraged with Jill and her memory, and then let these things go, but he was drifting in the opposite direction. He was becoming obsessed with what had taken place between him and this woman.

If his feelings were already twisted, they became even more so when his ex-wife contacted him early in 1992 and reported that she'd just given birth to a beautiful baby girl, named Lara. The baby, she said, had been born in Humboldt, Texas, and Jill's neighbors had been kept up all night by the infant's cries. The baby was prickly, she went on, and seemed to have the same personality as her father.

When Gerry's friends and family members heard about Lara's birth, they dismissed the news as absurd—one more outrageous lie, delivered to make Gerry feel even worse than he already did. Jill was more malicious than they'd given her credit for being.

If some of his acquaintances had been waiting for months to unleash their contempt for this woman, they now poured out their feelings: Jill was a scammer and a con artist, a person with no sense of common decency.

What if, Gerry asked himself, Jill had lied about everything else, but was telling the truth about Lara? Just hearing about Lara's existence was enough to give him a measure of hope that he'd fathered a child and the infant was alive and well. These questions caused him to become even more obsessed than he already was. He had to find out if Lara was real—and if she was, he had to see his daughter and hold her in his arms.

Gerry had now been presented with a challenge that was painful, but on some level appealed to him.

It was almost as if he had a new hobby. The core of that hobby was that he wanted to know the absolute truth about two things. The first was whether or not Lara had been born. The second was that he wanted to know all he could about the woman he'd married the previous April.

His desire for this knowledge was not merely an intellectual craving. He believed that what she'd done to him was fundamentally wrong. He'd already glimpsed, from the things that Vance Halvorson, Judy Prier-Lewis, and Thane Gilliland were finding out about Jill, that he was not the first person she'd lied to or the first man she'd attempted to scam. And he was determined that in the future no one was ever going to have to endure with her what he was now enduring.

He was not just going to figure out who she was; he was somehow going to put this information in written form and expose it to the world.

"He wanted the next man she met," says Judy Prier-Lewis, "to have access to what he'd learned about her. He wanted that person not to make the same mistakes he had."

He told Judy to keep digging into his ex-wife's background and to follow Jill in order to find out if she'd had a baby. He told Thane and Vance that he would not have any peace of mind until he knew what the facts were. He told his brother that he never wanted Jill to do to another family what she'd done to theirs.

When Gerry's friends and family members saw the change in him, they felt uncomfortable, but they were uncertain what to do about this.

"I tried to get him involved in other things," says Doug, "but he just wasn't interested."

"I tried to tell him that she might be dangerous," Thane says, "and he took that idea seriously for a while, but then he began to think he was safe."

Twelve

Judy Prier-Lewis could not quite believe where her legwork was leading her. The private detective soon came up with fifteen names for the woman she was investigating: Jill Lonita Billiot; Jill Johansen Coit; Jill Steely; Jill Steeley; Jill Coit-Steely; Jill Boggs; Jill Johanson; Jill Carroll; Jill Theresa Kisla; Terrie Kisla; Jill Inhen; Jill Brodie; Jill Metzger; Jill Moore; and Jill DiRosa. Each name, Prier-Lewis was discovering, was attached to a story or a series of stories.

Jill had been born in New Orleans in the early 1940s, although no one was quite sure which of her several birth certificates was the real one. By 1992, she was closing in on 50. Despite being well into middle age, she still clung to some bitter feelings she'd picked up as a child. Judy had learned something that Carl Steely had also discovered: Jill believed that her younger brother, Marc, was her parents' favorite child, and she thoroughly resented him for this. Because she disliked Marc and was drawn to adventure, Jill left home when she was a sophomore in high school and moved north, going to live with her maternal grandmother in North Manchester, Indiana. In 1961, when she was nearly 20, she married Larry Inhen, but they were divorced less than a year later.

By 1963, she'd returned to Louisiana and met a college student named Steven Moore. They were wed on May 5, 1964, and in March of '65, Jill gave birth to her first child, Steven Seth Moore. A few months later, she met William Clark Coit II, an engineer for the Tenneco Corporation in Houston. Coit was taken with her lively personality and her striking good looks—Jill had big brown eyes and was buxom but still thin, and more than one person described her as not only beautiful, but "voluptuous." She married Coit on January 29, 1966, although at the time she was still married to Steven Moore. In March of 1967, she and Moore were divorced and for the time being Jill was no longer bigamous.

She now entered a period of stability, which lasted for several years before coming to a sudden halt. Between 1967 and 1972, she changed Steven Seth Moore's name to Johnathan Seth Coit, and she had two more sons with her husband: Andrew was born in 1966 and William Coit III was born in 1968. Most of the people who knew the Coits assumed they were a happily married couple, but then came rumors of money problems (William II said that his wife was spending more than he made), and this was followed by even more troubling developments.

Jill liked to drop casual remarks to her friends and acquaintances about having an insatiable sexual appetite. She told more than one listener of the affairs she'd had lately with a scuba diving instructor and a training pilot. Her activities, and especially her talking about them in public, naturally angered and hurt her husband. At first, he tried to ignore his feelings and keep his family together, but that was becoming impossible. He began drinking heavily, retreating further inside himself, depressed by what was happening to him, his marriage, and his children. His wife did not seem to be the same person he'd met half a decade earlier. She'd turned into a stranger, totally unpredictable and capable of things that were not just unnecessary or in bad taste, but downright cruel.

In March of 1972, when things between them had grown intolerable, the couple filed for divorce, but their marriage would never be legally dissolved. The Coits separated, with Jill taking the children and the furniture. On March 29, 1972, the wife of one of William's colleagues at the Tenneco Corporation, B. B. McCurdy, went to his home to see if Coit was all right, after he hadn't shown up for work that morning. William was lying in a pool of blood in the hallway of his home, shot to death by a .22-caliber pistol. Police detectives who investigated the slaying concluded that there had been no forced entry into the house and that Coit had apparently let his killer in through the back door.

The first and only suspect in the murder was his wife, but by the time William's body was discovered, Jill had taken her children and gone to New Orleans. There she hired an experienced attorney, Louis DiRosa, to help her fight extradition back to Texas. In New Orleans, she checked herself into a psychiatric hospital and when homicide detectives arrived from Houston, anxious to ask her some questions about her involvement in her ex-husband's financial affairs, and perhaps in the murder itself, she refused to talk to them.

For months, the Texas authorities tried to get her shipped back to Houston and to place the case before a grand jury, but with DiRosa's help, she successfully foiled all their attempts. The murder eventually fell into the inactive file. Jill checked herself out of the hospital and once again was a free woman.

She left New Orleans for California, and in the Golden State she met a wealthy ninety-year-old man named Bruce Johansen. By now, Jill was approaching 30 years of age, the mother of three sons, and the ex-wife of a trio of men. At the moment, she wasn't married to anyone, but it was not a wedding date that she proposed to Johansen, once they'd become close. He was too old for that, so they decided to try something else. On August 1, 1973, Johansen adopted Jill and included her in the settlement of his estate. Back in New Orleans, Louis DiRosa, her extradition lawyer, handled the paperwork for Jill's inclusion in Johansen's will.

A few months after legal technicalities had been completed, Johansen died. In the settlement that followed, Jill received several pieces of property and an undisclosed amount of money.

Judy Prier-Lewis was not able to uncover any evidence linking Jill to Johansen's actual death, but the private investigator still found her arrangement with the man highly suspect.

By the time Johansen died, Jill had a new romantic entanglement. She'd met a major in the U.S. Marine Corps, Donald Brodie, and they were married in

California on November 3, 1973. Brodie did something with his wife that her earlier husbands had not done, which helps account for the fact that the union lasted only two years. He stringently oversaw all of their financial affairs and refused to let Jill handle his money. Still, he could not entirely avoid trouble.

Near the end of their marriage, Jill claimed that she'd become pregnant. Following their divorce, she said that the major had fathered a son with her, named Thadeus John Brodie, and as a result of this, she wanted child support. Prier-Lewis did find a birth certificate for Thadeus, dated October 18, 1974, but the investigator came up with no other evidence that the boy had ever existed. In her opinion, Jill had merely invented the baby as a way to generate cash.

"Thadeus John Brodie," Judy once said, "was nothing more than an idea, a scam to get money. Jill would find a woman who had a baby and ask if she could borrow the child for an hour or two. Then she would show up with it wherever she needed to be, in order to make it look like she'd given birth.

"She had insurance scams, where she would fake injuries and collect on her policies. And she had credit card scams, which were also useful for getting money, but borrowing babies was one of her more creative acts."

After Jill's divorce from Brodie, which came in July of 1975, she left California and went back to New Orleans. In the next two years, she married her resourceful attorney, Louis DiRosa—twice. In 1976, they were wed in Mississippi, and even though they were already married, she married him again in 1977 in Louisiana. In November of 1978, they traveled to Haiti and got a divorce, which was apparently for the first marriage, because in the mid-eighties, they got another divorce on American soil.

Before the Haitian divorce from DiRosa, she married Eldon Metzger, an auctioneer from Indiana. That wedding took place in March of 1978 and there is no known record, according to what Prier-Lewis uncovered, that the couple were ever divorced. Jill also claimed to have had a child with Metzger, named Tenley, a baby whom she said had died young and was buried in a crypt in New Orleans. One day that crypt would be opened—and found empty.

When Jill met Carl Steely in the early 1980s, she had at least one husband—Eldon Metzger—if not two, since the U.S. divorce to DiRosa had not yet been granted. In spite of these matrimonial engagements, she married Steely in January of 1983, then divorced him quickly, then married him again, and then married him at least once again, although she hadn't divorced him from the second marriage.

As Steely himself once said, "She just loved weddings."

While married to Steely and perhaps Metzger, she married Gerry Boggs. After her annulment with Boggs and after she left Steamboat Springs at the end of 1991, Jill was not finished with matrimony. She soon met a Texan in his mid-sixties, Roy Carroll, and they exchanged vows in Houston in February of 1992. While still married to Carroll, Jill eventually met a man roughly her same age from Greeley, Colorado, a telephone repair worker by the name of Michael Backus. In time she would live with Backus, and although she would tell people that she was married to this man, no record of this union has been found.

By the end of 1992, she had been married to nine men a total of eleven or twelve times, or perhaps thirteen, depending on how you added them up. From what Prier-Lewis had learned, Jill was still married to at least two of her husbands.

The private detective gradually conveyed this information to Gerry Boggs as her investigation went along, and he became more upset with each revelation—and more determined than ever before to expose her.

Part Four

The Lawsuits

Thirteen

After Gerry and Jill had first become intimate, she'd persuaded him to do the kind of thing he'd never done for anyone in the past. She'd talked him into signing what amounted to a bogus deed of trust, worth $100,000, on the Oak Street Bed and Breakfast. She knew that once Carl Steely realized that his name was not on the bed and breakfast's ownership papers, and once they began their divorce proceeding, he would attempt to get as much money from Jill as possible in their upcoming settlement. She believed that if she could produce legal documents showing that she owed Gerry Boggs $100,000—and therefore had no assets from the bed and breakfast to share with Steely—she had a much better chance of fending off Carl and his lawyers.

For a while, Gerry resisted this plan. He wasn't the sort of man who leaped blindly into questionable business ventures (Jill wasn't asking him to lend her any money, but even signing the deed went against his lifelong practices and principles). He had little interest in becoming entangled in anyone's—including his lover's—legal affairs. It wasn't until Jill told him she was pregnant that he started to change his mind. Once they were married and she began talking constantly about the child that was soon to arrive, he found her arguments more convincing.

If he didn't want to sign the deed of trust for her benefit, Jill said, then he should do this for the baby. Their child, after all, would grow up one day and need financial resources of its own. If Carl took everything she had, it would ultimately hurt their offspring, and it wasn't too early to begin thinking about such things. In time, Gerry capitulated and signed the deed.

After Vance Halvorson and Judy Prier-Lewis had determined that Jill was still married to Steely and had most likely never been pregnant with Gerry's child, her legal strategy shifted again. After leaving Steamboat and going to Texas, she now demanded that Gerry take his name off the bed and breakfast and release the deed of trust. Because they were no longer married, she told him, and because he wasn't going to offer her any financial support for the baby she'd just given birth to, he should immediately let go of his claim to the business. That was the least he could do for her and his newborn daughter.

Gerry, for his part, was not that attached to the bed and breakfast, but he badly needed some leverage with his ex-wife. He wanted this in order to prove something to himself and to others—something that had been haunting him ever since Jill had said that she'd given birth to Lara in late December. Even though he doubted that the child really existed, he'd asked Prier-Lewis to follow Jill down in Texas, to see if there was any evidence of a baby in her life. After looking into this, Prier-Lewis said that no such evidence could be found, but that still did not satisfy

Boggs. Even though there was no carseat in Jill's automobile, and no baby clothes or toys where the woman lived, and no record of Lara's birth, he retained a kind of blind hope, which was regularly fueled by his ex-wife.

Each time Jill communicated with him or with his lawyer, Vance Halvorson, she mentioned some new details about Lara and in June of 1992, she sent Gerry a Father's Day card—"signed" by the baby girl. The card enraged him, yet it gave him one more pulse of hope. Maybe the child was living in Texas and Judy just hadn't been able to locate her. Maybe she was alive and well and growing each day. Maybe they needed to keep looking . . .

The only leverage Gerry felt he had with Jill came by holding onto the deed of trust. If he could get his former wife to confess before legal authorities that there was no baby girl and never had been—if he could get her to do this in exchange for the deed—then he would have achieved his own peace of mind and resolved a very painful situation. So he refused to relinquish the document without a fight.

As a result of his decision, Jill found a lawyer and sued her ex-husband, in an effort to force him to give up the deed. She also wrote some long-winded letters to him and his attorney. The letters are a remarkable combination of accusation, self-flagellation, fragments of honesty, and deep self-pity. She bounces back and forth between blaming herself for everything and being the victim of others. Jill is excellent at picking up the weaknesses of others, and then using them as weapons.

97

Her mind is fervid, versatile, creative, and imaginative. But it's as if it constantly moves from one extreme to the other, and there is very little in between.

In one letter to Vance Halvorson, she begins by portraying herself as an overly trusting, guilt ridden victim, of sorts.

"Jerry (sic) says that he does not want me to contact him or his family, that my only contact is to be with you. I am really sorry this turned out the way it did. I did not mean to do any harm to Jerry, his family or myself, yet it seems I have made a major mess of everything . . .

Jerry says to tell the truth so I guess I need to apologize publicly for choosing Jerry Boggs as the father of my child. When Jerry and I first started dating he told me he could never love me in the way that I need or wanted, he said he could not love anyone that way. I didn't believe him, I should have. When he told me that he loved me it was just a whim, maybe it would happen and he would love me. He said he was not capable of loving anyone. I had hoped that if I gave him a child he could learn to love. I now realize too late that I can never teach him to love, that he totally hates me . . ."

Roughly halfway through the letter, the reader begins to sense that whether or not Jill is telling the truth is no longer the issue (at least for her). She believes in what she is writing. To her, it has become real. It is the game she is playing that is most important, not the facts.

"If Jerry wants joint custody of Lara, I am willing to share her with him. It is the least I can do considering all the heartache I have caused. He says that if he can get Lara he can maybe forgive me. Jerry says that I am a liar and he is correct, because my foolish pride would not let me admit to being pregnant before marriage. I am not an adulteress, however, the child is Jerry's. He is more than welcome to have her tested. I just do not want to know if he does. I will not take part in any way because then if I don't know, I can never tell Lara that her father had so little faith in me that he had to have her checked. I will drop her off, all that I ask is that I get her back. . . ."

When talking or writing or just making eye contact, there was one subject—sex—that Jill could never avoid for long. It was as if everything that she came in contact with or thought about passed through the filter of her own sexuality.

"People told me he [Gerry] was gay, weird, bisexual, had a mean temper, was never happy . . . I should have taken their advice. I said, Hey, I defended him through all of that, he is not any of those things. . . . I am not immoral. From the very first date with Jerry, I have not even thought or desired, let alone had intercourse with anyone else. . . ."

By the time Gerry had read this letter, his family members, his friends, his lawyer, and his private investigator were all telling him the same thing: Lara did not exist and he'd recently been married to the most elaborate liar any of them had ever encountered. Her writing to Halvorson, they said, was just more proof of the extent to which she would go to try to make her fantasies appear real. They were aghast that to Jill, a baby girl was nothing more than a prop in the latest drama that she had created for herself to star in.

Gerry himself wasn't so sure about that. He respected the opinions of those he was closest to, but he couldn't yet be certain that Lara was not alive—and he was not a father.

Fourteen

The most important people in Jill's life were male—yet all her difficulties seemed to revolve around the opposite sex. Her brother, she was fond of saying, was intolerable, and her father had been abusive. Whether these things were true or not didn't really matter (she invented her past as she went along). Men clearly annoyed her in ways she could not resolve. She'd married nine of them and fought with all of them, often moving from an old husband to a new one without bothering to get a divorce. She was almost never without a male companion, but she was hardly ever content.

Besides her father, her brother, her husbands, and her lovers, there were three other significant men in Jill's life. Her oldest son, Seth, had been born in Texas and then tagged along with his mother as she'd zigzagged across America, bouncing from one state and marriage to the next. He'd helped her run her bed and breakfast in Culver, Indiana, and he'd followed her to Steamboat Springs. Since adolescence, he'd suffered from what a neurologist had once diagnosed as a learning disorder. He had trouble reading, he wasn't always fluent of speech, and some folks found him to be a little "slow"—but most everyone felt that he had a good heart.

In the summer of 1994, the movie *Forrest Gump,* a story about a gentle but somewhat retarded man, became a blockbuster hit at the box office. Following the release of this film, a number of people both in and beyond Steamboat Springs began comparing Seth Coit to Forrest Gump. Seth not only acted something like Gump, he had a passing physical resemblance to Tom Hanks's portrayal of the fictional character on the silver screen.

Jill's middle son, Andrew, had once attended the Culver Academy in Indiana, and in time he became an analyst of crime patterns for the Denver Police Department. A bright young man with a blondish beard and sincere eyes, Andrew had managed to separate himself, to some degree, from his mother early in life. By his mid-twenties, he had a good job and was married. As a boy, Andrew, like Seth, had been dragged all over the nation by his mother and he'd grown up feeling torn this way and that by invisible forces that were hard to name. But they still pulled at his heart.

When Jill lived in Steamboat, she occasionally visited her middle son in Denver. He tried to avoid whatever dramas she was currently spinning around herself, but that wasn't always possible. In December of 1991, while Andrew was on a trip to Mississippi, his mother went through Denver and stayed at his apartment. While there, she later explained to her son, she'd given birth to a baby girl named Lara. The child, she told him, "was ugly because it looked like Gerry."

Not long after Lara was born, Jill also informed Andrew, she'd given the child away—to a community of Amish people in Indiana.

Andrew was not entirely surprised by this story. Back when his mother was married to another husband, Eldon Metzger, she'd told Metzger that she'd prematurely given birth to a girl who had died right after being born. Andrew remembered his mother saying that she'd locked herself in the bathroom for a week, because she'd felt too bad to come out and face the world.

If Andrew had suffered because of his mother's behavior, he'd kept most of that suffering inside and tried to manage it as best he could. If his family bonds had been fragmented over the years, he believed that the fragments were still worth holding together. He thought of himself as the peacemaker between his mother and brothers whose job was to keep the lines of communication open. As he grew older, keeping the peace would only grow more difficult.

William Coit III, Jill's youngest son, lived in Manhattan Beach, California, and was employed by a construction firm. If Seth was his mother's helper and Andrew was the family mediator, William played a different and more unpredictable role. In the early 1990s, William heard something so shocking that he could not quickly absorb it. When this piece of information sank in, it would change the course of his life and many other lives as well.

He was told that his father, who was William's namesake and who had died when William was 4, had been murdered not by a stranger, as the young man had always been led to believe, but by Jill.

William eventually confronted Jill and asked her if this was the truth. That was preposterous, she said, just one more lie designed to punish her and turn her own flesh and blood against her. How could William even ask such a question?

Dissatisfied with this answer, William decided to travel to Houston to see if he could learn anything more about the life and death of his father. Like the homicide detectives who had attempted to solve this murder twenty years earlier, he was not able to find out precisely how his father had died. But through contact with his father's relatives, he discovered some old movies of him and his father, made when William was a small child. Then a very strange and powerful thing happened. He watched the movies of his dad playing with him. He watched them again and again. He felt what was going on between the man and the boy. He had no real memory of ever seeing or being around this person who had obviously cared so much for him when he was little.

As William was studying these videotapes, he fell in love with his father—fell in love with the image of the man who was towering over him in these old home movies. He fell in love with the notion that he'd once had a father, and not just any father, not an indifferent or cold father, but the father who had been captured in the videos. He could have grown up living with this man and they could have done a thousand things together and he could have something inside him now that was very different from the hole he'd always felt when he'd thought about his father. The two of them could have shared secrets and gone places and taken vacations together. His father could have passed on some of his knowledge,

BORDERS®

Merchandise presented for return, including sale or marked-down items, must be accompanied by the original Borders store receipt. Returns must be completed within 30 days of purchase. The purchase price will be refunded in the medium of purchase (cash, credit card or gift card). Items purchased by check may be refunded for cash after 10 business days, or

Merchandise unaccompanied by the original Borders store receipt, or presented for return beyond 30 days from date of purchase, must be carried by Borders at the time of the return. The lowest price offered for the item during the 12 month period prior to the return will be refunded via a gift card.

Opened videos, discs, and cassettes may only be exchanged for replacement copies of the original item.

Periodicals, newspapers, out-of-print, collectible and pre-owned items may not be refunded.

Returned merchandise must be in saleable condition.

BORDERS®

Merchandise presented for return, including sale or marked-down items, must be accompanied by the original Borders store receipt. Returns must be completed within 30 days of purchase. The purchase price will be refunded in the medium of purchase (cash, credit card or gift card). Items purchased by check may be refunded for cash after 10 business days, or

the original Borders store receipt, or days from date of purchase, must be the return. The lowest price offered for prior to the return will be refunded

Opened videos, discs, and cassettes may only be exchanged for replacement copies of the original item.

Periodicals, newspapers, out-of-print, collectible and pre-owned items may not be refunded.

Returned merchandise must be in saleable condition.

some of his wisdom about being an adult and a man. All these things could have happened to him, if only . . .

William left Houston with a welter of new and contradictory feelings. He still loved his mother—he'd always loved her in spite of the fact that she'd once tossed him into and pulled him out of a series of military schools. He'd never known where he would be from one year to another, because that always depended on the next man who came into her life. He loved her despite her penchant for saying mean things to him and expecting him to forgive her for all of them. But now he also loved his father, and he grasped for the first time what he'd missed and what had been taken away from him, when he was much too young to understand. Without the videotapes, William would not have known about the kind of bond that can exist between a grown man and his children. He would not have felt the depth of it.

He couldn't be absolutely sure that his mother killed his father—and even if she had, he couldn't do much about that now. Yet there was one thing he could do, and when he left Texas and returned to California, he vowed to do it. He never wanted anyone to suffer the losses that he'd suffered in life. He never wanted another parent to be taken away from another child. If he could prevent that from happening in the future, he promised himself that he would.

Fifteen

While Gerry continued his research on Jill, she kept sending letters to his lawyer. The details about "Baby Lara" became more specific. One could almost see the woman sitting down in Texas and writing the letters, while imagining the reaction that Gerry would have when he read them at home or at his desk at Boggs Hardware. She knew precisely where his pockets of guilt lay and where his heart could be hurt. She knew just how to manipulate him into rage. His mind was no match for her kind of emotional warfare.

". . . He [Gerry] said no, go to the bed and breakfast and have the baby at Routt Hospital. I said no. I thought if you are kicking me out one week before I have the baby then you have no say so where I go. The next morning he was kind enough to load my TV, some clothes for me and Lara into the car. I was totally uncomfortable and my back hurt unreal. So he did load my things for me. In the driveway he must have been feeling guilty because he said, If you have no place to go, you can stay here . . . just until the baby is born. I said no, you have said all you need to say."

Vanity and sexuality, mixed in with a trace of tenderness and just a scintilla of truth, move in and around nearly all her letters:

"My only other question is how can Jerry tell people that he does not even know if I was pregnant. He will admit to my breasts getting even bigger. I am a 34D and then I ended up being a 34EE and my stomach growing about 10 inches in front of me, but he said maybe I was just fat. I was not fat anywhere else on my body, how could I control just getting fat in those two areas? I do not understand why he would say he doesn't think I was pregnant.

". . . Jerry told me that Saturday morning of her birth that if I did not go to the doctor with him and Thane that he would not see me through this thing with Carl, nor would he claim Lara as his. This was on the morning of her birth—December 21. She was born at 11:15 at night."

In a strange sort of way, after all of her experiences with men, Jill still retained a certain kind of innocence. In her letters, it never seems to occur to her that anyone would question her version of events or see them as nothing more than the creation of an overheated imagination.

"Well it is Christmas eve and Lara is ready to eat. Unfortunately she has Jerry's temper. She screamed so hard the night of her birth for her one o'clock feeding that the man across the hall heard her and asked me the next morning whose baby was screaming. I am not a neglectful mother who lets her baby scream. I always change her before I breast feed her. She is very impatient."

And in the end, everyone who knew Jill would agree that her possessions meant more to her than any human connection could possibly mean:

"One thing needs to be said. I am supposed to be doing a scam. I do not know how I can be accused of taking anything financially from them. I spent $28,943.17 in Boggs Hardware since I have been in Steamboat. Doug spent less than $1,500 in my bed and breakfast for his daughter's wedding. They broke my window on the T-Bird that I loaned them. Jerry burned up the new engine that I had installed in the Mercedes just a year and a half ago. By the way, when is he going to reimburse me. . . ."

She not only wrote Halvorson letters, but regularly phoned him at work. After a while, he told his secretary not to take any more of Jill's calls. Then Vance began receiving hang-ups on his home phone.

Gerry Boggs was a man who had never allowed himself to go in debt or spend money frivolously.

Now he was employing a lawyer and a private investigator to chase after a far more elusive opponent than he could have ever imagined.

Sixteen

After Jill filed her lawsuit demanding that Gerry release the deed to the bed and breakfast, he filed a countersuit, charging her with fraud. She'd lied to him, he said, by falsely claiming that she was pregnant. In a deposition that accompanied his lawsuit, Gerry said that in the months following Jill's departure from his hometown, "I believed there was no child, and yet every time Jill came to Steamboat, she would go around telling people that she had had a child and that I had kicked her and the child out of my home, and needless to say, this upset me greatly, and I guess maybe that since hope springs eternal, I thought, well maybe she did have a child."

His purpose in filing the suit was threefold: in return for releasing the deed to the bed and breakfast, he wanted Jill to sign a document stating that "Lara" had never existed. Second, he wanted his ex-wife to stop using and defaming the Boggs name in Steamboat Springs. And he wanted damages that would have brought his total claim against her to between $100,000 and $200,000.

Jill refused to sign anything concerning Lara—until Gerry had agreed to some other conditions. She wanted him to pay for engine repairs to her aging Mercedes, an engine which she said he had ruined. She wanted him to replace some furniture and personal items which she felt she'd lost as a result of their annulment. She also didn't want to pay him a nickel. Her divorce settlement with Carl Steely had cost her $100,000, and she now needed to sell the bed and breakfast in order to raise money. In addition to that, she felt that she owed Gerry nothing.

The upshot of all the legal wrangling was that no one could find a way to resolve the conflict.

For months, accusations and counteraccusations flew back and forth between Jill and Gerry and their attorneys. She was represented by a Steamboat Springs lawyer, Richard Tremaine, who worked on Main Street, just a few yards away from Gerry's attorney, Vance Halvorson. A few blocks farther down the street were Boggs Hardware and the bed and breakfast. All of the parties except Jill, who now lived in Greeley, saw one another on a regular basis. Their sidewalk greetings were chilly. The case soon generated a foot-thick stack of depositions, briefs, and other legal documents, kept on file at the Routt County Courthouse, also located on Main Street. While the briefs were piling up, Judy Prier-Lewis continued to look into Jill's background.

By the end of 1992, after tracking Jill through several states and even speaking with the woman's parents, Prier-Lewis concluded that Lara had never been born, and she'd more or less convinced Gerry of the same thing. He had been conned, his private investigator and Thane Gilliland kept telling him, just like many others before him.

"Jill," says Thane, "had gotten men to pay her child support for babies that had never been born."

To support her contentions about Jill's past, Prier-Lewis had put together five boxes of information, showing where Jill had lived, whom she had married, and when she had divorced. The boxes outlined her history of bigamy and polygamy, her insurance schemes, and her credit card scams. They gave the details of her previous false pregnancies and revealed her numerous social security cards, her multiple birth certificates, her aliases, and her attempts to transfer money from the accounts of her husbands into her own accounts. They showed that one of her husbands had been murdered, another had lost most of his life savings, and a third man, who had not married her, had perished soon after adopting Jill. They detailed that while she had lived this way for nearly three decades, she'd somehow managed to escape any serious run-ins with the law.

"She'd come to think of herself," says Prier-Lewis, "as almost like a Mafia leader, someone who was untouchable when it came to the legal system."

Stan Lewis, a private detective from Texas, who also looked into Jill's background, went further than that. "She's a psychotic, vicious, ruthless black widow," he once told the *Houston Chronicle*. "She takes a sadistic delight in preying on well-meaning men to facilitate her ultimate goal of furthering her financial welfare."

After Jill had left Steamboat Springs, a married woman in town put it somewhat differently. "Her kiss," she said, "was always the kiss of death."

* * *

The people who were uncovering Jill's past—Gerry, Prier-Lewis, Thane Gilliland, and Vance Halvorson—were both appalled and fascinated by what they were finding. Each time Prier-Lewis called or faxed or wrote the hardware owner, telling him something else that Jill had done to someone ten or fifteen or twenty years earlier, Gerry felt an even greater sense of indignation, yet he was driven to learn more. What other outrageous things had she done? What other men had been hurt or robbed by this woman? Who else had suffered at her hands?

Gerry's message to his private investigator was always the same: keep digging and placing more information into those boxes. Because he and his ex-wife could not reach an agreement on resolving their lawsuits out of court, Gerry had begun to feel that a courtroom battle would be necessary. And if it came to that, he wanted to be well prepared. By now he recognized that he was dealing with a clever and resourceful adversary, so he would need all the ammunition he could muster. But he also felt something else, which came out of two distinct parts of his character.

The first part was that he was very intellectually curious, and this was the kind of search that had always appealed to him. He craved new information, and now he was in a position where he could oversee a remarkably fruitful investigation. The story that Prier-Lewis was putting together was too good to turn away from. What would the next chapter be? In which direction would the plot turn? What set of ugly details about Jill had they not yet stumbled across?

Like many people who love books, Gerry had long

harbored the notion that someday he would sit down and write about his own experience. The war in Vietnam notwithstanding, his encounter with Jill Coit was easily the most disturbing thing that had ever happened to him. It needed to be documented and the process of book-writing had, in a sense, already begun. Prier-Lewis was doing the basic research, and in the future, when he had more time, Gerry would put it all together in a manuscript. He'd even mentioned this to Judy, in a joking sort of way, saying that American men needed a handbook for how to avoid involvement with Jill and women like her.

The other part of his character that this search appealed to was the one that believed deeply in the concept of right and wrong. If Gerry was not a conventionally religious man, he was someone who had always tried to live by a moral code—a code of honesty, decency, and respect for other people. He felt strongly that people who were engaged in illegal or illicit activities should be rooted out and exposed. That served the good of everyone.

Now he was in a situation to expose a woman who had skated away from responsibility for her entire life. Now he would get her inside a courtroom and bring in some of her ex-husbands to testify against her. Now he would open up the five boxes of damning information in public and show people who she really was and what she'd done to others throughout her adulthood. Now he would do to her what she'd done to him—and return the humiliation he'd received.

It was almost as if Gerry had been looking for something like this: a crusade that would combine his passion for learning with his desire for seeing justice rendered. In the strange way of such things, the events that had brought him so much pain were now also bringing him a kind of pleasure. This kind of work—the labor of a private investigator or an attorney in these circumstances—was far more interesting than being a bookkeeper in a hardware store. It was more fun to chase a legal opponent than to pay close attention to debits and credits and the other minutiae of running a business.

As he and Jill moved inevitably toward a courtroom showdown, Gerry's mind and his heart now had an intense focal point: whether she won or lost these lawsuits, his ex-wife would no longer be allowed to run away from her past.

Seventeen

By the end of 1992, nothing had been settled between Gerry and Jill. The two principals had become angrier with one another, while their lawyers just kept quarreling.

"In 1993," says Thane Gilliland, "before the case was scheduled to come to trial that summer, Gerry made her an offer and it was a good one. He asked her to sign an agreement saying that there was no baby, that she would stop using the Boggs name, and that she would obey a restraining order that would keep her away from his house. In return for these things, he would give up the deed he held on her property. When he presented the terms of this agreement to Jill, she laughed in his face.

"She would not let Gerry out of the lawsuit and she got a perverse pleasure in keeping him in this position. For her to have signed a document saying that there was no baby and she'd been wrong about Lara went against everything she stood for. She just couldn't do it."

The civil dispute between Jill and Gerry was set to go to trial before a Steamboat Springs jury in

June of '93, but it was postponed for several months after Jill decided to get a hip operation. Gerry saw the operation as nothing but a stall tactic. Because he'd been eagerly awaiting the trial's start and putting this long and painful episode behind him, he did not take the delay at all well.

"Before the first trial date in June," says Thane Gilliland, "Gerry had been very, very nervous. He was concerned that Jill might do something stupid or dangerous to prevent the trial from taking place. He and I talked about this a lot. I told him what she was capable of. Sometimes, I'd ask him to come down and stay at my house in the Denver suburbs for a while and he would. He was afraid of her. I even suggested that he move out of Steamboat or get a bodyguard, but he didn't want to do either of those things. I also told him that he needed a gun, but he already had one, and guns really weren't Gerry's way.

"He changed after she canceled that June trial date and had hip surgery. He went into a blind fury over this and lost his whole sense of being afraid of Jill. That was the turning point. He quit being fearful of her and became obsessed with this thing. He went berserko."

The great Midwestern flood in the summer of 1993 altered Jill's life. When the rains started to fall, she was living in Greeley with Michael Backus, the telephone repairman for U.S. West, and she was also attending classes at the University of Northern Colorado. As the waters continued to wash away farms and homes, creating a disaster in the heartland, prob-

117

lems developed with the phone lines in several states. By midsummer, sections of Iowa were in the midst of an emergency and U.S. West decided to send out some of its Colorado workers to help repair the damage.

When Backus was offered the opportunity to go to Iowa, he readily accepted it. He was divorced, had an eight-year-old daughter, Erin, and needed all the funds he could generate to make his child support payments. Money had never come easily to the forty-eight-year-old repairman, and if he now had to work overtime to earn more of it, and if he had to work in flood conditions, he would do both those things. His fantasy had long been to have more money—but not have to strive so hard for it. After twenty-three years at U.S. West, he had an excellent record with the company. He was skilled, solid, and dependable. He almost never missed a day's work. His colleagues liked him and his superiors respected his commitment to his job.

Backus was tall and rather trim, he wore glasses, and his features conveyed something serious. He looked more intellectual than he was. He looked like a political science professor at a community college or like an aging student radical in the late 1960s. The first thing some people noticed about him was the intensity in his eyes. He was a man who harbored things deeply, good things and bad things, but he seemed to be lacking some fundamental self-confidence. You could see it in the movement of his eyes and the shape of his mouth. It was almost as if he was just waiting to apologize for something.

Like Gerry Boggs, he was a Vietnam veteran, and the experience had marked him for life. Sometimes at

U.S. West, he talked about the war with one of his fellow employees, Troy Giffin, another veteran and one of his closest acquaintances on the job. Vietnam was a bond between the men. They'd been places and done things that most other people hadn't done and never would. They'd seen violence up close and knew what it did to people. They had something in common that was hard to put into words.

When U.S. West sent Backus east in the summer of 1993, he did not go alone. Jill took some time off from school and traveled with him to Ottumwa, Iowa, a town of roughly 30,000 people in the southeastern part of the state, near the Des Moines River.

Despite her lifelong fascination with the opposite sex, it would be wrong to suggest that Jill was drawn only to males. On occasion, she liked to flirt with women, and she slipped into that role just as easily as she became the seductress when meeting a new man. She was a thoroughly sexual creature who understood that people like to be titillated and that her own sensual identity was a very fluid thing. Whenever she had a new encounter, she focused on a person's sexuality before anything else.

It wasn't so much intimacy that she wanted—with either a woman or a man—but something that went beyond the act of making love. She wanted to see where intimacy led and to find out how much power it gave her over someone's life. She wanted to discover what somebody was willing to do for her after they'd become lovers. Her sexuality was like a weapon that could be loaded, aimed, and fired in any number of directions.

Ottumwa, Iowa, had a small but thriving lesbian community, and one of its most visible members was a middle-aged woman named Mohee Hanley. Mo had very short dirty-blond hair and a tattoo on one hand, and she liked to dress in Western-cut clothes and cowboy boots. She worked at the Excel Hog Producing plant and was in a committed relationship with a woman named Judy. At a yard sale in the summer of '93, while the rains were overwhelming Iowa, Judy met a talkative stranger by the name of Jill Backus. Jill said that she was living in Ottumwa while her husband worked on the telephone lines, and the couple were looking to meet some local people during their stay in town. Judy introduced Jill to Mo and the women became friends.

Jill told Mo that she was bisexual; and that she was a gay/lesbian psychologist, with a counseling practice in Greeley, Colorado; that she offered help to self-destructive people and was a clinically trained "suicidologist"; and that she would like to attend some lesbian meetings with Ottumwa women. She also told Mo and Judy that the two of them needed therapy and then suggested that she counsel them. When they accepted, Jill advised Mo that Judy was suffering from an attitude problem and that the women would benefit by putting some "distance" between themselves. The women took this under advisement.

Mo Hanley had led a hard, highly unpredictable life. She never knew her father and her mother was an alcoholic prostitute. As a child, Mo had been placed in a series of foster homes—when she wasn't living on the streets or under the bridges around Ottumwa. To survive, she begged and borrowed. She stole carrots and potatoes from grocery stores. One night when she was eight, a man tried to rape her, but she resisted with all her strength. He shot her in the leg with a shotgun; as a grown woman, she still wore the scars from this blast.

Remarkably enough, her childhood had not left her bitter or defeated. It had just helped her appreciate how much better her life had become since she'd grown to adulthood. When people met her, they were struck by her forthrightness and her obvious pride in who she was. She made no attempt to hide her sexual preference and she had a splendid indifference toward those who would judge her. After what she'd been through as a youngster, the opinions of others were of no consequence. If they could not accept her as she was, that was not her problem, and she did not have time to explain why this was so. In her appearance and in the way she carried herself, she commanded respect.

Jill introduced Michael Backus to Mo and Judy, and he was intrigued, coming into contact with a circle of lesbians in this small Midwestern town. This was a lot more interesting and stimulating than most of what he did in Greeley. He was away from home, away from his bosses at work, away from his past— and in a new place with new possibilities. He liked Mo Hanley, liked her toughness and no-nonsense view of life. He liked the way she dressed. He admired the prominent belt buckles she wore on her pants. After getting to know the woman, he suggested to her that he, Jill, and Mo make a movie together: a porn film featuring the threesome in bed.

To his surprise and disappointment, Mo turned him down flat. She just wasn't into cavorting with men, she said, in private or in public. The whole idea seemed to her, as she once put it, "derogatory."

After Jill became Mo's therapist, they had several counseling sessions together. Jill also attended some lesbian meetings with her new friend, and during one of them, she suggested that the other women who were present write down their sexual fantasies and give them to her; they complied. Once she'd had a chance to study these writings, she told the group, she might be able to provide them with some real insight into their lives.

As September approached, and as Mo and Jill became closer, the Iowa native told the visitor from the mountains about her experience of nearly being raped as a youngster. This prompted Jill to ask her a question.

"What would you do," she said, "if your daughter had been raped and you knew who did it? What would you do to the man responsible for that?"

"I'd kill him," Mo said at once.

"You would?"

"That's right."

Then Jill told her a story. She'd had a lesbian lover back in Colorado, she said, but the woman had died in a car crash not long ago and left behind her five-year-old girl, who was being raised by a relative. Jill explained that her husband, Mike Backus, had helped console her through the terrible period of grieving that had followed this woman's death. Now that her grieving had diminished, Jill was deeply troubled by what was happening with the five-year-old. Jill gave the child $500 a month to make things easier for her, but money wasn't the only issue involved in this tragic situation.

The girl lived in Steamboat Springs, and Jill had recently learned that the youngster was being sexually molested by a man in that town. He was a prominent member of the community whose family had owned a hardware store on Main Street for more than fifty years. Local people regarded him as one of their most upstanding citizens, but he had a hidden and passionate attraction to very small girls. Jill knew about his secret life, and it filled her with contempt for the man. She was so repulsed by his activities, she confessed to Mo, that she could not even bring herself to walk by his store in Steamboat Springs, let alone do business there.

This man was dangerous, Jill said to her friend, but no one had the courage to step forward and stop him. Even the police were paralyzed, because they did not have the backbone to arrest a town leader for child molestation—not when his family name was Boggs.

As Mo listened to this story, she, too, felt repulsed. It brought up anger and some deeply disturbing memories for her. She expressed her sympathy for the child and agreed with Jill that no man should be allowed to get away with such behavior.

After sharing this information with Mo, Jill asked her if she owned any guns.

Mo said she didn't, but her lover, Judy, did.

"What kinds of guns does she have?" Jill asked.

There was a .22-caliber rifle, Mo recalled, a .257-caliber handgun, and an old Winchester. There may have been one or two more at their home.

"Why do you want a gun?" Mo said.

"I just need a clean and untraceable weapon," Jill told her.

"What for?"

"I can't stand what's being done to that child in Steamboat Springs. I can't take it any longer."

Jill mentioned purchasing one of Judy's firearms, but Mo didn't think that was a very good idea. She had an alternate plan.

She took Jill to one of the livelier hangouts in Ottumwa, a topless bar called Chills 'n' Thrills—a tavern where bikers came together and a place where you might be able to make a contact to buy a handgun, if you knew the right people. In the bar, Jill asked her companion if someone there would sell her an untraceable weapon, but Mo said she didn't think so; Jill wasn't an insider here and could not be trusted, at least not yet. The women left Chills 'n' Thrills without attempting to buy anything.

Jill and Michael stayed in Ottumwa for several months, but by late September, they were planning to return to Greeley. His repair work was largely finished, and Jill had to get back for her upcoming trial, scheduled to begin on October 27. Before they left Iowa, Jill told Mo some of her suggestions for getting rid of the man in Steamboat Springs who was molesting the five-year-old girl. Mo went along with this talk and added some suggestions of her own, as if this were a form of recreation or a way of letting off steam—a fantasy about what should be done to people who harm children.

The women talked about blowing up the tall, balding, hardware store owner, but Jill said she didn't know where to get the explosives or how to make a bomb. They talked about burning him to death, but

124

Jill said she didn't have access to flammables. They talked about putting rat poison in his milk—and Jill said this was a distinct possibility, because she knew that the man left his back door unlocked and she could slip into his kitchen, open the refrigerator, and spike his milk carton. They talked about driving past the hardware store and shooting him.

When Mo said that Backus could help Jill carry out one of these missions, Jill said no, he was too weak and she needed a strong person for an ally, someone who was not afraid to take action. She wanted Mo herself to move to Colorado, and the two of them working together could figure out how to stop this man for good. When Mo resisted this idea, Jill asked if she knew anyone else who might be willing to help. Mo was taken aback by the seriousness of the question and said that her friends would give Jill a "backhand" for trying to get them involved in something so violent and deadly.

Jill offered Mo a plane ticket and $1,000 to come out to Steamboat and do what had to be done. If Mo wouldn't do this, Jill insisted, the man would just go on and rape other children, the same way Mo had been raped as a youngster.

Mo said she was sorry, but she couldn't possibly meet Jill's demands. For one thing, she hated to fly, and for another, this wasn't nearly enough money to kill another human being. Mo no longer wanted to have conversations about this with her friend, because it had stopped being amusing and had become entirely too real.

When Jill realized that Mo was never going to comply with her wishes, she told the woman that she owned a trenchcoat, which would conceal most of her body, and a long wig, which would hide all her hair. She didn't need any allies to complete this mission. She had a good disguise and could do it by herself.

Eighteen

Troy Giffin was a native of Greeley. Short, bearded, and spindly looking, Giffin had originally been named Charles before giving himself a new and more romantic moniker. From 1961 to 1966, he'd served in the military, as a U.S. Marine in Southeast Asia. He'd been honorably discharged, but the war had not ended for him when he'd returned to America. For years afterward, cancer kept showing up inside him and he needed one operation after another to have it removed. The disease might have been there for genetic reasons, or because of the way he lived, or because he'd been subjected to Agent Orange in Vietnam. Whatever the reason, he underwent five major surgeries to get the tumors out of his body.

Following his military duty, he went to Los Angeles and tried to establish a career as a photographer. Before long, he'd returned to Greeley. He'd grown up as a tough kid and had had some brushes with the law. In 1978, he was charged with armed robbery and attempted murder, but eventually the charge was reduced to reckless endangerment and he was fined

$1,000. He never served any time. With middle age on the horizon, he settled into a job at U.S. West, as a technician for the phone company. To keep himself stimulated, he read a lot of books and was an aggressive collector of antiques. It was a decent life and one that was devoid of trouble. He had every intention of keeping it that way.

In 1993, Troy had spent the previous four years working with Michael Backus. If they were not intimate friends, they were buddies on the job who could talk about the one piece of their past that was shared—Vietnam—and about what they hoped for their future. Giffin mostly wanted good health and security. In addition to his cancer operations, he'd fallen out of a tree in recent months, while checking a phone line. He'd landed on his head, breaking an elbow and fracturing his neck. Giffin lost considerable time at work recuperating from these injuries, and during his convalescence, Backus visited him and talked openly about his future plans and dreams.

By the summer of '93, Troy felt that his co-worker was becoming a different man from the one he'd always known. Backus had met a woman from Steamboat Springs, someone named Jill, and she seemed to have a profound influence on her new lover. Backus spoke about her all the time, talked about the bed and breakfast she owned up in Steamboat Springs, bragged about the money she had access to or could make, and fantasized about how he and Jill were going to be married someday and live a more luxurious life than any life that he'd ever been accustomed to.

His money problems and his difficulties in making his child support payments were soon going to be

128

behind him. Before long, his decades of laboring for U.S. West would be over. Troy listened to his friend, concluding that Mike had become obsessed with this woman.

Just one thing, Backus explained to Giffin, stood between him and prosperity—and that was a very prominent individual in Steamboat by the name of Gerry Boggs. This man owned a hardware store on Main Street, came from one of the best families in town, and lived a bizarre double life. By day he was a thoroughly respectable citizen with a pristine reputation, but by night he was something of a wildcat. He was bisexual and he was partial, Backus told his colleague, to threesomes. He liked to watch Jill make love to another man before jumping in bed with both of them. Mostly, he liked men and this was his way of connecting with them. Because of his prominence in the community, Backus said, Boggs usually had to travel outside Steamboat to find his lovers.

But Backus went further than describing Boggs's sexual proclivities. He told Giffin that the hardware store owner was "no good." He was an "SOB" and a "faggot"—the kind of person who would be "better off dead."

And the problem, Backus explained to his co-worker, was that Jill had married Gerry Boggs, before she'd realized who he really was. She'd even given him a piece of her bed and breakfast. Now she wanted that piece back, so she could sell the business and give part of the money from that sale to the man who was going to be her new husband: Backus himself.

Boggs was holding up the sale by refusing to release his share of the bed and breakfast. Jill and Michael had tried to be patient and reasonable about this, but their patience was running out and they'd grown tired of waiting. They were ready for action.

"I want him dead," Backus said to Giffin during one of their phone conversations in the summer of '93. "Do you know anyone in Greeley who would help me with this?"

Troy attempted to change the subject, but Backus repeated the question.

"Maybe you should look for someone in the Latin Quarter," Giffin said offhandedly, referring to one of the rougher parts of Greeley.

"How much money would it take?"

"I don't know. Why do you need someone to do this for you?"

"Jill and I are too well known in Steamboat. A lot of people up there have seen us together."

"Try the Latin Quarter."

"Is thirty-five hundred dollars enough to get someone interested?"

"I really don't know."

"Look, Troy. No one would suspect you if you did this for us."

"I'm not going to do it."

"Why not?"

"I don't need any trouble."

"There won't be trouble. After people in Steamboat find out about Boggs's sexual habits, they'll think that one of his gay lovers came to Steamboat and killed him. A jealousy thing. No one will ever know what really happened."

"I'm not interested, Mike, and I don't want to talk about it anymore."

Later that summer, Backus told Giffin that he'd

thought about it and realized that $3,500 might not be enough to get the job done.

"Would you do it for seventy-five hundred?" he said.

"No."

"Do you think somebody else would?"

"I don't know. I just don't want to be involved in this thing."

"But you know the kinds of people who would, don't you?"

"I told you to look in the Latin Quarter."

"Do you think seventy-five hundred dollars would do it?"

"It ought to."

"Do you think the killer would wait for the sale of the bed and breakfast before getting his money? Or would he demand it up front?"

"Up front, Mike. These are not the sort of people who sit around and wait to get paid."

"Are you sure?"

"Yeah, I'm sure. You're not going to find anyone to do this on contingency."

Part Five

October

Nineteen

By early October, Jill and Michael were back in Colorado, living together in Greeley. Neither of them had been able to come up with the kind of agreement they'd been seeking. Neither Mo Hanley nor Troy Giffin was willing to do what they'd asked them to. Out of frustration, Jill had even called her former husband, Louis DiRosa, the lawyer down in New Orleans whom she'd married twice in the 1970s. DiRosa had helped her with some legal problems in the past, and she thought he might be of assistance now. The lawyer also disappointed her. Jill would later tell people that DiRosa had said he wanted nothing to do with resolving her Gerry Boggs dilemma—because he was occupied with running for a judgeship in Louisiana.

The civil trial was only three weeks away and virtually everyone involved in the legal dispute was looking toward the end of October. For months, Doug Boggs had been nervously awaiting the autumn, hoping that the trial would come and go without trouble. On several occasions he'd warned his employees at the hardware store that if they ever saw Jill Coit coming in the front door, they were to stop whatever they were doing and immediately run out the back. There were no exceptions to this command: their safety was more important than any business transaction.

By the first week of October, Gerry knew that he and his legal team had backed Jill into a corner; under these circumstances, he believed, she would do what she'd always done. Either she would stall again, or she would run. If she stalled, by planning another operation or a similar tactic, he could wait for another trial date. If she ran away, he would have shown the people of Steamboat that she could not stand up to the revelations that were coming in the courtroom. If she surprised him and compromised, settling with him at the last moment and signing a document proving that she and Gerry had never had a child, that would also be a victory.

"He never felt there was going to be a trial," says Thane Gilliland. "He thought she'd skip the country. And by October, he no longer seemed so worried about what she might do to him. He felt that if she hadn't done anything yet, she certainly wouldn't do it right before the start of the trial.

"Around that time, Gerry and I had some very candid talks about what had happened between him and Jill. He would say, 'Why did she pick me?' I would just look at him and say, 'Why you? Don't you understand? You weren't picked arbitrarily, Gerry. You were picked precisely because of who you were.'

"He was a bachelor who was rather lonely. He hadn't had a lot of experience with women. He didn't owe anyone a cent and he had assets. Jill knew all of that. If she'd gotten her hands on a piece of Boggs Hardware and then told him that the baby had miscarried, she'd have walked out of Steamboat Springs with half a million to seven hundred and fifty thousand dollars. She was a totally unconscionable person."

Seth Coit was also thinking about the upcoming civil trial. Earlier in 1993, he'd given a deposition regarding the ownership of the bed and breakfast. Before he did this, his mother had told him to say nothing about the baby she'd supposedly had in late 1991 and to act as if he'd never heard of "Lara." Seth followed her orders well. He was good at looking bewildered and some of his befuddlement was genuine: he didn't know everything Jill was up to.

This complicated legal battle over the bed and breakfast, Seth liked to point out to others, was not his own. It was his mother's and Gerry Boggs's. Seth liked people. He liked Gerry Boggs. He and the man had eaten lunch or dinner together many times, and Gerry was not his enemy. Seth liked Doug Boggs, as well, and had always enjoyed going into the hardware store. He lived a simple life and wanted to keep it that way. He was content doing his chores at the bed and breakfast—preparing meals, cleaning the rooms, and helping the people who came to stay at the establishment on Oak Street—and these other things, he often told people, didn't concern him very much.

Some folks believed that Seth was naive and childlike. Others thought he was more calculating, and that his innocence was mostly a put-on. But almost everyone, no matter how much they disliked his mother, realized that parts of the young man's life were complex and uncomfortable; how uncomfortable, they had not yet imagined.

Jill had promised not just Michael Backus, but also her three sons (and primarily Seth) that when she sold the bed and breakfast, each of them would benefit financially. All of the important men currently in her life had a stake in seeing the legal matters resolved quickly and in her favor. If that happened, ten percent of the monies would go to one person and ten percent would go to another. The bed and breakfast, she was now telling people, was worth almost a million dollars.

If his mother made Seth's life more complicated, so did his relationship with his new wife. By the fall of 1993, he and Julie English had been married and were running the bed and breakfast. They managed the bed and breakfast while Jill moved from Texas to Greeley to Iowa, then back to Colorado, always going from one location to the next, one home to another, an old relationship to a new one, changing names and addresses and birth dates, jumping in and out of school, never staying anywhere for long, inventing herself and her future from one moment to another.

All of her sons seemed to crave the stability that she herself disdained.

Julie was the new woman in Seth's life, and she did not follow Jill's orders as easily as he did. Like many people, she had never met anyone quite like her mother-in-law. Conflict was inevitable, if not between the two women, then inside Seth himself.

Julie's own parents were from the South, and her

mother, Anne, had grown up in Atlanta. Anne now lived in Panama City, Florida, and on several occasions she'd come into contact with Jill Coit. These encounters had made a lasting impression on her.

"Jill liked to think of herself as a real Southern woman, but she really wasn't that way at all," Anne says in a strong Georgia accent. "For one thing, she had very little sense of privacy. I was with her once and she was still married to Carl Steely at the time. She got on the phone with him and began screaming and shouting at the man at the top of her voice. I was just taken aback. It was almost like I wasn't even there listening to her. I walked out of the room because I didn't feel that it was right for me to hear these things go on between two people I barely knew.

"Not long after I'd met her, we were having a conversation and she asked me to come upstairs with her, so I did. We walked into the bathroom and she began undressing right in front of me, taking off every bit of her clothing until she was nude. She jumped in the tub and took a bath. I guess you could consider something like that to be a compliment, but I thought it was very forward."

In October of '93, Jill and Backus began visiting Steamboat Springs and talking more openly to Seth and Julie about how Gerry Boggs had become an impediment to the sale of the bed and breakfast. Julie became worried and called her father, Larry English, who made some inquiries into Jill's background. He was particularly interested in her marital history and in the rumors that she might have been responsible for the death of William Coit back in

Houston in the early 1970s. English didn't uncover anything definitive about the murder of William Coit, but he was able to gather that Jill was phenomenally shrewd and possibly dangerous.

Julie told her father of her fear that Seth's mother and her boyfriend might hurt Boggs, or even kill him. In spite of his research into Jill's background, English considered this an overreaction.

"Don't worry, honey," he told his daughter. "I don't think she's so stupid that she'd do something like that again."

Julie wasn't alone in her concern. Seth had lately been calling Manhattan Beach, California, and talking to his brother, William, about their mother's current movements in and around Steamboat Springs. Seth told William about some of her recent demands on him. Jill wanted her oldest son to watch the back of the hardware store—Seth could see it clearly from the bed and breakfast—and report back to her when Gerry came to work and when he went home. She wanted to know where he parked his car. She'd been asking Seth to call Boggs's house and then hang up after he answered, just to make sure that he'd not left town. She asked him to drive by Gerry's house, asked him to tell her the best way to get into someone's home. Should she try the front door or the back? Should she break a window, or was that too obvious and noisy?

Jill had already done her own research on Gerry's residence. After her marriage to Boggs had been annulled, she made a point of going out with a locksmith in Steamboat. During one of their dates, he let drop that while he'd lately changed all the other locks at Boggs's home, he hadn't rekeyed the back kitchen door. Anyone with an old key to the house, he told the woman, could still get in that way.

Jill had mentioned some of her other plans to Seth. She'd told him about putting on a disguise, sneaking into Boggs Hardware, spraying WD-40 into the computer system, and destroying all the business records. What was the best way to do something like this? she asked her son. What was the best time of day for such a raid? Wouldn't that be the perfect revenge on Gerry Boggs—the man who was always working on his computer, his head buried in statistics, instead of paying attention to real life? Wouldn't that enrage him?

Seth patiently listened to Jill, answering her questions and complying with her wishes, just as he'd always done. No matter what she was suggesting, she was his mother, after all, and he was employed in her business. Hadn't she always looked out for him?

Seth knew that if you challenged the woman or resisted her, she could suddenly turn vicious. Watching his mother's mask slip away, Seth felt small and helpless and afraid, like a child who believed that no matter what he said or did, he could never do the right thing. If he said yes to her demands, he would be violating himself. If he said no, he would be hurting his mother. Either way, he would suffer. When she attacked him with harsh words and ugly looks, she wasn't like a mother at all, but like a force pushing against his chest and throat, telling him to do things that he could not stop himself from doing.

So it was always easier and more comfortable to say yes.

After Seth called California and told his younger

brother about Jill's activities in Steamboat, William became alarmed. His own research into his mother's background—like Larry English's and Judy Prier-Lewis's, like Gerry Boggs's, Vance Halvorson's, Carl Steely's, and Thane Gilliland's—told him that she'd been involved in things that may have gone far beyond financial scams or bigamous marriages.

It was common knowledge among those well acquainted with Jill that she had a number of firearms, mostly handguns. She liked to brag about keeping a small pistol in her "fanny pack"—the pouch she wore around her waist. She'd once told Sylvia Boggs that it was always loaded.

As October unfolded and the start of the civil trial on the twenty-seventh moved closer, everyone was thinking more and more about Jill Coit. People were watching her and talking more about her, too.

William told Seth to keep him informed of any new developments in Steamboat. Seth nervously agreed to do this, but he didn't know what his mother might do next. No one did.

Twenty

One morning in the summer of 1993, Michael Backus arrived at the bed and breakfast on a motor- cycle and offered to take Seth and Julie to lunch, but Seth declined; he had chores to do at the bed and breakfast and was insistent about finishing them. While Backus and Julie were eating, he told her that he was angry at Gerry Boggs for filing a countersuit against Seth's mother. He was angry at Boggs for holding up the sale of the bed and breakfast, which was keeping Seth and Julie from getting a share of the money the sale would bring.

"I can't believe that son of a bitch is doing this to you kids," he said, adding that he knew where Boggs lived and had driven by his home.

Gerry had lately been receiving bitter phone mes- sages on his home answering machine. One was from a man named Don Cole, who spoke as if he were a gay lover of Boggs's, a lover whose feelings had been hurt by a romantic encounter with Boggs. He threatened to expose their relationship to others.

* * *

On Friday, October 15, Seth received a subpoena ordering him to appear at the civil trial over the ownership of the bed and breakfast. He was annoyed and disappointed. He'd already given a deposition in this case and in the last week of October he and Julie intended to travel to Georgia to visit some of her relatives. Now they would have to reschedule their trip. His mother was always getting him involved in something that changed his plans.

The day that Seth was served with the subpoena, Backus came to Steamboat and stayed at the bed and breakfast. Before he arrived, Jill called her son from Greeley and told him to put Backus in bungalow number 8, because it had a back door and would allow him to come and go from the establishment inconspicuously. Seth agreed to do this for his mother.

Then she called back and changed her mind. She told her son to switch Backus to number 9, but then she said to put him in bungalow 1, because that room offered the best view of the rear of Boggs Hardware, which was just across the street. From number 1, he could clearly see the store's parking lot. Seth put Backus in number 1.

That evening, the young man was walking his two Dobermans near the bed and breakfast when he saw Backus coming toward him carrying a plastic grocery bag. The bag was weighted down and held what appeared to be a heavy object. The sight of the bag filled Seth with discomfort, but he didn't know what to say or do.

Jill had once told her oldest son that Backus had a "clean, untraceable" .22-caliber pistol. Seth knew that his mother herself had a 9 millimeter U.S. government-issue handgun; a stun gun; a couple of .38s; and a .32-caliber pistol. Jill had also told Seth that she knew someone who could kill Gerry Boggs, but this person lived a few hours from Steamboat and would have to drive a considerable distance before committing the murder.

"Do you want to see what I've got in here?" Backus said, holding up the bag.

"No," Seth said, "I don't."

"You know that we're doing this for you kids, don't you?"

"I gotta go," Seth told him, walking away from the man and pulling his dogs behind him, moving back toward the bed and breakfast.

He went into the house next to the bed and breakfast units and did something that his mother had strictly forbidden him to do. He told his wife the truth about what had just happened with Backus. He described the bag. He said something heavy was inside it. He spoke openly to Julie, even though Jill had insisted that he not even tell the young woman that Backus was in Steamboat Springs tonight.

The following morning, a Saturday, Backus left the bed and breakfast to attend a meeting of the National Guard (for years he'd been a member in good standing with the organization). A few hours after he departed, Jill arrived in Steamboat alone. She normally drove a red Paseo, but on this occasion she was in a gray Toyota Forerunner. Someone, she told her son when he asked about the Toyota, had punctured the gas tank of the Paseo and she was convinced that it had been Gerry Boggs.

Seth quickly realized that his mother was in a bad mood. She was angry at Backus, angry at his cowardice and lack of resolve. The telephone repairman, she told Seth, looked at her as his retirement plan, and someday she would have to get rid of him.

~~ "What's the best way," she asked Seth once again, "to get into Gerry's home?"

He shook his head, meaning that he didn't want to talk about this.

"Should I break the kitchen window?"

"No," he told her. "The neighbors would hear you."

"Should I go through the garage door?"

"Someone might see you."

"What about the back door?"

Seth shrugged. The hardest thing in the world for him to do was to ignore the person standing in front of him, asking him questions.

Jill told him that he had to get Julie out of the house for the coming week—get her out of Steamboat. She said she would buy the younger woman a plane ticket, so Julie could fly to Idaho and look for some real estate for her and her husband. The couple had lately been thinking of moving away from Colorado, and this was a good time, Jill insisted, for them to start looking for a home in the Northwest. When Seth hinted that his wife did not want to leave just now, Jill said that one day he would have to get rid of Julie, too.

That night, Jill stayed in unit number 7, and before going to sleep, she asked Seth to come to her room and fix her VCR. He complied and had soon repaired it so that his mother could watch a movie while lying in bed.

"Would you help me with the body?" she asked

him, while he was fiddling with the back of the VCR.

"What do you mean?"

"Would you help me remove it?"

He kept working.

"Would you put his body in his car, after he's dead, and drive it to the airport?"

"The airport?"

"Yes. The Steamboat airport. Just leave it there. In his car."

"I . . . uh—"

"Would you do that for me?"

He bent over the VCR, studying it more closely.

"You don't have to do anything else. Just take his body to the airport."

The next morning Seth told Julie that no matter what his mother said or offered her, he did not want her to fly to Idaho and be gone during the week ahead. He needed Julie there with him, at the bed and breakfast, every day, talking to him and helping him resist his mother's demands. He couldn't trust what he might do—or not do—if Julie went away. She promised not to leave.

Jill left on Sunday at noon. She drove back to Greeley but would soon return to Steamboat. She was in motion now, gathering speed. She was always in motion, but rarely in such a focused way, zigging and zagging across Colorado, driving over mountains and through valleys, changing cars and making phone calls to her son and her lover, refining plans and sharpening words. She'd put together some disguises—wigs and bulky men's clothing, a mustache, and a long, scraggly brown beard that she liked to attach to her chin and wear as a kind of joke. It was fun to pretend that sometimes she was a woman and sometimes she was a man. She enjoyed changing her identity by merely altering her apparel. This appealed to her sense of humor and her creativity. It made her laugh and feel as if she was getting away with something naughty.

Jill was skulking now, scurrying around. She was talking faster and harder. She was trying on wigs. She had a base in Greeley and a base in Steamboat, and she moved quickly from one to the other. Everyone was watching her, but nobody could see what she was doing. Not Gerry or Thane or Judy or Vance or Doug Boggs. Not William Coit (he badly wanted to prevent anyone else from being hurt by his mother, but he was too far away), and not Andrew Coit, and not even Seth. Not Larry English. Not Carl Steely or any of her other living ex-husbands.

Jill was slipping through back doors at the bed and breakfast and sneaking through the alley behind the hardware store. She was talking about guns. She was looking for keys. She was trying on bandanas and telling Julie that she looked like Aunt Jemima. She was ready to break windows or jimmy doors—to drive a body to the airport. She was laughing and telling Julie about putting a bunch of snakes in Gerry's car, because he hated snakes most of all. She was planning her wardrobe.

Once before, back in the fall of 1992, she'd donned a blond wig, borrowed from a Greeley beautician, and worn it in Steamboat during the course of a weekend to see if anyone recognized her. No one did, she later told Seth. On another occasion, she said, she'd put on a wig, a mustache, and overalls, then she'd walked into Boggs Hardware, looked at the merchandise, and spoken to several of the employees. They hadn't recognized her, either.

Some people often see things coming, or feel them, or sense them in a way that is difficult to explain. Maybe it's nothing more than a feeling in the bones or a charge along the skin, a hint of the future in the air. No one in Steamboat Springs was more receptive to such things than Cathy McCullough.

"I feel cheated," Cathy once said, "because once Gerry became involved in the civil suit, we saw less and less of him. He was so busy with that and with all the investigating and legal work that led up to it. Because of this, we lost out on some time with him, time that we never got back. He no longer dropped by our house. He no longer came over for dinner or spent time playing with our kids. He didn't participate very much with us anymore. I feel really robbed because I saw so little of him the last couple of years.

"When I would go into the hardware store and see him, he was in his own little world. You could see that in his eyes. My husband kept saying to me, 'I can't wait until this is over, so we can get Gerry back.' One day, I said to Bob, 'I'm scared. I think she might do something crazy.' We knew she was hiding behind the dumpster in back of the store.

"I saw Gerry in the store in early or mid-October. The court date was a week or two away. I went up to him and said, 'Be careful.' He just looked at me and said, 'She can't do anything to me.' "

Twenty-one

On Sunday, October 17, Jill called Seth and told him that she and Backus were going camping during the upcoming week. They would be staying out-of-doors—a statement that struck her son as highly unusual, if not downright improbable. His mother was not the sort of person who'd ever enjoyed roughing it in the woods. She liked warm baths, cozy rooms, and the indoor luxuries that money could buy. She liked pampering herself, especially when she was in a feminine mood. She'd also recently had painful hip surgery, which made her an even less likely candidate for the travails of autumn camping in the chilly high country. But Seth wasn't one to quibble with or question his mother's plans.

On Monday morning, the eighteenth, after Jill had returned to Greeley, Seth went into number 7 of the bed and breakfast, where his mother had just stayed. She'd told him not to clean the room because she would be coming back soon, but he looked around to see if there was anything—leftover food or drinks—that needed to be removed before they spoiled. Finding nothing, he left the unit and resumed doing his other chores. That evening, his mother phoned again, and he expected her to ask him to do something for her. She surprised him by simply saying that she loved him very much.

On Tuesday morning, Jill called Seth and told him to drive up to Gerry Boggs's house and see if the man was at home. A few hours later, Seth called her back and said that he'd gone to Boggs's residence, but Gerry's Jeep was not there.

"Where is he?" his mother asked.

"I don't know."

Gerry and Thane were hunting elk in the back country around Steamboat Springs. They enjoyed being outside together and it gave them time to talk about the upcoming trial. Thane was planning on returning to Denver soon, but he would be back next week when the proceeding began. The men, along with Vance Halvorson and Judy Prier-Lewis, were fully prepared for the courtroom, with charts and graphs and other documents that would show precisely where Jill Coit had been during the past three decades and what she had done. In a few more days, Halvorson would open their five boxes of information on Jill and let out her past.

Being in the woods together also gave Thane and Gerry time to sit down under a tree and argue some more.

"He was my best friend for forty years," Thane says, "and we had no competition between us, but we didn't agree on anything. Not on religion, not on politics, not on women. Nothing. He loved to sit around and sip brandy and argue about anything. Arguing was a sport with Gerry, like mental exercise. Gerry would take the opposite side of any issue and argue it just for fun. His friends understood how much he enjoyed doing this and never took it personally."

During the week of October 18, the men went hunting several times and shot an elk, but it wandered off into the woods and they were never able to locate it.

While hunting, they spoke openly about their fear of Jill, but Gerry was more worried for Thane, and for Thane's wife and daughter, than for himself. Gerry had once suggested that his friend should find another place to live, but Thane hadn't acted on this suggestion.

This doesn't mean that Gerry felt peaceful when he thought about his ex-wife.

"One time he told me," says Harold Boggs, the white-haired patriarch of the family, "that he was more afraid of that upcoming civil trial than he was when he went over to serve in Vietnam, twenty-five years earlier. He knew the situation was risky, and maybe we should have offered him more protection, but what can you do?"

On Tuesday evening, the nineteenth of October, Seth called William in California. He told his younger brother that he was very concerned about their mother and her boyfriend.

"I think she's going to kill Gerry Boggs," he said.

William didn't know how to respond. He was half a continent away and wasn't certain that Seth was perceiving things accurately. Their mother talked a lot about what she might do to others, but most of it was just talk. He told Seth that it was very important now to keep him closely informed about any new developments.

Jill did not phone her older son on Wednesday, October 20. She did not call him again until the following afternoon.

Twenty-two

Thursday, October 21, was warm in Steamboat, almost balmy for this late in the year. Rain had come earlier in the week, but it was gone now. A few translucent clouds hung on the face of the mountains and a breeze shook the stands of fading aspen. The trees were yellow and gold, and from a distance, they resembled patches of frozen sunlight. In autumn, signs welcoming deer hunters to this part of the Rockies were prominent. So were ranch hands wearing black hats and big mustaches. So were muddy pickups. This morning, traces of Indian summer were on the wind and local people felt they were stealing one more day from the harsh winter to come.

Gerry Boggs went to work as usual on Thursday, arriving at the store well after his brother had opened the doors at 7:30. Gerry went into his office and spent some time on his computer, gazing at the screen and taking in the statistics that reflected the state of affairs at Boggs Hardware. He liked studying numbers, playing with them, moving them around. They were clean and neat and manageable; they lined up in rows and did what you expected them

Jill with her ninth husband, Gerry W. Boggs, at a social function in Steamboat Springs, Colorado.

Gerry Boggs was one of the most eligible bachelors in Steamboat Springs before he met and married Jill. (*Courtesy of the McCullough family*)

Known as "Uncle Gerry" around town, Boggs was universally liked because of his caring heart and gentle demeanor with children. (*Courtesy of the McCullough family*)

The front of Boggs Hardware in Steamboat Springs. (*Courtesy of Joyce Jacques Singular*)

The Oak Street Bed & Breakfast, formerly owned by Jill and Gerry Boggs. (*Courtesy of Joyce Jacques Singular*)

Doug Boggs, Gerry's brother, and his wife Jan.
(*Courtesy of Joyce Jacques Singular*)

Bob McCullough, long-time friend and employee of Gerry
Boggs, and his wife Cathy in their Steamboat Springs home.
(*Courtesy of Joyce Jacques Singular*)

Gerry Boggs shared this home with Jill until they separated. He was found murdered in the kitchen on October 22, 1993.
(*Courtesy of Joyce Jacques Singular*)

Gerry Boggs as the police found him after his murder.

The gravestone of Gerry Boggs in a small cemetery outside of Steamboat Springs. *(Courtesy of Joyce Jacques Singular)*

A photo taken of Jill Boggs disguised as a man in Steamboat Springs shortly before the murder.

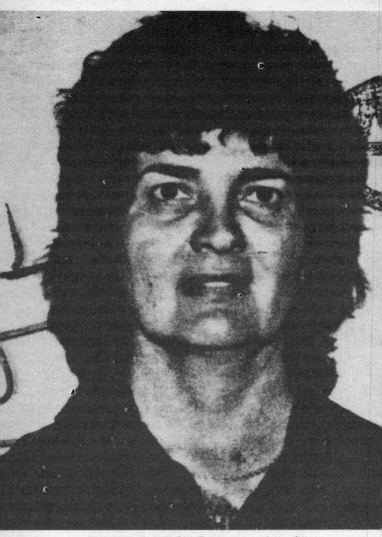

This photo of Jill Coit Boggs was taken after
she fled the United States.

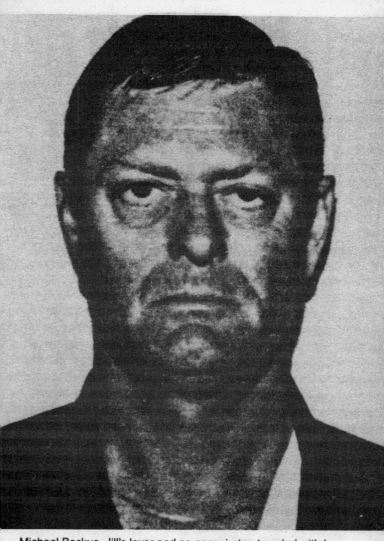
Michael Backus, Jill's lover and co-conspirator, traveled with her after they committed the murder.

Routt County District Attorney Paul McLimans (*left*) and
Assistant District Attorney Kerry St. James successfully
prosecuted Jill Coit Boggs and Michael Backus.
(*Courtesy of Joyce Jacques Singular*)

The tiny mountain town of Hot Sulphur Springs where Coit and
Backus stood trial. (*Courtesy of Joyce Jacques Singular*)

Grand County Courthouse in Hot Sulphur Springs.
(*Courtesy of Joyce Jacques Singular*)

Routt County Investigator Tim Garner (*left*), Steamboat
Springs Homicide Detective Richard Crotz (*center*),
Colorado Bureau of Investigation Agent Susan Kitchen.
(*Courtesy of Joyce Jacques Singular*)

Jill Coit Boggs immediately after being sentenced to
life in prison for the murder of Gerry Boggs.
(*Courtesy of Joyce Jacques Singular*)

to do. They didn't fight with you or defy logic or act in ways that could only be called perverse. They weren't cruel. They gave him satisfaction and aesthetic pleasure. They made sense to Gerry, and being around them was almost always comforting.

He stayed at the store until 1 P.M., then walked down the street a few doors to a casual restaurant known as the Shack. He ordered eggs, potatoes, and toast, eating his food while glancing at a newspaper and nodding hello to a few familiar faces. After paying for the meal, he left the Shack and got into his green Jeep, which was parked where it always was, behind Boggs Hardware. He wasn't feeling particularly well this afternoon—he had too much on his mind—and decided to take the rest of the day off. He drove away from the store slowly, not paying much attention to this stretch of road because he'd driven it so many times before, moving up a long and winding incline at the edge of town and steering in the direction of home.

At 8:30 that morning, Debbie Fedewa had seen something startling. She lived on a hillside east of town, just across the street from Gerry's residence. Both their houses sat on a cul-de-sac on Hillside Court West and both offered a magnificent view of the Yampa Valley and the surrounding mountains. As Debbie was coming home and approaching her driveway this morning, she noticed two people walking together along her street, two people whom she'd never seen before and was certain did not live in the neighborhood. One was a white man, roughly 45 years old and six feet tall, with a slim build and light-colored dirty-blond hair. He had on a tan canvaslike jacket, blue jeans, and a brightly colored cap.

His companion was also white and approximately the same age, but stood about five feet five and had a much stockier build. Wearing a blue jacket, light-blue jeans, and a blue cap, the individual had a mustache and a ponytail hanging down from the back of the cap. At a glance, Debbie was convinced that the mustache was not a real growth of hair, because it was much darker than the hair on the person's head. And while the shorter figure was obviously dressed to resemble a man, Debbie instinctively felt that it was a woman in men's clothing. The lines of the body were all wrong for a male. The hips were too wide, the shoulders too narrow. The buttocks were flat, Debbie noticed, and all in all, the shape was decidedly female.

As she stared through her car window at this woman in disguise, the odd figure stared right back at her. When their eyes met, Debbie started, a rush of fear jabbing her chest. She looked away but then glanced back, so upset by this silent interaction that once she'd parked her car and walked into her home, she immediately locked all her doors, something she'd never felt compelled to do in Steamboat Springs. Moments later, she looked out the window, scanning the cul-de-sac and gazing across the street, anxious to see what the strangers were doing. They'd disappeared.

At 2 P.M., Debbie was out in her yard, stacking firewood, when she glanced up and saw the duo again. They were walking along her street once more, strolling in the cul-de-sac, looking out of place on Hillside Court West. They walked with their hands in their pockets, as if the day were cold, but it was warm for late October. They were overdressed for the weather. This time Debbie was so alarmed by their presence that she stopped what she was doing, went inside the house, and was afraid to look outside again for several minutes. When she finally did so, the couple had vanished, but she was still not comfortable enough to go out and resume piling firewood.

Two hours later, a pair of young girls, Andrea Thorne and Alyssa Re, walked up to the back door of Gerry's home, eager to sell him some "Girl Scout nuts." The girls knew from experience that he was a notoriously soft touch for such products: he could not drive by a lemonade stand in the summertime without stopping his car, getting out, and buying at least one drink for himself. He was known throughout town as someone who left generous tips for kids selling treats.

Andrea and Alyssa were disappointed this afternoon, because when they rang the man's doorbell, they received no response. Alyssa thought this was unusual, because she'd noticed that one side of Gerry's two-car garage was open and his Jeep was parked inside. The girls tried the door several times before turning away and walking toward another house.

Seth spent Thursday afternoon visiting a printshop, talking with a friend of his named Matt Modica, and washing his car in the parking lot of the bed and breakfast. At 4 P.M., he was still working on the vehicle, while Matt stood by and watched him. Seth had scrubbed the car and rinsed it meticulously, the same way he did many things. Now he was carefully drying it off and making sure that he'd removed as much of the dirt and grime as he could, before winter came again and covered the car with mud and ice and snow.

The phone rang and Seth went inside to get it.

"Oak Street Bed and Breakfast," he said into the receiver. "Can I help you?"

"Hey, baby," the familiar voice said in his ear. "It's over, and it's messy."

He recoiled as the words penetrated, a surge of panic rising up from his stomach and spreading through his whole body.

"Don't fucking talk to me like that over the phone!" he said to his mother.

"It's over," she said, hanging up.

He went back to the parking lot, trying to act as if nothing had happened. He didn't want Matt or anyone else to know anything about his mother. Maybe she'd been lying, he told himself, but from the tone of her voice, Seth believed she was serious.

Matt soon left, and by 5:30, Julie had returned to the bed and breakfast. She'd gone biking earlier in the day, before taking their Dobermans to the veterinarian. When Seth told her about the phone call, her first reactions were shock and disbelief, but these were quickly followed by a more practical response: they needed to make some plans for this evening, plans that would give them an alibi and make them look innocent. They decided to go out to dinner and then to a bar, so that people would see them and realize they were not hiding from anyone. They were acting perfectly normally, just as they'd done on many other nights, but tonight they wanted to be seen by as many people in Steamboat as possible.

They ate dinner at a local restaurant and then went to the Smokehouse Tavern, where they ran into Mindy Miller, a woman who'd worked at the bed and breakfast. They made small talk with her and had similar conversations with other people in the bar. After going home, they'd tried to sleep, but it had come only fitfully, as they lay in the dark and wondered when they might receive another call—this one from the police.

Early the next morning, Seth went outside and stood in the front yard of the bed and breakfast, looking across the street, straining his eyes and watching the parking lot behind the hardware store, hoping to see Gerry's Jeep pull into the lot. Seth knew the man's schedule. He knew when Gerry arrived for work, knew when he left for lunch, and knew when he went home. He knew how long it took Gerry to drive from his home to downtown. Seth had stood here before, on his mother's orders, and seen the man come and go. He knew when Gerry was early and he knew when he was late.

This morning, he was late, and then he was later, and by noon Seth doubted that he was coming in at all.

Twenty-three

Twenty-three and a half hours after Jill called Seth on the afternoon of October 21, Doug Boggs pulled up in front of his brother's house. He'd driven out to 870 Hillside Court West after not being able to reach Gerry by phone on Thursday evening or Friday morning. He'd come here because he was starting to get worried. It wasn't like his brother to miss the appointment they'd scheduled this afternoon with an architect. And even if Gerry was out hunting with Thane, he would probably have called the store by now.

When Doug arrived at 3:30 P.M. and stepped out of his Ford Bronco, staring up at Gerry's home and then gingerly approaching it, he had a bad feeling that only grew worse when he saw Gerry's Jeep parked in its usual spot in the half-open garage. Doug couldn't help wondering where Jill Coit was at this exact moment.

It would not have been at all comforting to the man to know that Jill was more than a hundred miles to the east, having her nails done at a manicurist's shop in Greeley, chatting nonstop with Sue Heiser.

Jill was telling Sue that her ex-husband was homosexual, that he liked to have sex with men who lived outside Steamboat Springs, and that because of all this, she was involved in a suit with her former spouse. Her trial was set to begin next week and the legal issue was slander. When Jill asked Sue if she knew a good attorney in town, the manicurist mentioned a lawyer named Bob Ray.

While the women talked, Michael Backus went about his job as a repairman at the phone company. His appearance at work this morning at 7 A.M. had come as a big surprise to his colleagues and his superiors, because just a few days earlier, he'd asked for and received the rest of the week off. When he returned to U.S. West on Friday morning, he told some of his co-workers that he and Jill had stayed outdoors the night before at the Kelly Flats campground in the Poudre Canyon, located between Greeley and Steamboat Springs. Backus said they'd used some new camping equipment and had filled out a card at the campground that stated that the couple had spent the evening at Kelly Flats. They'd left the card in a box at the campsite, Backus said, along with four dollars for the use of the facilities.

Doug tried two doors that were locked before climbing the few steps that led to the back door of his brother's home. This one was unlocked, but something heavy was blocking it. He pushed on it hard, until the door gradually gave, allowing him to step inside the kitchen. What he saw was not just horrible, but something surrounded by the residue of extreme cruelty.

Gerry was stretched out on his side on a throw rug, which covered a section of the parquet floor. He wore blue jeans, tennis shoes, and a blue jacket. Bullet holes had ripped his chest. Blood had been splattered on the parquet, on the walls, on the floor, and on a plastic bag near the man's body. Doug saw blood on one of Gerry's hands and blood near his brother's head.

Dried blood was caked on Gerry's face. His eyes were partially open and bloodshot. His brow held a deep gash—a long, ugly dent that had fractured his skull. He had been viciously beaten.

A propped-up shovel in a small bathroom, just off the kitchen, had blood on its handle. A discharged bullet lay five feet away on the floor. Gerry was cold to the touch. The house was unbelievably quiet.

Doug saw everything and understood everything in an instant, but he could not take all of it in. He felt numb and for a moment or two, he froze, unable to take another step, before running toward the phone and dialing 911.

After the police came to 870 Hillside Court West, Doug was asked to go downtown and answer a number of questions about how he and Gerry had been getting along lately. Then he was forced to give blood and strip naked in front of one of the cops.

Officer Kevin Parker drove to the murder scene first, arriving at 3:39 P.M. Detective Richard Crotz came next. Crotz had worked as a policeman in San Diego for several years before moving to Steamboat Springs and becoming a detective. He would be the lead investigator on the case.

As Crotz studied the body, he found three gunshot wounds and a deep bruise on the victim's right cheek. He saw the bloody shovel in the bathroom. There were no signs of a forcible entry into the home, no indication of ransacking. Boggs's TV and stereo were intact, but it looked to the detective as if a struggle might have taken place in the kitchen.

Before he was taken downtown by Officer Robert Del Valle, Doug told Crotz about the longstanding civil suit that Gerry had been involved in with Jill Coit. His brother, Doug said, had discovered that woman had a deep criminal past, full of bigamies, financial scams, and false claims of pregnancy, and she could have even been responsible for the murder of an ex-husband in Houston two decades earlier. At least some of these things, Doug explained, were to have been revealed at the upcoming trial.

Doug also told the detective that Gerry had lately been receiving—and recording—harassing phone calls from the woman. Tapes of those calls should have been in his brother's answering machine, but when Crotz located the machine, he saw that the tapes were missing.

Dr. Michael Dobersen soon arrived at the residence, but the police decided to do a thorough search of the house before letting Dobersen inside to examine the body more closely. While conducting that search, the officers found no murder weapon, no fingerprints, no footprints, no trace evidence of hair or fibers or other material, and no obvious clues of any kind. In the upstairs of Boggs's home, they did see two used condoms. They would be booked into evidence and the semen would be studied closely.

It was 1 A.M. on Saturday morning before Dobersen

was finally able to start examining the victim. He learned that "gunshot wounds to the trunk" had killed Gerry Boggs and that the dead man had suffered "large lacerations and a skull fracture." He also noticed some mysterious marks near Gerry's right ear, small red impressions that the doctor did not initially consider all that relevant to the murder investigation. He would later change his mind.

Twenty-four

At 4:30 that Friday afternoon, while Doug was sitting at the police station, a phone call came into Boggs Hardware. A local woman who listened to Steamboat's police radio band had just heard about a death at the residence of Gerry Boggs, and she thought the people at the store should know this at once. The employee who took the call, Judee Duerst, told Bob McCullough and then ran to the bathroom, crying and holding her stomach, barely able to speak. When she came out, McCullough suggested that she leave work and go find her husband, because she was in shock and needed help.

"Even after Judee told me about the call," says McCullough, "we weren't sure who was dead. Gerry's dad, Harold, was in the store with us, but I didn't know whether to go talk to him or not. I didn't know what to do. Then Doug's wife, Jan, called and told me that Gerry was dead. She asked me if Harold was there and I said he was. She said they were coming down to tell him.

"I waited and didn't talk to any of the other employees until the immediate family members arrived.

I just hung out in a back room and tried to find something to do. It was a long wait. Harold's wife, Sylvia, and Jan arrived at five o'clock. They took Harold outside and told him.

"We close at five-thirty. At quitting time, I told the other employees what had happened. People were just totally stunned. So was I. I'd never had a feeling like that in my life. It was like giving birth, I suppose. I've always respected what women go through in childbirth, because I know that I can never feel that.

"After hearing about the murder, I never experienced anything like the sickness that went through my body and settled into my stomach. I can still feel it there, months and months later. I worked with Gerry for more than twenty years. He was the godfather to my son. He treated him like he was his own. To take what's in your heart after you lose someone like Gerry and try to put that into words— it's just very, very difficult."

Seth didn't hear from his mother on Friday, but late in the day, he went back into number 7 at the bed and breakfast, the same one Jill had stayed in earlier. He carefully looked around. The room smelled a little funny, but there was nothing unusual on the bed, nothing in the toilet. He glanced in the bathroom sink and saw what he took to be drops of blood, several of them, and he found a towel that also appeared to have blood on it. On top of the television was a cap—his cap—with the words "EADS Bulldozer" sewn on the face of it. The last time he'd been in the room, the cap had not been there, nor had the towel, nor the drops that looked like blood.

Seth furiously began cleaning number 7. He swept the floor, he wiped down the furniture. He got some Comet and scrubbed the toilet. He scoured the tub and the sink. He bleached all the towels. He dropped his baseball cap into a coffee can that he'd filled with water and bleach. After strenuously washing the hat, he removed it from the can and tore it into small pieces. Then he dug a hole on the side of the bed and breakfast and buried the pieces in the ground.

The next morning at 11:30, a local real estate agent called the bed and breakfast and asked Seth if he'd heard the news that Gerry Boggs had been murdered in his home. Seth said no, he wasn't aware of that.

His mother called several times that day and left messages on his answering machine. She told her son that in the past few days she'd gone to a movie in Denver with her latest husband, Roy Carroll, and she'd also shopped at a Denver mall with a friend. She gave very specific times for when she'd done these things, and she told Seth not to talk to the police about anything.

Several officers came by the bed and breakfast on Saturday around noon and asked Seth to accompany them to the police station in downtown Steamboat Springs. He was cordial and did as they'd requested, but after going to the station, he told them that he knew nothing whatsoever about the death of Gerry Boggs. And he knew nothing whatsoever about where his mother had gone after her most recent visit to Steamboat. Seth tried to act calm around the authorities, but inside, he was quaking, terrified of being blamed for something he hadn't done—and something he also hadn't prevented from happening.

That night he again called his brother, William, from a pay phone in Steamboat, certain that his own phone was now tapped. He told William about Gerry's death and about their mother's phone call on Thursday afternoon. He mentioned that she'd used the words "over" and "messy."

If it was too late for the brothers to stop their mother from acting on her rages and her whims, and too late to keep Gerry alive, it was not too late to talk about whose side they were really on. Did their loyalty belong to Jill, finally, or did it belong to something that was larger than their mother?

For William, the answer was becoming more and more clear. Others had suffered enough at her hands. Others would keep suffering until someone did something to bring her reign of terror to a halt.

For Seth, the issues were far more complicated. He was still living in the bed and breakfast, still working for his mother, still receiving phone calls from her telling him exactly what he could—and could not—do. He wasn't quite ready to make the crucial separation from the person who had raised him. That separation would not simply involve distancing himself geographically or emotionally from the woman, as many adult children were forced to do with their parents. The process would go far beyond that. If he came forward and spoke the truth, he had the power to take away his mother's life.

On Sunday morning, the twenty-fourth, Jill arrived at the bed and breakfast with her ninth husband, sixty-eight-year-old Roy Carroll. She was driving her red Paseo. When she and Seth were alone at the bed and breakfast, she spoke to him as she always had in the past, when she wanted to make sure that he was following orders.

"You didn't talk to the police, did you?" she said.

He nodded sheepishly, afraid to say yes.

"Why did you do that?"

"They came here and . . ."

"Don't fucking talk to them," she said. "Don't do that to me."

"Why did you call me Thursday afternoon and tell me that it was over?"

She glared at him.

"I didn't want to get involved in this."

"You *are* involved in it," she said. "Did the police say when the time of death was?"

"No."

"Are you sure?"

"I don't know anything about the time of death. I went into room seven and—"

"Room seven? Why did you do that?"

"I cleaned it."

Now she smiled at him. "That's good. That's very good. What else have you done since I've been gone?"

"Nothing."

"Good."

At noon, Detective Crotz went to the bed and breakfast and spoke to Seth. He asked if his mother was in town, and the young man hesitated before responding, trying to think of the answer that would be least painful. He wanted to cooperate with the officer, but he didn't want to hurt his mother. Yet

169

he'd fabricated enough lies on her behalf. If she wanted to avoid questioning by the police, why had she come back to Steamboat Springs? Why couldn't she have just left town and stayed away? Why did she always put him in these impossible positions? Seth knew only one thing for certain: he wasn't nearly as gifted a liar as his mother was.

"She's in unit four," he told Detective Crotz.

"Go get her," the man said.

Reluctantly, Seth walked out to room number 4 and knocked on the door. When he informed his mother that a police officer was at the bed and breakfast and wanted to talk to her, she exploded, swearing at her son and demanding to know why he'd told the detective that she was in Steamboat Springs.

He tugged at one of his earlobes, something he often did when he was uncomfortable.

"Tell that detective," she said, "that I'm not coming out to speak to him. He can talk to my lawyer if he wants to. My attorney's name is Randall Klauzer, and his number is in the phone book."

Seth walked back into the house and reported her message to Detective Crotz.

The officer wasn't sure what to do. Ever since Gerry's body had been found two days earlier, he'd been learning more and more about the ongoing conflict that had existed between Jill Coit and the dead man. He'd been told about this by Doug Boggs, Vance Halvorson, Thane Gilliland, and other sources. By now, he realized that the person with the strongest motive for getting rid of Gerry was not his brother or anyone else in the Boggs family. It was most likely the woman in unit 4. Yet Crotz had no physical evidence linking her to the crime; he had no witnesses, no solid information from anyone who knew her, nothing that was at all tangible. He just had some ugly rumors that had been flying around the civil suit—rumors that had only grown uglier since the murder.

Crotz wasn't ready to charge Jill with anything and he thought that perhaps he should wait before approaching her directly. If she was in Steamboat now, she would probably stay in town a while longer. He didn't want to scare her away, and he was going to need much more than rumors to make his case, so he decided not to go to unit 4. He quietly left the bed and breakfast.

Seth felt momentarily relieved.

That afternoon, he felt even better when his mother told him to leave town tomorrow, to go ahead and take the driving trip down to Georgia that he and Julie had been planning for weeks. Jill would stay on in Steamboat, she said, and handle any problems that arose. Seth was very grateful that she wanted him to go away.

That evening, Vance Halvorson and his wife, Sharon, were driving around Steamboat when she glanced through her windshield at an oncoming car and was struck dumb. She did a double-take, looking once more to make sure that she wasn't hallucinating. The vehicle that had just passed her, a red Paseo, was indeed real, and the driver had looked strangely familiar.

"That was Jill!" she said to her husband. "She was dressed up in that disguise!"

Both Sharon and Vance turned around and stared at the car that was moving away from them in the distance.

"I can't believe she would do that," Sharon said.

By Sunday evening, Debbie Fedewa had already come forward and told the police that last Thursday afternoon she'd seen two suspicious-looking figures walking near Gerry Boggs's residence. She'd reported that one of them was tall and male, while the other was shorter and female, with a stocky build and wearing what appeared to be a fake mustache. This information had been passed along to the Boggs family, the Halvorsons, and others who were close to the investigation.

Sharon knew that Jill owned a red Paseo, but what had struck her this evening was that the person behind the wheel of the Paseo was wearing a long, phony mustache. The driver was Jill, Sharon was convinced, dressed up in a man's disguise.

That same evening, Doug Boggs was paying his respects to Gerry at the Shearon Funeral Home, located right across from the courthouse, when he glanced out the window and saw a red car go past. The driver wore a long, scraggly mustache. Doug stared in utter disbelief. Was Jill driving around town in the costume that she'd worn to kill his brother?

Twenty-five

On Monday morning Doug Boggs again put all of his employees on alert—beware of a man or a woman lurking in the alley behind the store or standing on the front sidewalk or coming in the door. If you see anything unusual, get out at once, just turn and run . . .

Doug was afraid for his family, and in the first days after the murder, he and Jan had friends stay all night at their house, which is a few miles outside of town, in an isolated wooded area near the foothills. Alternating with their friends, an off-duty police officer came to their residence and spent the night, so the couple could get some sleep. On one occasion, Jan arose in the dark hours of the morning, got out of bed half-awake, and saw the officer standing in her living room—momentarily forgetting who he was.

The man scared her stiff.

"We lived in total fear from the moment I found Gerry in his home on Friday afternoon," says Doug. "We didn't know what she would do next. I kept calling the police and telling them to arrest her now—get her while she was still in Steamboat or Greeley, get her before she killed someone else—but they didn't believe me for a while."

Jan and Doug locked their windows and doors, precautions they'd never had to take while living in the countryside. They had friends looking out for their house, when they were not at home. They had a gun handy, in case they noticed anyone menacing near their property.

In the morning, when Doug went to work, or at noon when he went to lunch, or in the evening, when he was leaving the store for the day, he frequently looked across the street and saw Seth lingering in the front yard of the bed and breakfast, staring at the back of Boggs Hardware and gazing at Doug in silence.

"I think," says Jan, "that Seth just wanted to say he was sorry."

"I thought," says Doug, "he wanted to kill me."

Thane Gilliland was so frightened for his family that he moved his wife and daughter out of the house for a month after the murder. Thane knew that Jill was always armed, and in the days following the killing, he told the police about seeing two guns in a car she'd once driven to his home.

Judy Prier-Lewis would have been more fearful had she not been a private investigator. Fifteen years of experience in her field had left her less naive and innocent than most of the people she knew. She'd looked deeply enough into Jill's past to know that she was dangerous, yet she was shocked by what had occurred in Steamboat Springs.

"By mid-October," she says, "I was somewhat nervous, but I thought if Jill did anything, she'd hire someone to beat the stuffing out of Gerry on a country road. I didn't think she was stupid enough to kill him five days before the start of the trial."

Following the murder, Vance Halvorson began receiving hang-up calls. He and his wife, Sharon, had become increasingly wary of the strangers they saw driving or walking in Steamboat; wary of going out in their car; wary of picking up the phone, of answering the door, of performing their everyday rituals. They weren't at all used to feeling this way in their community.

Bob and Cathy McCullough were in a state of alarm. It was extremely difficult for them to try to explain to their children, Colleen and Mark, that their father's business partner, one of the family's best friends and Mark's godfather, had been shot to death.

"Our son," says Cathy, "was devastated by Gerry's murder. He became silent and didn't want to talk about any of it. But our daughter was just the opposite. She wanted to talk about it. We made a point of telling them everything, so they would hear it from us and not hear the lies and half-truths that were going around town. People in small towns talk a lot, so you need to be very honest with your children."

The McCulloughs were worried about more than their kids hearing falsehoods.

"After the murder," Cathy says, "we screwed the windows of our home down tight. Bob slept with a baseball bat. We locked everything we had. We didn't allow the kids to walk down the street by themselves. We called their school and told the teachers and administrators to be extraprotective of them. They were to take no phone calls from anyone except Bob and me, and no one was allowed to come there and visit them."

If fear ran rampant in Steamboat, an enormous amount of anger was also stirring, and much of it was directed toward the bed and breakfast.

"Seth's role in all this never bothered me that much," says Cathy, "but Julie's did. I thought that she might have been able to stop what happened. She knew what Jill was capable of and she had heard things for a long time, but she was frightened of her mother-in-law. But still . . . if I found out that someone was going to be murdered, I would call the police, whether they listened to me or not."

The discomfort that virtually everyone in Steamboat had felt around Jill Coit for years was finally being acknowledged and vented. No one had to pretend any longer that she was just an eccentric middle-aged woman—with a penchant for marriage. No one had to look the other way or hold his tongue—out of concern for Gerry's feelings. No one had to deny that with her sweet smile, her instant charm, her constant banter, and her faded Southern accent, Jill was utterly terrifying.

Some of the local citizens began taking up a collection for the Boggs family. It was not to be used for Gerry's funeral expenses, or for his headstone in the cemetery, or for anything having to do with the settlement of his estate. There was money enough for those things. It was to be spent on finding Jill (rumor had it that she'd disappeared), on arresting her, and on bringing her to the Routt County courthouse on Main Street, where she could be tried, convicted, and given the harshest possible sentence. If the death penalty was an option, they were ready to exercise it.

If the townspeople had thrown away the principle of the presumption of innocence and already declared her guilty of first-degree murder, that was just the way they felt. They'd been indulgent and forgiving long enough. They'd pushed their own values aside to accommodate someone who made them feel squeamish. As a result of their indulgence, a native son had been taken from them, a gentle man who purchased lemonade from kids and bought other people's children expensive Christmas gifts.

Gerry might have had some unusual or cantankerous notions, he might have read some peculiar books, he might have been argumentative or ponderous on occasion, he might have held inflammatory political opinions, but his death confirmed one of the strongest of all feelings that run through small towns: if he was different from other people, he was still one of theirs. If he thought too much, he was Steamboat's thinker. The town felt his loss bitterly.

"A lot of folks around here hate Jill Coit and everything she represents," Bob McCullough said, after the murder. "That's a perfectly natural reaction for them to have, because Gerry never did anything but good in his life, and she never did anything but bad. Calling him a bisexual or a homosexual like that— how ugly can you get? When you're finally trapped and caught in your own lies, you just blame everything on the homosexuals, right? Gerry wasn't gay. He was just an intelligent man who felt things deeply.

"I don't hate Jill, per se. I try to understand her. I look at her as a rabid dog that has to be put down so that you can get on with the rest of your life. You can't change her or fix her, so you just put her down."

On Tuesday, October 26, the day before the civil trial had been scheduled to begin, Gerry's funeral was held just off Main Street in the United Methodist Church. The church is located next door to the Oak Street Bed and Breakfast, no more than fifty feet away. Boggs Hardware is visible from the church's front lawn. The sanctuary was crowded with local people and with out-of-town visitors who had come to pay their final respects to Gerry and to offer comfort to his family.

The funeral would have been wrenching for the Boggses under any circumstances, but it was made even more painful by a phone call Doug had received a few hours before the afternoon service commenced.

It was from Jill's lawyer, Richard Tremaine, and he wanted to discuss with Doug the possibility of the Boggs family now releasing the deed that Gerry had held on the bed and breakfast. Jill was anxious to sell the business, and with Gerry's demise, Tremaine indicated, there was no reason to hold her up in putting the bed and breakfast on the market.

Doug was stunned by the timing of the call. And his answer was a resounding No! He didn't want to discuss releasing the deed then, or at any time in the near future.

"Tremaine phoned me," Doug said, more than a year after the funeral, with incredulity still in his voice, "three hours before I'm going to put my brother in the ground. He wanted to talk business. Can you believe that?"

Thane Gilliland gave the eulogy at the funeral.

"I talked about how much Gerry liked to argue and people laughed," he says. "I told them that he was one of the finest people I've ever known, just in the way he was put together. In March of 1991, my four-year-old daughter, Jenna, died. We had a funeral, and then she was cremated. A lot of small children came to our house after the service for her. Gerry was here, too, but for a while we couldn't find him. He wasn't with the adults. I found him in a back room, sitting with the kids on the floor and telling about Jenna. He wanted to be with the children."

Gerry was buried in a hillside cemetery on the northwest edge of town. From the top of the hill, you can see parts of the huge mountain—Mount Werner—which now draws in skiers from all over the world, its high slopes covered with champagne powder eight months of the year. You can see distant peaks of the Rockies, which surround the Yampa Valley and tug at your chest and create the impression that you are standing near the top of the world.

Gerry's headstone was of handsome marble and read:

BOGGS
"Uncle" Gerry W.
OUR BELOVED SON & BROTHER
May 27, 1941 – Oct. 21, 1993

Next to the headstone was the grave of the child of Doug and Jan, Van Douglas, who had died in his second year.

A late autumn breeze comes down off the mountains and blows hard across the hillside. Few trees and no leaves are left to break it or take away its damp penetration. The grass is dead and the graveyard is barren now, and sitting atop the hillside and looking out over the valley, you feel cold.

Twenty-six

As Gerry was being buried on Tuesday, Jill was in Greeley, speaking to a young tenant of hers named Ricky Mott. He worked at a local Pizza Hut, attended the University of Northern Colorado, and lived with a roommate in the basement of the house that Jill and Backus shared at 1309 Eleventh Avenue. The previous Thursday, Jill had made a point of going down to the basement and giving Mott a freshly baked dessert, then telling him that she and Backus were leaving town for the day.

A note accompanying the dessert read, "Here's a Boston cream pie. We've gone camping. Luv ya, Baby." The note struck Mott as unusual for two reasons: Jill was still recovering from hip surgery and had never seemed to him like the outdoors type; and Backus was suffering from the flu. The couple left the house that morning but were back in Greeley the next day.

Mott, a husky blond baby-faced young man of 20, was taking a shower on Friday when Jill knocked on his door and asked him to come outside. Through the door, he told her that he needed a few more minutes to make himself presentable, but she insisted that he talk to her—now. He did as she'd asked, appearing before her wrapped in a towel and shivering.

"We're back from camping," she said, looking up at her young tenant and smiling flirtatiously. "How was the Boston cream pie?"

"Good," he said. "Very good. I shared some of it with my roommate."

"You really liked it?"

He nodded, wondering why she was so concerned about his response to the dessert. In the past, she'd never been this solicitous about anything.

"I'm going to get my hair fixed," she said, "and I've got to run some other errands. I'll be back in a few hours."

Mott didn't see her the rest of that day, or during the next three days, but on Sunday, the twenty-fourth, she called the house and spoke to Backus. She told him to put Mott on the phone and he did.

"If anyone suspicious shows up there," she said to the young man, "don't tell them anything."

"Why would someone suspicious come here?" he said. "What are they looking for?"

"My ex-husband has died, and some people may come around asking questions. Don't say anything more than that you live in the house with me. That's all you know. All right?"

"Yeah. Is there a problem?"

"No."

Two days later, Officer Robert Del Valle of the Steamboat Springs police department came to the Pizza Hut where Mott worked. Mott was upset because Del Valle had tracked him down at his place of employment, but he agreed to speak to the officer. Resisting Del Valle would not have been easy. He is a compact middle-aged man with dark hair and a very solid build. He always looks tough, and at times he looks dangerously serious. If you were creating an image of a police officer who can appear deeply intimidating, it might resemble Robert Del Valle.

Mott told the man that he lived in the basement of the home of Jill Coit and Michael Backus. And he added that he thought Backus worked in Greeley for the utility company. He didn't tell the officer that Jill had made a point of dragging him out of the shower last Friday, so that she could ask him about the Boston cream pie and announce that they were back from their camping trip. He didn't mention being told about the death of her ex-husband or that he was supposed to be on guard against anyone who looked or acted suspicious.

Later that day, when Mott had returned home from work, Jill came to his door and said the two of them needed to take a walk. As he stepped outside, she grabbed his elbow and steered him slowly in the direction of a sidewalk that led toward Twelfth Avenue. She looped her arm through his. She leaned her body against his side, complaining about the pain she still felt from her hip surgery.

To Mott, the woman seemed unusually nervous, talking fast and clinging to him a little too hard. Her breath came in spurts, as if she could barely walk with him, even at this pace. And she kept repeating herself. When he told her that he'd been visited by

183

a policeman earlier in the day, she stopped walking and gave his arm a tug.

"What did you say to him?" she asked.

"Nothing. Just what you told me to. Just that I live in your basement and you're my landlord."

"My ex-husband up in Steamboat Springs was killed."

"Killed?"

"He was murdered. He was a homosexual, and he was killed by one of his gay lovers. If the police come to the house, shut the fucking door, Ricky. Do you understand me? Shut the fucking door and don't talk to them. Tell them they can call my lawyer."

Mott was gazing at her in amazement, taken aback by her tone of voice. "Who's your lawyer?"

"I have two attorneys in Steamboat Springs. The one to call is named Randall Klauzer. He's in the phone book. Tell them to call Klauzer."

"All right."

"If you need a lawyer, he can represent you, too."

Her words scared the young man. "Why would I need a lawyer?"

"Just tell them to call Klauzer. He can answer all their questions."

They'd walked a couple of blocks and then Jill paused to catch her breath. She pulled Mott around until he was looking right at her.

"As long as you don't do anything to harm me," she said, "I won't do anything to hurt you."

He'd never heard this harshness in her voice before or seen this expression on her face. She no longer had a Southern accent, no longer wore the pretty smile of the woman who'd given him the pie. She looked mean, and her words carried a menacing edge.

"My momma and daddy," Mott said, "always raised me to tell the truth."

"I'm really sorry you feel that way. I'm sorry you were brought up like that."

They walked back to the house, the woman still holding his arm and keeping a gingerly pace. He wanted to go much faster, because he was anxious to be alone, but he didn't want her to know that.

When he was by himself in the basement, Ricky decided that he had to call someone and tell them what had just happened, but before he could dial a number, Backus came to the door and stepped inside. He gave Mott Randall Klauzer's home phone number in Steamboat and told him to call the attorney immediately. Backus left and Ricky felt overwhelmed by fear and confusion. He was just a tenant in this house who didn't know what was going on; he didn't want any trouble, and he'd never realized that the people upstairs could be so threatening.

He called his girlfriend and told her he was afraid. He called his parents to ask their advice, but they were out for the evening. He called his sister and she told him to call the police at once.

"The police," she said, "are always right."

He called a Greeley detective he'd met and gotten to know, but the man was out, so he left a message on his phone.

The next morning, Wednesday, the twenty-seventh, Jill called Mott and her voice was again friendly and soft. She said that Ricky would always be welcome to live in their home and that he shouldn't be concerned about paying November's rent. She and Michael might be going away for a while, and if they did, he could live there free for a while and help himself to the food they were leaving behind upstairs.

"You're a very good tenant," she said, "and we won't ever evict you from the basement."

Mott thanked her and hung up.

Michael Backus's supervisor at U.S. West was Neil Wilson. Like virtually everyone else at the phone company, Wilson had long been impressed with Backus's employment record and his dedication to his job. When Backus had asked for a vacation the week of October 18, the supervisor had granted it without asking many questions. Because of the flooding in Iowa, Wilson acknowledged, the repairman had put in considerable overtime, and he deserved some days off.

Backus did not show up for work from October 18 to October 21 and Wilson did not expect to see him on Friday, October 22. Yet the supervisor wasn't entirely surprised when his employee arrived at the phone company at 7 A.M. that morning; these days, people who labored as diligently as Mike Backus were very hard to find.

That weekend Backus had stayed in Greeley, spending part of Saturday and Sunday with his eight-year-old daughter, Erin. On Monday, the twenty-fifth, he reported to his job as usual, but then he asked Wilson if he could have some more time off. The supervisor said that would not be a problem, but the repairman changed his mind again and decided to go in the next two days.

On Wednesday, he was assigned to ride with Troy Giffin, his colleague and the war veteran who had also

186

served in Vietnam. At 8:30 A.M., they got into the company vehicle that Giffin normally drove and began riding through the streets of Greeley. Backus was more talkative than usual and fidgeting in the passenger's seat. He looked anxious and drawn, as if he hadn't slept much lately. He took a knife from his pocket, opened it, and rested it in his lap. The exposed blade caught Giffin's eye and made him a little nervous.

"Did you hear about the death of Gerry Boggs up in Steamboat Springs?" Backus said.

Giffin turned to him, remembering the numerous conversations the men had had during the past summer about finding someone to kill the person who was holding up the sale of the bed and breakfast in Steamboat. He remembered Backus saying that the bed and breakfast was worth nearly a million dollars and that Michael himself would get ten percent of that when the sale went through. He remembered all the times that Backus had said that he needed more money, because of his divorce and his daughter and his child support payments. Giffin remembered telling Backus, as something of a joke, that he should look in Greeley's Latin Quarter for a gunman for this kind of job. He remembered Backus offering $3,500 for the murder and then, as time went on, $7,500 for the execution.

"There is no evidence," Backus said vaguely, looking out the window, "none at all."

"What do you mean?" Giffin asked.

"They say that Boggs was shot multiple times. There is no evidence of that."

Giffin stared at him.

"They say that the murderer had blood on his shoes."

Giffin looked out at the road, keeping his silence.

"You could be burned, if you didn't dispose of the shoes, couldn't you?"

Troy nodded, glancing down at Backus's feet. The man was wearing a new pair of boots.

"I would never keep evidence around. You've got to get rid of all the evidence."

Giffin pulled the truck into the parking lot of a Hardee's restaurant. They went inside the café and sat down, giving their order to a waitress. Backus had become very quiet, but he was still fidgeting.

Giffin attempted to make eye contact with him but could not. Backus kept looking at the table, out through the window, down at the floor. He seemed badly distracted, and more than anything else, sad.

"Mike, you spoke to me about all this last summer. About Steamboat Springs. About that man up there and the bed and breakfast."

Backus said nothing.

"We talked about it, Mike. Several times."

"I wish you had forgotten that."

"I know, but I haven't."

"That's about the only thing that could hang me."

Giffin shook his head.

When Backus spoke again, it was in a different, almost pleading, tone of voice.

"Vietnam buddies," he said, "don't tell each other's secrets."

Giffin looked away from him.

"They don't rat on each other, Troy."

He paused and said, with more emphasis, "They don't rat on their buddies."

Twenty-seven

By that Wednesday, Detective Crotz, Officer Del Valle, and the Steamboat Springs police department were not alone in working on the Boggs case. The Routt County district attorney's office was now represented by Assistant D.A. Kerry St. James, and by its lead investigator, Tim Garner. The Colorado Bureau of Investigation had also been called in, and two of their agents, Robert Sexton and Susan Kitchen, were following a series of leads that had been generated from Steamboat.

Ballistics tests demonstrated that Boggs had been murdered by gunshot wounds from a .22-caliber pistol (the same caliber of weapon that had killed William Coit two decades earlier in Houston). The authorities had also interviewed Thane Gilliland, receiving from him some .22-caliber bullets that Gerry had given him in the spring of 1993. Boggs had found the bullets in a vehicle once driven by his ex-wife. The slugs were tested and had the same coating, the same color, and the same kind of depressions as the bullets that had entered the victim.

When the police learned that Jill now lived in

Greeley and shared a home with a man named Michael Backus, they soon discovered that Backus was employed by the phone company.

On the morning of the twenty-seventh, while Giffin and Backus were driving around and having coffee at Hardee's, CBI agent Sexton and Officer Del Valle decided to pay a visit to the U.S. West offices in Greeley. They spoke to Backus's superior, Neil Wilson, and asked him about any recent changes in the repairman's work schedule. Wilson told them how Backus had taken off most of the previous week but then mysteriously shown up at U.S. West on Friday. Wilson said that Backus had asked for more time away from his job this week but then continued coming in to work. This was highly unusual, Wilson said, for someone as steady and predictable as Mike Backus

They asked Wilson to locate this employee in the field and tell him to come to the office. The supervisor put out a call and within the next hour, Backus had returned from his ride with Giffin. Wilson led Agent Sexton, Officer Del Valle, and Backus into a small room at the phone company, introduced the men to one another, and left them alone. It was clear to Wilson that his employee was greatly agitated and embarrassed by the presence of the visitors.

The interrogators sat down next to Backus and told him that he'd been seen at Gerry Bogg's residence in Steamboat Springs last Thursday afternoon, October 21.

"That was the day of the murder," Sexton said.

"I wasn't in Steamboat last Thursday," Backus replied.

"You weren't at work that day, either, were you?" the agent asked him.

Backus made no response.

"Your boss told us that," Del Valle said. "Where were you?"

"I went camping."

"Camping?" Sexton said.

"Right. All day and all that night. I went to the Poudre Canyon."

"Why did you come back to work on Friday?" Del Valle said. "Wasn't that your day off?"

"I felt like it. I like to work."

"We've got a witness," Sexton said, "who saw you walking in front of Boggs's house that afternoon. Your guilt is a done deal, Mike. You might as well tell us what happened."

"There's nothing to tell. Nothing happened."

"Are those new boots, Mike?" Del Valle asked, gazing down at the man's feet.

Backus said nothing.

"Those are very nice boots," the policeman said. "They look brand new."

"When did you get those?" Sexton said.

"A while back."

Sexton leaned in closer to Backus and spoke right into his face.

"Jill Coit is going down," the agent said quietly, "and you're going with her."

At 2 P.M., Backus took another ride with Troy Giffin. They talked about the police coming to U.S.

West and Backus brought out the same knife he'd shown Giffin earlier in the day—a knife that had been designed to cut phone cable. This time Backus did not keep it in his lap, but scraped the blade against a small metal box that was used in the repair of telephones. He scraped it back and forth, back and forth, metal against metal, the sound grating on Giffin's ears and filling him with tension. He wanted to tell Backus to stop doing this, but he was afraid to. Troy had the impression that his passenger was now wielding the knife as a threat—a demand that Giffin keep quiet about their earlier discussion, or he would put himself in danger.

"They're going to tell my parents," Backus said. "Those cops are going to talk to my mom and dad."

Giffin kept driving.

"I told them that I wasn't in Steamboat on Thursday. Both Jill and I went camping."

"That's no alibi, Michael. It doesn't cover anything."

"Someone destroyed all the evidence. They burned it or buried it."

Backus moved the knife back and forth across the face of the metal box, scraping the edge of the blade harder. The sound was maddening.

"How closely can they determine the time of death?" Backus said.

"Pretty close. Probably down to an hour."

"An hour? I'm sure they can't do that."

Giffin glanced over at the knife.

"How can they do that, Troy?"

"They just can."

Backus looked down at the floor of the vehicle.

"I got these new boots last weekend. I got them for work."

"Good."

"When that bed and breakfast sells, I'll be getting a lot of money. At least ten percent of the total amount. If you leave the country, can the police come and look for you?"

"It depends on where you go."

"Which countries are safe?"

"I think Brazil and Argentina. They can't extradite Americans back to the U.S."

"Pull over."

"What for?"

"Just pull over." He scraped the blade again.

Giffin steered the truck to the curb and parked it, but kept the engine running.

"Troy?"

When he turned to look at Backus, he noticed that the man had tears in his eyes.

"What is it, Mike?" he said.

"They say there was blood on the shoes."

"That knife is making me very nervous. Can you stop doing that?"

Backus looked at the object in his hand, as if he weren't sure what it was. "All right," he said, putting it back in his pocket. "Maybe I'll go to Mexico. Can they come to that country and get you?"

"I don't know."

Backus rolled down his window. He reached into his pocket, taking out his wallet. He removed some business cards from the wallet and began ripping them into small pieces, tossing them out the window. Tears were on his cheeks.

"I want you to slap me," he said.

"What?"

"I want you to hit me."

"Mike, come on."

"In the face."

"Mike—"

"Now, damn it! Hit me!"

"I don't understand."

"I want you to kick the hell out of me. Like they taught us to do in the military."

Troy didn't move. He'd never seen anyone act the way Backus was acting, not even in Vietnam, when he and other soldiers were under extreme duress. He'd never been asked to punish another man for something he'd done.

"Please," Backus said. "Hit me in the face."

"I can't, Mike."

"Why not? Use hand-to-hand combat. Do whatever you want."

"Look, I've got to go back to the office. I left some papers there that I'm supposed to have with me."

He slipped the truck into gear and pulled away from the curb, driving toward U.S. West.

Backus stared out the window in silence.

Troy had been married for twenty-two years. That night when he arrived home from work, his wife, Terry, asked how his day had gone.

"Awful," he said. "It was the day from hell."

He told her about riding around Greeley that morning with Michael Backus. He told her how his colleague had asked Troy to beat him up.

In recent months, Backus had visited their home

and Terry had also heard him talk about his relationship with Jill Coit, about marrying this woman, and about the bed and breakfast in Steamboat Springs.

Terry asked her husband what he planned to do next.

"I don't know," he said.

The people who worked at U.S. West, especially those like himself and Mike Backus who'd put in a number of years with the company, were like an extended family. They belonged to the same union. They looked out for one another. They took care of each other when there was a problem on the job. If he went to the police about Backus, he might face repercussions at work. But if he didn't, he might be an accessory to the crime after the fact. He already had a criminal record from a second-degree assault charge in the past.

After thinking about it for a while, he contacted an attorney, who advised him to talk to the police in Greeley. Giffin followed this suggestion and the local authorities in turn called the police department in Steamboat Springs, who then informed the CBI. Within days, Agent Susan Kitchen was in Greeley, asking Troy to tell her everything he could remember Backus had said.

By then, she couldn't ask the phone repairman himself, because Mike Backus and Jill Coit had vanished.

Twenty-eight

On Saturday evening, October 23, Andrew Coit
had received a call from his mother. Virtually every
time she visited or phoned him, he felt discomfort
and instability, and tonight would be no exception.

"Gerry's dead," Jill told her middle son, "and I'm
the number-one suspect."

"He's dead?" Andrew said.

"Yes. Have you talked to the police about this?"

"No."

"They haven't called you?"

"No."

"Don't talk to the fucking cops!"

"What happened?"

"I'm going to turn myself in. Don't talk to anyone
about this."

Andrew didn't know what to say. He'd never known
what to say to his mother.

"If you need to talk to someone, talk to my lawyer—Randall Klauzer, in Steamboat. He'll advise
you."

"About what?"

"The bed and breakfast will get sold now, Andrew.

When the sale goes through, part of that money will go to you. You'll get a share if everything goes smoothly. But don't talk to anyone about this."

In the weeks ahead, when Detective Crotz and CBI Agent Kitchen came to Denver and asked Andrew what he could tell them about his mother, he mentioned this call, but he said he didn't know where she'd gone after she disappeared.

Backus and Jill had flown to California, and when they reached Los Angeles, she phoned her son, William, in the nearby town of Manhattan Beach.

William had also received a call from his mother on Saturday, October 23. She'd told him that Gerry Boggs had been killed, that he was not to speak to the police under any circumstances, that he was to phone Randall Klauzer in Steamboat Springs if he needed legal advice, and that she would contact him later. After speaking to his mother, William called Seth and relayed the substance of their conversation.

Seth told his brother that he did not want to talk about this—not now, and not over a phone that someone was surely listening to, or recording.

That evening, Seth called William from a pay phone and said that if the police asked him any questions, William should pretend that they had not spoken earlier in the day.

William agreed with this plan, but he didn't tell Seth that he himself was recording their phone calls.

Four days later, on Wednesday, October 27, William received another call from his mother. She was flying west with Michael Backus and wanted her youngest son to meet her at the Los Angeles airport. She gave him no flight information and said those details would be conveyed only after they'd touched down in California.

On Friday afternoon, the twenty-ninth, she phoned William at his job at a construction company and asked him to come to the airport to pick up her and Backus. He did as she'd requested and then drove them toward his home in Manhattan Beach. Jill was riding in the front seat beside him. When she asked William if he'd spoken to the police, he told her the truth: a detective from Colorado had called and he'd answered a few questions.

His mother reached over and hit him on the arm.

"Stop the fucking car!" she said, hitting him again.

He kept one hand on the wheel, guiding the vehicle through L.A.'s rush-hour traffic, while fending off her blows and ignoring his pain.

"I told you not to talk to them!" she said. "What's the matter with you?"

"I didn't tell them anything."

"Stop the fucking car. They're watching us right now."

He slowed down but kept driving.

"They're watching this car," she said.

Two blocks from her son's address, Jill decided it would be better if the couple did not stay at his home, but at a local motel. William's residence, she was certain, was being monitored by the police. William took them to the El Camino and before they checked in, his mother said she would call and set up a place for them to meet and talk again. That evening, she phoned and told him to meet her and Backus at a mall in Manhattan Beach.

William drove there with his wife, Robin, and their four-month-old boy, Conner. Backus and Robin stayed outside the mall, while William, his mother, and his infant son went into the mall and stood on the concourse, talking.

Jill was holding the baby, but in William's opinion, she was doing a very bad job of this, carrying the child under her arm as if he were a football. This upset William, but he was worried about creating a ruckus in public.

His mother was telling him that she had an airtight alibi regarding the time frame for the murder of Gerry Boggs, because she'd gone camping that day with Backus. They could prove where they'd been.

"My attorney," Jill said, "is going to split up the money once the bed and breakfast has been sold. He's going to divide it between you three boys."

William watched her awkwardly holding his son. He was half listening to what she was saying and fighting the impulse to grab the infant, run outside, and find his wife. But he wondered if they were being followed by the police right now—and this was a bad time for a fight with his mother.

"You'll get a third of what comes from the sale of the bed and breakfast," Jill was saying.

He nodded, certain that if she sold the business, he would never receive any money.

"I'm selling it soon."

"Okay."

"That's why it's very important that you don't talk to the police."

In the distance, William saw his wife coming toward them with Backus at her side. He felt deeply relieved.

His mother kept talking until Backus and Robin had joined them. As all of them stood in the center of the mall, William gently retrieved the baby from Jill and held him in his arms.

"We've got to get out of here," Backus said, glancing around nervously.

"Where are you going?" William asked.

"We're taking a boat from San Diego to Mexico," the man told him.

Jill and Backus backpedaled away from her son, his wife, and her tiny grandson.

"You guys walk that direction," she said to them, "and don't look back at us. I'll call you."

William soon told Susan Kitchen of the CBI about this meeting with Backus and Jill. He informed the agent that the couple were on their way to Mexico and he said that in her purse his mother usually carried a small, pearl-handled, silver-framed .22-caliber pistol.

Part Six

November
and
December

Twenty-nine

They went to Tijuana and then flew to Mexico City, arriving on November 2. The following day, Jill visited the American Embassy and, working through the office of the U.S. vice-consul, Elise Paterson, she signed over power of attorney to Seth. This gave her oldest son the authority to sell the bed and breakfast and to oversee her other financial affairs. Jill and Michael had purchased airline tickets to Madrid and a Eurorail pass. They flew to Spain and made preparations to ride the train across the Continent.

No one in Colorado knew where the couple had gone, but everyone believed they'd fled the country. CBI agents and Detective Crotz continued speaking with the Coit brothers, Troy Giffin, U.S. West management in Greeley, Ricky Mott, the Boggs family, and other contacts and relatives of the fugitives, but as the days passed and the first week of November came to an end, the sense of frustration in Steamboat Springs was tangible. The police, many people felt, had waited too long to look at Jill Coit as not merely the prime suspect, but the only suspect in the murder of Gerry Boggs. And they'd given her time to slip away.

203

Hadn't she been seen driving around Steamboat in her murder disguise two days after the body had been found? Hadn't she flaunted her outrageous indifference to public decency and her belief that she would never be arrested for anything? Hadn't she given the police the best opportunity they'd ever have to catch her—and hadn't they failed to act on it?

If she and Backus were hiding in Mexico or South America or Europe, and if she had as much money stashed away as some of the research into her past indicated she might, the couple never needed to return to the United States.

The thought of that not only sent Doug Boggs into a rage, it made him and his family consider putting up wanted posters of the duo in Mexico. It also made them consider sending a private investigator after the couple, but ultimately, they didn't do either of these things. They waited and hoped and prayed, remembering that Jill had a propensity for returning to places—especially for returning to Colorado and for returning to Steamboat again and again, not just after her marriage was over, and not just after she'd stopped living there, but even after her ex-husband had been shot to death. Maybe she would come back once more.

Thane Gilliland knew a private detective in Southern California. After he heard that the fugitives were heading south of the border, Thane alerted this man and told him where the couple might be found. The investigator began calling his Mexican connections.

Jill and Michael traveled from Spain to Switzerland to Germany, riding the train through Europe and enjoying their sense of freedom and escape. It was exhilarating to be out of America. It was fun to be thousands of miles away from trouble. Visiting foreign lands, eating exotic food, and sleeping in new beds were much more enjoyable than working at the phone company or sitting in a courtroom, listening to boring testimony about deeds, liens, and legal disputes. Jill was certain that they were safe as long as they stayed out of the United States.

Yet it wasn't like her to keep things safe for very long. Her mind worked fastest and keenest when planning a new intrigue or maneuver, and it was difficult, if not impossible, to do what she did best on foreign soil. She already had a man with her, so she didn't need to find another one—at least, not at the moment. She wasn't familiar with the insurance industry in Europe, or with most international businesses, so they didn't stimulate her to find novel ways of generating cash. And beyond these things, she liked to observe the effects of her work on other people, especially those she was close to. Travel was interesting, but it was no match for beating the system and everyone who represented it.

Contrary to what some people believed, Jill also needed money. After losing $100,000 to Carl Steely in their divorce settlement, and after employing a lawyer on the civil suit for years, she found her assets dwindling. She wanted Seth to sell the bed and breakfast as soon as possible, and she wanted him to liquidate some of her other possessions. She'd faxed him the power of attorney from Mexico for just that reason, but she was worried about his ability to consummate the sale without her involvement. He'd always been dependent on her, and she'd never been very comfortable placing her trust in him. He constantly needed to be given orders. So she sent him more faxes.

After a week in Europe, she was restless and concerned, no more able to find contentment or stay put in that part of the world than in Colorado. She began talking about returning to America and started laying plans.

Backus went along with her, as he always did. What other options did he have? They weren't traveling on his money, or even his dreams. He'd never made the important decisions in this relationship, and he wasn't going to win any arguments with her. He was living far outside the normal bounds of his experience, and if the feeling was exciting, it was also unnerving.

He was used to getting up every day and going to work at the same job, as he'd done for the past twenty-three years. He was used to a routine, a paycheck, a defined sense of his future, even if it wasn't a very happy one. Now, he was riding a train across Europe with a woman who was far stranger and far more imaginative and far more flighty than he was. Now, he was running away, seeing new things and hearing odd languages, remembering the past. Now, he was listening to her tell him what they were going to do next.

They flew back to Mexico City and made their way toward California, where they picked up a car and began driving east across the United States. They went through Arizona, New Mexico, and Texas, moving north now, up through southern Colorado, toward Denver and Greeley and Steamboat, returning to where they'd been.

The private detective who was also a friend of Thane Gilliland's had learned through his contacts that the couple had flown back to Mexico City. The investigator told Thane that he'd picked up their trail by noticing Jill's inclination to send faxes to America; more specifically, she liked to send them to her son in Steamboat Springs. What was odd about this was that Seth did not have a fax machine himself at the bed and breakfast, but relied on a local office to receive them for him and then alert the young man once they'd come in.

It wasn't long before Thane (and the Steamboat police and the CBI) discovered which office this was. It wasn't much longer that this office began sending Jill's faxes to Thane and to the authorities before passing them along to Seth.

One came in from Denver on November 20. This was after Jill and Michael had driven from Colorado Springs up to Lowry Air Force Base, which sits on the eastern edge of Denver. Backus, who was in the National Guard, had access to a room at Lowry, and he and Jill stayed there on their trip back home.

Thirty

On Sunday, November 21, Jill arranged to meet Seth and Julie at some factory outlet stores in the small Colorado town of Silverthorne, just off I-70 and roughly an hour west of Denver. Since returning from Georgia early in the month, Seth and his wife had gone to his mother's house in Greeley and collected some of her papers and other business documents. They'd found a very messy home, full of rotting food, a discarded wig, a .41-magnum firearm, and a stun gun that could be used on animals or humans to send a powerful electric charge into the flesh. Seth was not surprised to find so many weapons at his mother's residence. He knew that over the years she'd amassed a minor arsenal and he owned a .20-gauge shotgun and several rifles himself.

When Jill phoned her son and asked him to meet her in Silverthorne, she told him to bring along the titles to a few of her possessions, including the Mercedes. She wanted to liquidate these assets, talk to him about selling the bed and breakfast, and clear up some other financial matters before leaving once again. When Julie asked what her next destination

208

would be, Jill announced that she and Backus were "going south." They had to go away, she told the young couple, "because after someone is murdered, they always blame the spouse."

If she hadn't killed Gerry Boggs, Julie asked her mother-in-law, then why had she made the call to Seth on the afternoon of October 21? Why had she told him that it was over and it was messy?

Jill looked at her daughter-in-law and smiled before sending forth another wall of chatter about her upcoming travel plans.

Months later, when Julie recalled posing these questions in Silverthorne, she said that it was her impression that Jill hadn't simply ignored them; she hadn't heard them.

Following this rendezvous with his mother, Seth didn't call the police and tell them she was back in Colorado. He did something else, something that for him was much easier to do. He phoned his brother, William, and informed him of these developments. A short while later, it was William who called the authorities and said that Jill was briefly returning to Greeley to put her monetary affairs in order so she could flee again. If they were going to catch her, they had to act now.

For weeks, the CBI and the Steamboat Springs police department had been observing the home on Eleventh Avenue, which Backus and Jill had occupied before going to Mexico and Europe. On Monday, November 22, they increased their surveillance of this house and several other locations in Greeley, including the residence of Gary Bolton, a close friend of Backus's from the phone company. While out of the country, Backus had contacted U.S. West to ask about taking an extended leave of absence or early retirement, but nothing had come of these efforts. On October 27, he'd left his job without warning, and in the eyes of his employer, he was now a fugitive from justice.

By the first hours of Tuesday morning, November 23, the police were aware that Backus was staying at Bolton's home. They were also aware that Jill was back in Greeley, driving a blue Ford Tempo, and had just paid a visit to her old house. At 4 A.M., she came out of her residence, got into the car, and drove away slowly. CBI Agent Robert Sexton and Steamboat Springs Officer Robert Del Valle followed her for several blocks before pulling her over to the side of the road. As they approached her vehicle and asked her to step outside, she smiled up at them and did as they'd requested.

When they told her to lean against her car so they could frisk her, she complied. But she protested when they asked her to spread her legs. She'd recently had hip surgery, she explained to the men, and parts of her lower body were still sore. She also said that she suffered from hypoglycemia and if she didn't eat something very soon, she might become too weak to function.

The police told her to spread her legs anyway, and this time she reluctantly did as she was told, while offering more words and more resistance. Jill wasn't used to being treated this way. She'd never been arrested before, never even been seriously questioned by the police. She seemed astonished that it was happening now, as if the thought had never occurred to her that rules existed or that anyone cared enough to enforce them.

While some other officers were arresting Backus at Gary Bolton's home (the phone repairman did not put up a fight), Jill was taken to Greeley's Weld County jail and escorted into a small interrogation room by Sexton and Del Valle. They read her her Miranda rights, informing her that she had the option of having an attorney present for their discussion and the option of not speaking to the police at all. She was noncommittal on these issues and seemed very curious about what the authorities knew and had to say.

Sexton is a large man with sad eyes that turn down at the corners. He didn't look nearly so intimidating as the deep-voiced, dark-complected Del Valle, who in the right mood could chill people with one frown. These were the right circumstances, and a big part of his job just now was to stare in a withering fashion at the woman sitting across from him.

The conversation among the three of them was rambling and disjointed. The suspect appeared mostly worried about what all this would do to her public image.

"I want to get this over as quickly as possible," Jill said, "because the Steamboat paper is gonna come out and say I've been arrested. And it's gonna be on the front page. And then, when I'm released, it's gonna be on the little bitty back page. Nobody is gonna notice it."

Her attorney in Steamboat, Randall Klauzer, had

already advised her not to talk to any police officers, she said, at least not until Gerry Boggs's time of death had been publicly announced.

Del Valle explained to her that the time of death was uncertain and that Boggs's death certificate had been marked only "Friday, October 22."

"Okay," she said, "so I have to provide an alibi for four or five days before, right? From Wednesday to Friday, correct?"

Sexton told her that Boggs had been seen alive on Wednesday and on Thursday morning.

"Okay, good," she said. "I have nine people [who saw me] from Thursday to Friday. I mean, every time frame is not covered. My attorney said, 'You give them nothing, because as soon as you don't have an alibi, guess what? That's when it happened.' "

Del Valle asked her to explain these remarks.

If she mentioned a time period in which she didn't have an alibi, she told the policeman, he would say that that was when Boggs had been killed.

"If nine people saw me in Greeley," she asked the men, "do I have to worry?"

"It's important," Sexton said, "if you have an alibi on where you were at that time. Our job is to find the facts."

"Right. You guys are under pressure. You have to pin this down."

She turned to Del Valle and asked him how long he'd been living in Steamboat Springs.

"Fifteen years," he said.

"Oh, then you knew he was gay. All of a sudden, he isn't gay anymore. Your CBI people told people that I was lying and that he was not bisexual and not gay. They told people that Gerry got the annulment, but I did. I got it."

When she discovered that she was still married to Carl Steely, she told the men, she informed Gerry of this. They then both went to Vance Halvorson, who declared that they had to get an annulment to avoid the embarrassment they would suffer in Steamboat Springs. It was she who demanded the annulment, she told Del Valle and Sexton, because she was the one who was at fault.

And the only reason Gerry had married her, she went on, was because he was homosexual and local people talked about him in humiliating ways.

"Gerry didn't marry me 'cause he loved me," she said. "It was all surface."

Sexton and Del Valle exchanged looks, startled by the direction the interview had taken. They hadn't expected to be discussing the dead man's sexual preferences.

"Did you," the agent asked her, "get the annulment because he was gay?"

"It was twofold. I discovered that he was gay about two weeks into the marriage. His mother is the one who told me."

The men nodded.

She got the annulment, she added, because she wasn't yet legally divorced from her previous husband and because of Gerry's bedroom proclivities.

Sexton said that neither he nor his partner believed that she was the one who had actually killed Boggs. He just wanted her to tell them the truth now, the whole truth, and if someone else had committed the murder, they would find that person and arrest him.

Jill began arguing with the agent, saying that she

was certain they wanted to put her in prison because she was "the one that has been married so many times."

"That's very, very important," she said.

"Why?" Del Valle asked.

"Because Vance built the whole thing of bigamy up and it went in the paper."

"Hey," Sexton said, "we're talking murder, not bigamy."

"Let me tell you, I have enough witnesses that are normal people. They saw me and there is no way in hell I could have killed him on Thursday or Friday . . . until you get the time of death, I'm screwed."

Del Valle asked her why.

"I have a four-hour period that is not covered. That's where I'm vulnerable."

"When is that four-hour period?"

"I'm not telling you, because that's when Gerry's dead."

"I don't think we can come up with an exact time."

She denied committing the murder and said that a person is truly innocent until proven guilty. The police just wanted to arrest somebody in this slaying, she told them, in order to quiet things down in Steamboat.

"How can I prove I'm innocent," she asked Del Valle, "if we don't have an exact time of death?"

Sexton repeated that the time of death could only be estimated. Then he said, "You're blaming us now, saying we need to pin the case on you."

She agreed with the agent. "Did you even check his former lovers?"

"Who are they?" Del Valle said. "You got names?"

"Look in his little address book. Gerry usually listed people by their initials. Look there."

"Initials," Del Valle replied, "don't tell us anything."

"They have phone numbers. Gerry and a boyfriend . . ."

"How do you know he had a boyfriend?"

"Number one, when we first got married—no, I don't want to leak that. Never mind that, okay?"

"You give us a piece of something," Del Valle said, "and then pull back."

"Okay. Our relationship wasn't quite right. I've been married enough times to know what relationships are supposed to be. Mrs. Boggs told me that Gerry was sexually abused in high school by one of his teachers. How many psychologists does it take to put two and two together? If a person can only have sex from the rear with the lights out, then . . ."

Sexton and Del Valle again exchanged looks.

"When I first came to Steamboat," Jill said, "I had hair to here."

"Uh huh," Del Valle said.

"Gerry made me have it cut off like a boy, okay? Totally like a little boy."

"Is that the first time," Del Valle said, "that you ever had your hair that short?"

She smiled at him. "I'm French. I've always had long hair."

Sexton told her that they'd already obtained a search warrant for her Greeley home and found a .45-caliber handgun inside the house.

She said that the cops had planted the .45 next to her dildo, just "to be funny."

215

When neither interrogator started laughing, she told them that she carried a .45 for protection because she was once punched and raped.

The men said nothing.

Because her attacker had been unable to get an erection, she told them, he'd beaten her very badly. Ever since then, she'd had seizures and had also needed the hip surgery as a result of that assault.

"You ever solicit anybody to kill your ex-husband?" Sexton said.

She frowned, and when she spoke again, her tone was no longer so breezy.

"Let's stop the questions, okay?" she said. "No, I did not."

"Okay," the agent said.

"Let's stop them, 'cause that's just ridiculous."

"We can stop at any time."

"Let's stop, 'cause that's just tacky!"

"That isn't tacky," Sexton said.

"That is tacky."

"There's a reason I asked it," the agent said.

"Why?"

"Well, obviously I have a reason, or I wouldn't ask you."

She gave him another smile.

"I wouldn't," he said, "waste your time and mine."

In three weeks, she told them, she would be tried, and in a month, she would be back on the street.

Sexton shook his head. A speedy trial in Colorado, he said, would take at least half a year.

"Okay," she replied. "Am I still allowed to have my glasses and reading material? Or do I just have to sit in this fucking jail?"

"I would think you're allowed your glasses," the agent said.

"Good. As long as I can have my glasses and my computer, I'm in good shape. I can spend six months in jail."

Thirty-one

By late November, the two murder suspects had been transferred from Greeley to the Routt County Jail, located on the western edge of Steamboat Springs. Each defendant was being held on $5 million bond, and Jill especially was the object of local gossip and scorn.

Near the end of November, Richard Griffith, a special agent for the U.S. Air Force, executed a search warrant on the room at Lowry Air Force Base, which Jill and Michael had occupied after returning from Mexico. He also searched her red Toyota Paseo, left behind at the base as the couple made their way back to Greeley. Griffith found credit cards for "Jill Coit" and "Jill Steely"; shares of stock from Tenneco and the Philadelphia Life Insurance Company; promissory notes and a deed of trust; two shoulder-length dark wigs, one curly and one straight; two used Aero Mexico airline tickets from Mexico City to Tijuana; two Eurorail passes, issued to Jill Coit and Michael Backus; a photocopy of the Power of Attorney document from Jill to Seth; two international driver's permits, a map of Mexico, a pamphlet from Zürich, and another pamphlet entitled "Temporary Military Lodging around the World." Griffith also found a pair of plastic surgical gloves.

The authorities had collected other pieces of evidence, which the couple had scattered in their travels from one continent to the other and back again. The CBI and the Steamboat Springs police had put together numerous facts about Jill's marital history, her disreputable past, and the details of her lawsuits over the bed and breakfast. The detectives had become familiar with the conflict between Jill and Gerry Boggs and with how it had intensified during the two years prior to his death. William and Andrew Coit were cooperating fully with the investigators, as were Judy Prier-Lewis, Thane Gilliland, Vance Halvorson, Doug Boggs, Troy Giffin, Mo Hanley, and others who'd come forward to talk about Jill's deviousness, her false claims of pregnancy in Steamboat in the summer of 1991, and her threats against the hardware store owner.

As November came to a close, the Routt County district attorney's office had just about everything it needed to prosecute the two inmates, except the one thing that is usually most critical in obtaining a first-degree murder conviction: physical evidence. Not one trace of it had yet been found. The murder scene had revealed nothing but some spent .22-caliber shell casings, a bloody shovel, a plastic bag smeared with blood, and the two used condoms that were found well away from where the body had been discovered. The semen in the condoms did not belong to Michael Backus, and DNA tests would show that it had most likely come from Gerry Boggs.

If the hard evidence was nonexistent, what made

things even more complicated was that there was no reliable way to determine when the man had been killed. Almost twenty-seven hours had passed from the time he'd left Boggs Hardware on the early afternoon of October 21 to the moment when his brother had walked into Gerry's kitchen and seen the victim lying on the floor. Another eight hours went by before a medical examiner was let into the house to do a cursory check of the body, and Gerry was then transported to the Denver suburb of Golden, where Dr. Michael Dobersen performed the autopsy (Steamboat Springs lacked the necessary facilities to do this operation). Dobersen began his examination at 2:15 P.M. on Saturday afternoon, October 23, and by then, Boggs might have been dead almost two full days.

Dr. Dobersen reported that Gerry had a skull fracture and a large laceration on his forehead, both of which could have been made by a shovel or a spade. The victim had black eyes—"raccoon eyes," as Dobersen put it—as a result of being severely beaten about the face. From Boggs's left chest cavity, the doctor removed a .22 slug, and the cavity itself contained three liters of blood. Although Boggs had been shot three times in the torso, it was this particular bullet, the examiner believed, that had created the fatal wound and caused Gerry to bleed to death.

Boggs had scratches on his knuckles and on one knee—defensive injuries, according to Dobersen, that had occurred while the man was being attacked. The doctor couldn't tell if Gerry had been shot and then hit repeatedly in the face, or whether the shovel attack had come first.

Dobersen also observed a circular area of redness

near the victim's right ear and some minor abrasions on the ear itself. At the time of the autopsy, these markings did not take on any great significance, but in the months ahead, they would become increasingly important—if not the single most important set of facts about the corpse.

Based upon Boggs's stomach contents, Dobersen concluded, the man might have died within two hours of eating his last meal, but the doctor acknowledged that this was only an estimate. Gerry probably did not die any earlier, but he could have died later. How much later was difficult to say, but if it was considerably later, the D.A.'s office had a serious problem in supporting its theory of when the murder had taken place.

Michael Backus had reported to work at U.S. West on Friday morning, October 22, at 7 A.M. sharp. Jill had had her nails done in Greeley at Sue Heiser's manicure shop that afternoon. If anyone could clearly demonstrate that the time of death was on Friday as opposed to Thursday, the couple had credible witnesses to establish their alibis.

If Dobersen's autopsy revealed much about how Gerry Boggs had died, it showed very little about when the murder had happened and virtually nothing at all about what had gone on inside Boggs's home during the assault.

At the beginning of December, all the evidence CBI and the Steamboat Springs Police Department had that might convict Jill and her lover were Debbie Fedewa's remembrance of seeing two strange people walking on her block on October 21; the words of Mo Hanley and Troy Giffin; Jill's behavior toward Gerry during the course of the lawsuits; and, most of all, the bad character that she had displayed all over the United States for the past three decades. While that character was well documented in the five boxes of evidence that private investigators had lately gathered on her, it was entirely possible that a judge would admit none of that at a murder trial. Not one piece of it, after all, was forensic evidence that connected either her or Backus to the murder of Gerry Boggs.

The detectives working on the case clearly needed something more—or someone else, someone who had been close to Jill in the months and weeks and days leading up to the murder. They needed someone knowledgeable and credible, who not only knew the truth but would be willing to speak it under oath in a courtroom. They needed one more witness who could add things that were still missing. They needed her oldest son.

Since his mother's arrest, and since she'd taken up residence in a small cell at the edge of town, Seth had become more and more uncomfortable. Like many other males in Jill's life, he'd long believed that although she was capable of doing all sorts of cruel things to other men, she would make an exception of him. Their interwoven lives and her maternal feelings for him, he'd always assumed, would naturally prevent her from doing anything vicious to him. Seth was no longer so sure about that.

In the aftermath of the crime, he'd discovered that his mother had held a secret life insurance policy on him for years and that she was the beneficiary. This piece of information shook him badly and made him think. If she became desperate enough or ever needed more money for her legal bills or could only buy her way out of jail or . . . maybe he wasn't so different from Carl Steely or William Coit II down in Houston, or from her other husbands or Mike Backus or the late Gerry Boggs. Maybe he was just another pawn . . .

Seth had already spoken to the local police several times and given them some of his mother's documents, but he hadn't begun to divulge what he and Jill had talked about in the days before the murder. He hadn't told them about seeing Backus walking near the bed and breakfast on the night of October 15, walking and carrying a bag with a heavy object inside. He hadn't told them that after he and Julie had returned from Georgia, he'd driven over to Greeley and removed a .41-caliber weapon from his mother's house, plus a .32, some wigs, and a stun gun.

Seth hadn't told the authorities that on the day before Thanksgiving, he'd taken two other handguns that were in his possession at the bed and breakfast to Jill's attorney in Steamboat, Randall Klauzer. He did this because he thought that at least one of them might have been used in the murder—and he wanted them off the property.

For many reasons, Seth was very reluctant to come forward and cooperate with the police. For one thing, he was afraid of his mother, even though she was incarcerated. He knew that she had connections, money, and the willpower to remove almost anything that was standing in the way of her freedom.

At the same time, Seth was also afraid of the police. He didn't know how much trouble he was in now, or if he was in any trouble at all. Was he an accessory to a capital crime, or was he an innocent bystander? And had his mother even committed this crime? Or had someone else who was working for her? He didn't know what Jill had done—or not done—to Gerry Boggs, and he didn't want to know.

Seth wasn't quite ready to believe that his mother would blame him for the murder, if her life was on the line, yet this thought had also crossed his mind. Was she capable of telling the police that he and Julie had killed Boggs? What would she say in order to save herself? Seth wasn't sure of anything.

He and Julie considered their options, then contacted a Denver attorney named Nathan Chambers. After listening to their story, Chambers told the couple that in his opinion they'd done nothing illegal and would be well advised to go to the CBI and the Steamboat police, make a full confession, and ask for an immunity agreement: in exchange for their cooperation in the ongoing investigation of Jill and Michael, and in exchange for their testimony if the suspects came to trial on first-degree murder charges, Seth and Julie could not be prosecuted for any involvement in the crime. The young couple thought about Chambers's recommendation and wondered if the Routt County D.A., Paul McLimans, would accept it. By year's end they still hadn't reached a decision.

Thirty-two

Around Christmastime, Steamboat takes on a different feel, another personality, losing some of its Western flair and becoming more of an international playground. Money—not so evident in town the rest of the year—arrives in force with the holiday season. You see it in the fashionable cars and the busy restaurants that offer sophisticated food at urban prices. You see it in the clothes that women wear when they shop on Main Street: the brown and silver minks that almost touch the ground, the fur hats and chic black outfits, the long leather boots that were made in Italy. You hear it in the voices of people from all over the world.

In the last week of 1993, the Oak Street Bed and Breakfast was charging $140 a night for a small room with a very low ceiling, but for that price you also received a loaf of fresh bread, baked each morning by Seth Coit himself. He and Julie were still running the bed and breakfast and still contemplating an immunity agreement with the Routt County D.A.'s office, just a few blocks to the east. Seth desired to sell the bed and breakfast and leave Steamboat far behind, but Gerry Boggs, even in death, continued to hold a deed on the business. Until a judge was willing to release that deed, the enterprise could not exchange hands.

Immediately following the arrest of Coit and Backus, Steamboat had been filled with rumors of Jill trying to sell her story to the tabloids or to the book world or the movies and make a fast bundle from her cell. This notion had gone down very hard with the Boggs family and other local people—about as hard as Jill's comments to the police that Gerry had been bisexual or gay.

Folks in Steamboat had spoken very reluctantly to the press, if at all. They did not want to interfere with the courtroom issues surrounding Coit and Backus, and they did not want to say one word that would further damage the feelings of the Boggs family. Everyone close to that family and to the hardware store was more or less hunkered down for the entangled legal process that lay ahead. They were prepared to wait in silence, no matter how long it took, for the justice system to decide the fate of the two people locked up on the outskirts of town. At that time, the Boggses had no idea just how long that could be.

On a pole near the cash register at the front of the hardware store, employees had placed a glass-encased tribute to Gerry Boggs, written by Judy Prier-Lewis. It contained a poignant, gentle-looking photo of the dead man, and it read in part:

"Gerry's life has been a testimonial to the individual who possesses unconditional love and an outstretched helping hand. We shared a love of books, flowers, diving spots, good coffee, and a silly sense of humor. We talked for hours about politics, religion, and things of the heart. . . ."

Bob McCullough was in the store during the last week of 1993. He was working straight through the holiday season, and his cheeks were redder than ever. His eyes were also red, and his whole face appeared strained. He spoke gingerly about the past two or three months at Boggs Hardware, willing to talk, but choosing his words very carefully. He seemed deflated, as if he'd lost not just a co-worker and a friend, but a piece of his trust and his innocence.

"Every time I go by that bed and breakfast," he said, "I have a bad reaction."

When a visitor asked him about speaking to Doug Boggs, who was busy in another part of the store, McCullough considered the request but offered some words of caution, clearly not wanting to start trouble of any kind. The Boggses were highly sensitive about strangers coming into Steamboat, he said, and looking at their tragedy as a "story" for the papers or the evening news. At the moment, things were very touchy.

Bob left to get Doug and ask him if he would mind talking to someone from out of town. A few minutes later, Doug appeared in the middle of the store, speaking without being prompted and shaking with anger. He looked like a man who was doing everything in his power not to explode—not to lash out at people who raised difficult questions, not to jump in his car and drive out to the jail with a loaded gun.

"Gerry died," he said, "because he wouldn't give in to the bitch. Other men paid her off to get rid of her, but he wouldn't do that. He stood and fought her, and it cost him his life."

His eyes were damp and he still looked stunned.

"My brother," he said, "didn't let the bitch have her way, and she killed him."

He started to say something else, but his voice faltered and he stared down at the floor. Then he excused himself and walked away.

In December, Gerry's house looked cold and utterly empty, as bleak as the Yampa Valley in the dead of winter. Long, sharp icicles hung from the eaves, and a fresh snow lay on the deck. The wooden siding had begun to weather, and without care, it would start to crack. The tall, imposing residence conveyed the odd silence of a place that was no longer occupied, no longer filled with telephones ringing or voices in the hall. Staring at the closed two-car garage and the stairs leading up to the back door, one couldn't help wondering exactly what had unfolded inside the kitchen after Gerry had come home from eating lunch at the Shack around 2 P.M. on October 21.

Lawyers in the Routt County D.A.'s office were trying to penetrate that mystery and making preparations for a preliminary hearing for Coit and Backus, initially scheduled for January 17 of the new year. While the attorneys searched for clues and evidence, both prisoners were adjusting to life inside their cells. Backus had become profoundly quiet, speaking to no reporters, causing no problems inside the jail, and assuming an air of complete resignation, as if the punishment he'd once asked Troy Giffin to give him was about to be delivered and there was nothing he could do to stop it. He'd grown a beard. His expression indicated that he didn't want to avoid punishment, but to embrace it.

And yet he wasn't totally resigned.

If he knew exactly what had taken place inside Gerry's home on the afternoon of October 21, then he had at least a sliver of hope that he could use that knowledge to help himself in the weeks and months ahead. If the D.A.'s office wanted to convict Jill more than anything else—and most people agreed that it did—and if they had no physical evidence on which to build their case, would they consider offering Backus a deal in exchange for his testimony against her to help put her away forever?

This was a long shot, of course, but people sitting in jail awaiting a hearing on first-degree murder charges devote hours and days to weighing such odds. Unless D.A. McLimans could come up with something more than he had, it remained a remote possibility.

It wasn't in Jill's nature to be as quiet as Backus, not even when she'd been advised by lawyers to hold her tongue. When a reporter for the *Rocky Mountain News* came to the jail, she gave the woman an interview. Asked about her marriage to Gerry Boggs, she said, "Intellectually, we were fine. Steamboat does not have that many eligible people who are intelligent. Most of the men here are ski bums.

"Two weeks after we were married, he [Gerry] goes to Belize, scuba diving on our honeymoon, without me. He told me he couldn't spend two weeks in a confined area with one person. He had never been married and probably never should have gotten married."

She had wed Gerry, she told the journalist, despite hearing ahead of time that he was bisexual.

"I'm very outgoing and like people," she said. "He didn't like people. He didn't really like to live life. Now he's portrayed as the great white savior, friendly, good old Uncle Gerry who everyone loved. What a joke. He wanted to get married and have a baby so people would stop laughing and saying things about him."

While Jill was telling her story in jail, her legend in Steamboat was starting to grow. Tourists who visited the town that winter heard tales about a woman who had killed seven other people besides the hardware store owner; she'd shot them and knifed them and poisoned them in the night. They said she'd gotten rid of half a dozen husbands and she was now referred to by many people (and in the media) as the "Black Widow." Folks were saying that she'd forced her own son, the friendly young man who ran the bed and breakfast on Oak Street, to commit the most recent slaying for her. They said that Seth had helped her plan the killing and was as guilty as she was and should be in the cell next to hers. The gossip was as pervasive as it was colorful.

But not everyone found it so entertaining. At 6 A.M. each morning in the El Rancho Café on Main Street, ranchers, farmers, and other locals gathered at the community table and talked in low, bitter voices about the town's most famous prisoner. They fondly remembered Gerry and made ugly comments about Jill. They shook their heads and spoke about the virtues of the death penalty.

"I hear that Coit is looking for a witness to help her out," a barrel-chested man in overalls said one morning, while glancing around the table at his companions.

"Is that right?" said another man who was wearing an old wide-brimmed hat.

"She needs someone to give her an alibi."

"Good luck, lady, finding anyone in this town who is going to save you."

"You bet."

One of the details that Debbie Fedewa had noticed about the pair of strange-looking people she'd seen walking along her street on two different occasions on October 21 was the "flat butt" of the shorter person. Debbie had told the murder investigators that she was a practiced observer of the human body, and especially of that part of the anatomy, so she'd made a mental note of the fact that the individual with the ponytail—who also wore a fake beard and was dressed like a man—didn't have much of a posterior. This detail eventually made its way into police reports, and those reports found their way into the jail, where Jill had a chance to read them. She was so fascinated and offended by Fedewa's comment that she decided to take action.

Another inmate at the Routt County Jail, Brandy Ranshaw, was being held on DUI charges, and while incarcerated, she'd made something of a name for herself as a snitch. Talking to the authorities had earned her favors at the jail and made life behind bars more interesting. After Jill was imprisoned and Brandy got to know her, the women began speaking on a regular basis. One day Jill asked her new friend if she would mind doing something for her. Brandy said of course not.

Jill dropped her pants and demanded that the woman tell her if she had a flat butt. Brandy was noncommittal on the issue, but afterward she ran to her police contacts and described what had happened. Jill was upset, she said, because she didn't think anyone would find her posterior unshapely. And if she could just demonstrate to the people who'd arrested her that it was round and full and attractive, she could easily prove that Debbie Fedewa had seen someone other than her walking on Hillside Court West last October 21. Then she could go free.

Thirty-three

"I'm a Southern woman," Jill said at the end of December, while sitting behind a glass wall inside the visiting section of the jail.

She was speaking on the phone to a stranger on the other side of the glass, and as she talked, she pulled at a strand of her short brown permed hair, wrapping the locks around her middle finger and twisting them above her head in a girlish gesture.

"If you understand and appreciate Southern women," she said, offering a wide, sweet smile, "you and I will get along just fine."

She was asked what part of the South she came from.

"Louisiana," she replied, with a stronger Dixie accent than she'd had before. "I was a beauty queen once, years ago, but you'd never know it by looking at me now, would you? They won't even let me have a hairbrush in here, or makeup, or anything decent to wear. These prison clothes are so drab and I look awful. Just awful."

She tugged at more strands of hair and frowned, clearly disturbed and embarrassed by her appearance.

Jill seemed surprised at finding herself looking this way, and at finding herself in jail.

"Southern women are different," she said. "We were raised to get married and have babies. That's what I did. We were brought up to cook and be polite and entertaining. I've always been a good wife. People will tell you that."

She smiled again. "I really appreciate you coming here to see me."

The previous afternoon, her visitor had driven out to the jail on a very cold winter day and asked those at the front desk of the facility when the inmates were allowed to have company. He'd been informed that Jill Coit, if she agreed to meet with him, would be available the following evening for thirty minutes. The visitor then sent a handwritten note in to the woman and quickly received back the response that she would be glad to speak with him tomorrow.

Why, she was now asked, did she want to speak to another reporter?

"I decided to talk to you," she said, moving closer to the glass, "because of your handwriting. It was very interesting, but I had a hard time reading it. It reminded me of the way I write. You scribble more than you write. I wanted to know what you looked like and who you are."

She offered another smile, this one warmer and more coquettish than the others. Her face looked softer and more receptive now; her eyes were very lively. She began chattering about the weather. She seemed bubbly, almost playful, swiveling around on her chair, but then she stopped talking and smiling, as if suddenly remembering where she was.

Light and darkness constantly moved across her

features, as if they were chasing each other in a footrace.

What, she was asked, did she do all day long inside the jail?

"I'm not a person who watches much TV," she said. "I don't find the things on TV to be very intelligent. I spend my days reading, mostly psychology books, because I'm intrigued by how the human mind works. What makes us who we are? What makes us act the way we do? When I get out of here, I'd like to be a therapist."

She stared directly through the glass.

"Do those things interest you?" she said. "You look like the kind of person who reads a lot."

She was asked what she thought was going to happen to her next.

"I'll be out of here soon," she said at once. "Probably in just a few more weeks. All of this will be over, and then I'll tell you everything. We can work out some kind of deal between us."

Did she receive many visitors at the jail?

She contorted her face into a childlike glare.

"In this town?" she said. "Are you kidding? After what they put in the paper about me and Gerry? Are you going to write about me? If you do, you better tell the whole truth."

As she continued talking about her life in jail and how the media had distorted everything that had happened between her and the murder victim, Jill conveyed enormous reserves of energy and a certain kind of intelligence—just the opposite of the kind of intelligence that had belonged to Gerry Boggs. Both of them never stopped thinking, but if Gerry had liked debating abstract ideas and concepts, Jill liked plotting concrete strategy and then putting it into action. You could see all that in the constant movement of her eyes.

"I can't wait until I can leave this place," she was saying. "I'll prove to everyone that I had nothing to do with this murder. The things people have said about me are just ridiculous. Do you know that? You seem like a nice person, a smart person. Someone I can trust. When they let me go, I'll tell you what really happened between Gerry and me."

Her face had become brilliant with hope.

"I'm guilty of only one thing," she said.

"What's that?"

"I married nine men. Other than that, I haven't done anything wrong. You believe that about me, don't you?"

"Why did you marry nine men?"

"Because I refuse to have sex with a man unless we're married. I don't believe in it. That's just the way I was raised in the South."

"Do your sons come to visit you?"

She glanced to the side and her expression fell. The breezy conversationalist who was there just a moment earlier had gone away, replaced by someone else. She looked incredibly old and sad.

"Oh, no," she said. "This has been very difficult for them, with all the things that have come out in the press about me. I feel really bad about that. You have to remember that I'm their mother."

Something very forceful moved across her face and hardened the set of her jaw. For a moment or two she looked frightening, but this also passed and her eyes held something that wasn't there before—a surge of genuine emotion and pain.

"I don't expect my sons to come out here and see me," she said.

She was asked if she'd hired a lawyer.

She brightened again and mentioned a prominent attorney from Denver.

"This will all be over soon," she said, "and things can get back to normal."

A prison guard arrived in the visiting area and told Jill that her time was up. The half hour had gone by very quickly.

She smiled at the guard, as if asking for just a few more minutes, but he repeated his command.

"I'm really glad you came to see me," she said, as she stood up, still clinging to the phone she was speaking into. "I hope you'll come back. I want to tell you more."

The guard hovered over her and she hung up. Looking through the glass, she put her fingers in her hair and twirled the strands once again, a provocative gesture. She grinned mischievously and blushed, making a movement like a curtsy, before turning back toward her cell and disappearing around a corner.

Leaving the jail and walking out into the cold, late-December air, her visitor recalled having read once about the behavior of black widow spiders. They're quite unpredictable. Sometimes, the creatures dance with their mates in elaborate rituals before killing them. Sometimes, they kill without much of a dance. Other times, they just wound the males, so that they can crawl away, though they are severely mangled. Either way, the desire to kill remains intact until the next encounter.

The visitor felt strangely touched by the meeting in the jail. He wondered if he'd ever spoken with anyone who'd had a more desperate desire to be liked. In everything she did, from her words to her smiles to the movement of her hands, she'd shown a tremendous need for his approval.

He was struck, as he often was after being inside a prison, by how smart and how stupid people are at one and the same time. And how pleasant and how terrifying they can be from one moment to the next. And by how much people want to be loved. He was moved because of how deeply she'd wanted him to believe in her innocence. And because of the sheer violence that was right behind the woman's eyes.

He shivered, recalling that the only real thing that had passed between him and the woman had come when he'd asked about her sons. That question had stung. At that moment, she'd seemed like flesh and bone and feeling. Like something more than ceaseless chatter. She'd seemed like someone's mother. But it hadn't lasted.

Stepping into his car, he realized that if Jill was going to be convicted of first-degree murder, and either executed by lethal injection or sent to prison for life, her sons, especially Seth, were going to have to come forward and tell the police what they knew about her. If at long last she was going to be put down like a rabid dog, as Bob McCullough had once said, it would not be done by the men who had married and divorced her, but by her own blood.

Part Seven

Courtrooms

Thirty-four

CBI agent Susan Kitchen is a broad-shouldered woman who conjures up the term "no-nonsense." A former cop in Colorado Springs, she has a commanding presence, a strong voice, and the kind of serious demeanor that can grab your attention—even if you aren't sitting with her in a small room and aren't potentially in a great deal of trouble. She's the sort of person who, through persuasion and intimidation, might very well make someone more inclined to tell the truth.

In mid-January of 1994, she interviewed Seth Coit for ten hours and he told her much of what he remembered about the events of the previous October. Slowly, painfully, and fearfully, he unwound the tale of watching the back of the hardware store for the comings and goings of Gerry Boggs. He spoke of driving past the man's home, of calling to see if Gerry was in town, of giving certain rooms at the bed and breakfast to Michael Backus. He told of seeing Backus carrying a heavy bag on the night of October 15.

He told of being asked by his mother how to get into Gerry's home and how to get rid of the dead man's body; of retrieving guns from Jill's home in Greeley; of scrubbing and cutting up the cap he'd found in room 7 at the bed and breakfast; and of burying the pieces in the ground near the bed and breakfast.

Whether Seth was saying all these things just to stay out of prison or because he felt genuine remorse over the killing of the man who worked across the street was the subject of a great amount of debate in Steamboat Springs. Some people felt sorry for him because he was Jill Coit's son; they saw him as one more of her male victims. But others could not forgive him for what they believed he had done—or failed to do—to save Gerry's life.

Seth's confession was more than an effort to help the authorities solve a murder. It was also a purging. This was his chance, as he neared the age of 30, to come forward and publicly begin the process of freeing himself from his mother. It was also an opportunity to avoid legal difficulties that could have been severe. In the end, Seth made a choice to help himself and to hurt the woman who had raised him.

There were people in Steamboat who were very pleased that he was going to provide information to the police about his mother, but they questioned his motives from another direction, besides just wanting to avoid prison himself. If Jill were convicted of murder, and then spent the rest of her life in prison, Seth would be in a position to take over some of her remaining financial assets, including the bed and breakfast. He would, in effect, be rewarded monetarily for testifying against her. After three decades of living directly beneath her thumb, the young man found himself at one of those rare and invaluable moments in life. By doing the right thing for others, he would also greatly benefit himself.

In a fumbling, nervous, and almost childlike manner, he spoke to Kitchen for half a day, trying his best to remember and reconstruct the past. When he finished, the prosecutors were elated. They knew that virtually nothing would be more damaging for a defendant in a courtroom than a son testifying against his own mother about the most heinous of crimes. Seth was inarticulate, but that could also be seen as useful: it would be difficult to accuse someone like him of having created an elaborate, polished act for the witness stand. He just wasn't that clever.

On the twelfth of January, Seth and Julie struck a deal with the Routt County D.A.'s office. In exchange for their testimony against Jill and Michael at a future trial, the young couple would receive full immunity from any charges related to the murder of Gerry Boggs. There were folks in Steamboat Springs who were not happy with this arrangement, but they would learn during the next fifteen months that the legal system was rarely about absolutes; it was about compromise. Deals were made with some people in order to avoid worse deals with others. Justice found its own level.

With the immunity agreement in place, Seth became very helpful to the police. He gave them some wigs his mother had once worn. He gave them some firearms he owned. He gave them several weapons his mother had given him—guns which he felt might have played a role in the murder. He got a shovel and dug up the buried cap that he'd found in unit 7 of the bed and breakfast, the cap that he'd washed with bleach and cut into small pieces. Even though he was worried because this was his hat and might have been at the murder scene on the day of the crime, he turned the pieces over to Detective Crotz.

Seth told the authorities about all the phone calls his mother had made to him right before and after the killing. He told them about the questions she'd asked him regarding the murder of Boggs and the time of death. He told them about the lies in his deposition in the civil lawsuit—lies that his mother had insisted he tell about the baby, Lara, and about his owning ninety percent of the bed and breakfast (so that Gerry Boggs would have access only to the other ten percent, if his mother lost the suit).

He told the police that his mother had talked scornfully about Gerry after she and the man had separated. She said that he was very prissy and liked to prance around the house in silk underwear.

Thirty-five

The preliminary hearing for Coit and Backus was originally scheduled for January 17, but then it was postponed so that all parties could have more time to prepare. Both defendants now had attorneys, and if Jill and Michael were bound over for trial after the hearing, they would be tried together. This was a source of much concern and much irritation for their lawyers, who were already lobbying Judge Richard Doucette to separate Coit and Backus and have two trials.

The attorneys also wanted any future legal proceedings moved out of Steamboat and sent to another, larger venue, where people are theoretically more open-minded. No one had any illusions about the kind of jury that would be selected in Steamboat Springs. The local paper and the Denver dailies had been filled with colorful stories about Jill's past and about her alleged connection to the murder. Everyone driving past Boggs Hardware or the Oak Street Bed and Breakfast was reminded of Gerry's failed marriage, of his phantom daughter, and that his brother had found him dead on his kitchen floor. Any potential juror who encountered Doug Boggs in his store or on the street would have had difficulty in keeping an open mind.

Michael Backus was now being represented by a broad-chested, talkative, controversial Denver attorney named Leonard Davies. Born in England in 1939, Davies had come to America at age 7 and grown up in Albuquerque, New Mexico, and Durango, Colorado. He was an excellent storyteller, and his indignation factor could rise from zero to ten in less than two seconds. Although Judge Doucette had already put a gag order on anyone associated with the Boggs case, Davies didn't mind talking about himself and his legal career.

"My parents were divorced when I was young, so I spent time in both New Mexico and Colorado," he once recalled, while sitting behind a massive wooden desk in his office near downtown Denver. He worked on the main floor of a restored Victorian mansion, which had been designated as a national historical landmark. Davies's office was cluttered and his desk was ornate, with huge pillars on the corners, adorned with carvings of lions with golden rings in their mouths.

"I come from a very poor background," he said. "The southwest valley of Albuquerque is a terrible place to grow up. It was then, and it is now. Full of gangs and violence. You got no education there, and I fought a lot. Fighting was impossible to avoid. One time, my brother got in a fight and got cut rather badly."

Davies leaned back in his chair and put his hands behind his large head, as if remembering some of the distant scraps he'd been in. Classical music softly filled his office. Something about the man made him look massive, bigger than he was. His pot belly rode proudly in front of him, almost like a flag, and he tousled his graying hair as he spoke.

"I got into the law for many reasons," he said. "My father was a Welsh coalminer in the same valley where Richard Burton was from. My father's father had died in a mine in Wales. I was raised on these stories that you had nothing when you got to the mines and no place to live. You ate in the company store. I grew up on fervent union oratory about justice. Justice! I had a passionate desire to defend the downtrodden and the working class against the haves of the world."

He sighed. "I was very naive. I'd never met a lawyer before going to law school. I didn't even know that attorneys dealt with things like trusts and wills and banks. I thought they were all out there righting wrongs, like Clarence Darrow. People at law school thought I had a leaky roof."

In December of 1965, he was admitted to the Colorado bar. He was instrumental in getting money from President Johnson's War on Poverty program in order to open a legal aid office for the poor in Denver. He was friends with radical lawyer William Kunstler. In the late sixties, Davies successfully represented impoverished migrant workers, student protesters against the Vietnam War, and a local Black Panther leader named Lauren Watson.

"I had the confidence of the Black Panthers," he said, "and I believed in them. I thought we had a terrible civil rights problem here. They never convicted a Panther that I represented in this town."

Since the seventies, he'd done mostly criminal law and personal injury work, handling roughly a dozen murder cases. Over the decades, he's lost his naïveté and much of his faith in the American legal system.

His view of contemporary lawyers and judges was withering.

"I think many attorneys have become greedy, un-idealistic money grubbers who say, 'Let's win at any cost. Let's not seek the truth, but be clever and hide the ball.' The low esteem in which lawyers are held today is not just because of their fees, but also because people recognize what's going on and they don't think that attorneys are being square. I'm cynical about lawyers who bill people at three hundred dollars an hour. What the fuck do we do that's worth that much money? My father never made that much in a week. It's outrageous. People work hard and bust their ass and we charge them those kinds of fees. It's lunacy.

"I haven't lost my idealism, but I don't think the system is amenable to change. I don't have the energy for it anymore, and I've lost the belief that I can make a significant difference. I see judges abusing people, and I'm horrified by it. Giving Coit and Backus separate trials in this case is the right thing to do, but Judge Doucette won't do that. The prosecution is also going to bring in Coit's past for the last twenty years and blow what she has done in those years over onto my client. It's totally unfair."

Why, he was asked, was the judge so bent on trying the defendants together?

"It would cost a lot more money for Routt County to try them separately. The county doesn't want to fly in its witnesses twice. That's not just fairness, but expensive fairness. And they probably can't convict Mike Backus if they didn't try him with her. How am I supposed to defend him when they bring in all the things she was doing two decades before she even met him? I'm outraged by this and I've let the judge know that, but what can you do?"

He was warming to his argument. "The defendants are charged with a conspiracy to commit murder in this case, a conspiracy that runs from June first of 1993 until October twenty-second of '93, when the body was found. Jill Coit was possibly involved in the murder of another man in Houston in 1972. That may come into the case, even though it doesn't quite fit in with the June-October of 1993 conspiracy theory, does it? They're going to use that against my client. He's just dead meat. You know that and I know that, but who cares?

"The whole legal issue here should be whether Backus went into Gerry Boggs's house and murdered him, not whether Jill Coit was a liar, a bigamist, or married a lot of times. They're trying to prove her bad character, not these murder charges. If he killed the man, let's convict him on that, not on her reputation."

He paused and drew a breath. "This case will be a challenge to my rhetorical skills."

At the preliminary hearing, Jill would not be represented by either of the local attorneys, Richard Tremaine or Randall Klauzer, whom she'd engaged earlier. The two men had generated enough hostility in Steamboat by having her as a client even before the killing of Gerry Boggs. Common sense dictated that she now needed a lawyer from outside of Steamboat—a tough-minded, experienced criminal attorney who would not be cowed by bad publicity or by the prospect of arguing the woman's case in front of a jury made up of people from in and around the victim's hometown.

Initially, she spoke with Walter Gerash, one of the most renowned criminal lawyers in Denver and the Rocky Mountain West. In decades past, he'd represented the world-class heavyweight boxer Ron Lyle, who one evening had gotten into an argument over money with a former trainer, Vernon Clark. A gun went off in Lyle's home and Clark lay dead. Lyle's story to the police was very muddy, and he looked guilty of murder. Against considerable odds, he was exonerated. More recently, Gerash had represented James King, a former security guard at Denver's United Bank. In June of 1991, a man wearing a disguise had walked into the bank one Sunday morning, stolen several hundred thousand dollars, and shot four bank employees to death. At King's home, the police found a detailed map of the bank, and several eyewitnesses to the killings identified King as the shooter. He was found not guilty and the crime remains unsolved.

Gerash ultimately decided not to take Jill's case, but passed it along to Joseph Saint-Veltri, one of his protégés and another well-known Denver attorney. With a high forehead and dark hair combed straight back, a tasteful wardrobe and a fastidious manner, a New Jersey accent still coloring the edges of his voice, fine features, eyeglasses, and a haughty yet streetwise air, a stellar vocabulary, and an attitude that often seemed to border on contempt for everyone, Saint-Veltri had the perfect facade for criminal defense work. He looked indifferent to everything on earth except the interests of his client.

For years, he'd worked right across the foyer from Leonard Davies in the Victorian mansion they shared with some other enterprises. His office was much tidier than Davies's and had a marble desk, louvered windows, and an impressive fireplace. It also featured two memorable quotes. The first said that the only justice found in the halls of justice was out in the halls. The second came from Al Capone and made the point that you could go a lot further in life with a kind word and a gun than with just a kind word.

Like Davies, Saint-Veltri had begun practicing law in the sixties as a left-leaning political activist, and he still retained some of the ideals that were prominent among many young attorneys at that time. Thirty years after the start of his career, he was quite eloquent when talking about the recent erosion of constitutional rights for criminal defendants; and about how the legal system worked for the rich and powerful, but against the poor and minorities; and about the brutality of the death penalty.

Listening to him, you were reminded of something that often arose when hearing socially conscious lawyers speak about their profession. Saint-Veltri waxed brilliant on the subjects of racism, economic oppression, and the foolishness of America's war on drugs, but the reality of his work was that he'd lately been offered $100,000 to represent a terribly unpopular client in a Steamboat Springs murder case. The money was attractive and he took the job.

Interviewing Saint-Veltri in his office, you constantly had the feeling that you were boring him to death and that he was about to stand up and pitch you out the door. Yet he didn't. He was polite, even gracious, and once you'd gotten past his severe exterior, he spoke freely and with feeling about the things that interested him. When he was interrupted by a phone call from one of his legal investigators, he said into the receiver one thing and one thing only: "Go hunt." Then he hung up and returned his attention to Jill Coit.

"In terms of the circumstantial evidence," said the lawyer, who'd tried a handful of other homicides before this one, "this is a classic murder case. But what's unusual here is all the adverse publicity my client has received. I think she will be tried on evidence from her past, evidence which the law contends is inadmissible. You can't try the character of the accused, but the prosecution will attempt to do just that under the rubric that her bad behavior during the civil suit was the motive to murder the victim. A rather tenuous notion, but . . ."

It was Saint-Veltri's contention that Jill would never have killed Gerry Boggs in order to protect her reputation in Steamboat—and to avoid the coming revelations about her in the civil trial—because she was not the sort of person who cared about how she was perceived in the small town. She'd left Steamboat behind and, according to her attorney, the local gossip meant nothing to her.

Like Davies, he would have much preferred a separate trial for his client.

"It's very tough," he said, "when the prosecution charges a conspiracy and there is more than one defendant sitting in the courtroom for the jury to look at, especially if a trial lasts for a number of weeks, as this one could. That appears very conspiratorial."

Would the absence of physical evidence help his client?

"It should," he said. "They have absolutely nothing to tie Jill to the crime, and this is after executing eighteen different search warrants. They also have no accurate time of death. The DNA tests on the semen in the used condoms at the murder scene do not match the defendant's DNA. They have no blood evidence that can be connected to my client.

"What they have is Seth Coit's testimony, and Seth is very vulnerable. But if I beat him up too badly on the witness stand, the jury will turn on me for being cruel. Seth is very confused when he talks to the police, until about his nineteenth or twentieth interview. He's confused about dates, places, and times. Then, he suddenly remembers everything—after he's been offered a very good deal. He's very susceptible to having his version of the events structured to suit his needs. The fact is that they threatened him with being an accessory to the crime and he talked."

Was Saint-Veltri looking forward to trying the case because of the legal challenges it presented?

"No," he smiled. "Of course not. Trying a bad character case is very hard, because it's difficult to get the jurors to look beyond all that. They tend to think that even if they're wrong in convicting her, she is not a good citizen."

He was asked if he and Davies, his colleague of many years and many legal wars, would be allies in this instance.

"Oh, no," he said at once. "In this venture, one has no allies. Leonard's defense will collide with mine at times, and he has no concern about what I'm concerned about. So that will be interesting. We've done this before, but with different clients. It gets a little testy, but then, it's supposed to. This isn't golf."

He smiled again and said, "By the way, did Leonard tell you about the great pig experiment?"

Thirty-six

In late October of 1993, while conducting his autopsy of Gerry Boggs, Dr. Michael Dobersen had noticed some reddish abrasions near the right ear of the victim. At that time Dr. Dobersen didn't pay much attention to the marks and neither did the police nor the prosecutors who read his autopsy report. But in the months ahead, as investigators were repeatedly confounded in their efforts to find any physical evidence linking Coit and Backus to the murder, the abrasions began to take on more and more importance. Months after CBI agents had retrieved a stun gun from one of Jill's vehicles, the authorities asked themselves if there was any connection between this gun and the marks on Gerry's face.

The strange-looking piece of equipment resembles a black, flattened flashlight with four small prongs on top of it and is called an "Omega Super Stunner." Activated by batteries and a button on the handle, it creates a crackling arc of electricity that travels a short distance through the air, and this charge causes an involuntary muscular reaction that can temporarily incapacitate an adult human being.

What kind of wound does it leave on the skin, the detectives wondered, and more precisely, what sort of wound would it leave next to the right ear? Was it possible that this gun had been used in an assault on Gerry Boggs?

During the first half of 1994, investigators in the Routt County D.A.'s Office, under the direction of Paul McLimans and Kerry St. James, put the recovered stun gun under intense scrutiny. They did this over the vehement protest of the defense attorneys, who pointed out that no fingerprints on the gun or its batteries matched either of the defendants'; that there was no accurate way to determine if it had ever been fired since leaving the factory; and that the search warrant that had led to the discovery of the gun did not mention that detectives were even looking for such a weapon. They also made it clear that Seth Coit himself had also been in possession of a stun gun at the time of Gerry Boggs's murder. The authorities weren't interested in testing Seth's gun, and the defense's protests were brushed aside.

The investigators examined the stun gun for blood smears or other trace evidence but found none. They measured the distance between the prongs and tried to surmise if these would match the abrasions on Gerry Boggs. They came up with an expert in stun gun testing, Dr. Robert Stratbucker, a cardiologist in Omaha, and sent the weapon out to Nebraska. Dr. Stratbucker told them that if they were serious about proving that the victim's wounds had been caused by this particular gun, they were going to have to pursue the matter further. He suggested that first they anesthetize a full-grown pig (because a swine's flesh is the closest in the animal kingdom to human skin) and then test the gun on the unconscious creature. With that accomplished, they would be able to tell exactly what kind of marks this stun gun left on that kind of flesh.

But if they were truly committed to finding a match, Dr. Stratbucker said, they needed to exhume Gerry Boggs from the cemetery and look at the abrasions again. If the marks on the pig were the same as those on Boggs's skin, they could be fairly certain when telling a jury that this gun had done this damage to this victim. And if the results turned out this way, they could also present as evidence that Gerry Boggs had not simply been murdered by three bullets from a .22-caliber pistol—but tortured with the stun gun before he died.

With all this in mind, the D.A.'s office gently approached the Boggs family to see how they felt about an exhumation, almost nine months after Gerry had been laid to rest.

In July, Dr. Stratbucker and Dr. Dobersen ran some tests on an anesthetized pig, performing this operation at the Large Animal Clinic in the Denver suburb of Littleton. They placed a hog on its back, shot it with the stun gun held slightly away from the skin, and carried out some other examinations on the critter, which was later destroyed. Their work revealed that the gun used on this animal caused a series of red spots that were similar to the ones on Boggs, but without more testing they could say nothing more.

In early August, the Boggs family, after thinking

it over and deciding that the procedure was absolutely necessary, agreed to have Gerry exhumed.

Dr. Dobersen examined the body again, closely studying the circular areas of redness, like small burns, near the right ear. He concluded that the spacing of these wounds on Boggs was consistent not with the muzzle of a .22-caliber weapon, but with the spacing of the wounds made by the stun gun on the pig. He also concluded that Boggs had most likely been alive when the stun gun had been used on him, and that he'd endured bursts of electrical shocks that had lasted between two to five seconds apiece. The gun, Dobersen believed, could have been applied to Boggs's skin for a total of one minute or longer.

While these experiments were being conducted, both the prosecution and the defense were greatly concerned with trying to establish a more accurate time of death. All that was known to either side was that Gerry had left the hardware store at 1 P.M. on Thursday afternoon, October 21, and been found at 3:30 P.M. the following day. Following the discovery of the body, no one had examined the victim's postmortem temperature or tested for lividity or rigidity until early the next morning. The autopsy had not been done until mid-afternoon.

An exceedingly long time had passed, the defense was fond of claiming, in which no one could be certain of what had happened. Under these circumstances, pinpointing the time of death was virtually impossible.

Dr. Dobersen felt that Boggs had died roughly two

hours after eating his last meal, but both defense attorneys, and especially Leonard Davies, found this conclusion to be highly questionable. In almost every courtroom appearance Davies would make in this case, he would declare that guesswork—and not hard scientific research—was the determining factor in the prosecution's opinion regarding the time of the murder. He would say over and over again that this was not just a matter of sloppy detective work or wild speculation. This was fundamentally the wrong way of doing things.

In February of 1994, four months after Dr. Dobersen had performed his original autopsy on Boggs, the CBI enlisted the services of Dr. David Norris to help support the autopsy's conclusions. A professor of biology at the University of Colorado, Dr. Norris ran some tests on Bogg's stomach contents, which had been removed during the autopsy, but which had not been very well preserved in the intervening period. After examining these contents, Dr. Norris reported that starch was still present in the hash browns Gerry had eaten with his last meal. The doctor also reported finding onions (which the Shack restaurant served with its potatoes) in the man's stomach. Because starch takes a considerable amount of time for humans to digest, it was Dr. Norris's opinion that Boggs had died many hours before his body had been found. He also corroborated Dr. Dobersen's finding that Gerry had probably died within two hours of finishing his final meal.

Thirty-seven

The preliminary hearing was held on February 17, 1994, exactly one month after it was originally scheduled. Entering the front door of the Routt County Courthouse, you see the head of a large moose mounted on the wall. Some writing below it says that the moose charged two hunters one day in the woods, so they shot the creature to death—a classic case of Western justice. If there is great tolerance in mountain communities for some kinds of behavior, involving drinking or general rowdiness or narcotics, there is also an underbelly of rigidity and moral rectitude.

Cross a certain line and almost no one will give a damn whether you live or die. Serious threats to human life must be dealt with seriously. In the small and crowded courtroom in Steamboat Springs, where a hearing was being held to determine if two people should be tried for murdering a respected native, every word and glance was deeply personal.

Four chandeliers hung from the ceiling and the courtroom was understatedly handsome, with pale blue walls and gold-and-green trim. Judge Richard

Doucette, a red-faced man with a quiet voice and a solemn, firm demeanor, moved things along quickly. He was not given to long speeches himself and not much interested in hearing lawyers carp and squabble. If the two urban attorneys, Saint-Veltri and Davies, with their many years of defending Black Panthers and drug dealers, thought they would come to Steamboat and ride roughshod over a provincial judge, they soon discovered that he was nothing like a patsy. He ran an exceedingly tight ship that would only grow tighter.

The Boggs family sat in the front row, no more than ten feet away from Jill Coit and Michael Backus, who were handcuffed and who never turned around to look at them. Harold Boggs's hair was thin and white. He wore old-fashioned horn-rimmed glasses. His chin trembled throughout the proceeding and he had difficulty hearing much of what went on. His elderly wife, Sylvia, sat next to him, folding her hands over his and occasionally weeping. It was as if this were the last place on earth these two people had ever expected to find themselves. And as if, in old age, they'd looked down into the abyss and been totally unprepared for what they'd seen. Their faces held not just disbelief, but shock that had not yet fully settled in.

Doug and Jan Boggs sat beside them. Jan was well dressed and looked coolly attractive, as she always did, but you sensed the rage pouring from her husband each time he gazed at the backs of the defendants. His hatred for Jill was tangible, and there were moments when it seemed as if he might jump up and shout something to her about his brother, but he always restrained himself. Sitting in court, waiting and listening, Doug was learning more about the

American legal system than he'd ever imagined he would or had ever wanted to.

During a break, he stood out in the hallway, looking very hungry for a cigarette.

"We don't have any rights in this situation," he said. "I don't and my family doesn't. Gerry doesn't have any rights, either. Only the criminals have rights."

Bob McCullough was also in the hallway, offering Doug his support, unable to stay at the hardware store and work while the hearing was taking place. He looked ready for revenge.

Judy Prier-Lewis had driven up from Denver for the day, and when the private investigator was asked if she thought the judge would dismiss the charges or bind the two defendants over for trial, she laughed, but it was not an amusing sound.

"If he doesn't bind them over," she said, "I'm getting out of this business. I'm throwing away twenty years of work and starting over in something else."

When court resumed, Jill sat at the defense table perched alertly on her chair, listening carefully or constantly whispering to her lawyer, her posture suggesting a fighter who was ready to go fifteen rounds. Conversely, Backus looked as if he'd already surrendered. His shoulders were not held squarely and his head was bent forward, as if his neck had lost some of its strength. His eyes had retreated into what appeared to be a pervasive gloom.

One couldn't help wondering if Backus had begun to question some of the words and feelings of the woman sitting next to him. Had it ever occurred to him that Gerry Boggs might not have been greedy or vicious, might not have been bisexual or homosexual? Had it ever crossed this defendant's mind that Gerry may have been a decent, hardworking man (not unlike what Backus had been before meeting Jill Coit)? Had it occurred to him that both he and Gerry had been charmed by the same woman and that both their lives had been forever changed by her?

While the Boggs family may have felt that they had no rights in the courtroom, they did have something that not everyone in their position could claim. They had a prosecuting attorney in Kerry St. James, the assistant D.A. for Routt County, who brought the kind of fervor to his job that cannot be taught or coached or implanted or even encouraged. It's either there or it isn't. In St. James's case, it came with breathing in and breathing out. A small man with wavy hair and a resonant voice, he looked so thin inside his dark suits that he seemed to have no body at all. His appearance was very misleading.

He was not just mentally rigorous and emotionally tough; he was also physically courageous. His hobbies were downhill skiing and competitive car racing, and he was one of those people who finds enjoyment in extremely tense circumstances. When there was good reason to panic, he often noticed himself becoming strangely calm.

Growing up in various parts of America and Europe, St. James had two heroes above all others. One was Frank Serpico, the New York City cop who exposed police corruption, and the other was Atticus Finch, the fictional defense lawyer in *To Kill a Mockingbird.*

"I just like people who fight for justice," he says. After studying literature at Duke and taking a law degree from Florida State, he began his career as a prosecuting attorney in Palm Beach County in Florida. For the next seven years, he handled a number of high-profile drug cases and homicides.

"I always wanted to be a prosecutor," he says. "It never even occurred to me to be a defense attorney. My interest is in helping people who have been hurt, and this job is the most direct way of doing that. I like murder cases the best. They're the only ones to try, after you get over your initial fear, because there's so much at stake. My dealings with the victim's family and friends is the most rewarding thing I do. To be a murder victim's friend or family member is unbearable, so I try to connect with these people and make a difference.

"I explain to them in plain English what's happening and what to anticipate. Things get ugly in the courtroom, and I want to let them know that in advance and to be prepared when they hear the victim being attacked. You try to tell them that it isn't personal. I put myself in the victim's place and fight for him or her as if I were fighting for my life. That gives me inspiration."

In his youth, he'd become an accomplished skier in Europe, and in adulthood he'd always wanted to live in the mountains.

"In 1987," he says, "the moon, the stars, and the sun all lined up to allow me to get this job in Steamboat. I came here in part for the skiing, but then the Boggs case came along. The ironic thing is that ever since it started, I've had almost no opportunity to be on the slopes. But next year . . ."

Between 1987 and 1994, he prosecuted half a dozen local homicides, none of them nearly so prominent as the murder of Gerry Boggs. St. James believes strongly in the death penalty and while working in Florida, he was successful in getting the court to award it in two of his cases. Because Colorado had not put anyone to death by lethal injection since 1967, and because of the difficulty of getting capital convictions in the state, and because of the complexity of charging two defendants in this murder, the Routt County D.A.'s office intended to ask for life without parole for Coit and Backus, should there eventually be a conviction.

If St. James was disappointed with this decision, it had done nothing to blunt his enthusiasm for the case.

"My moral commitment to my job doesn't waver," he says. "As a prosecutor, it's very easy to become an institutionalized government lawyer, but when you're dealing with victims' families, that's the very last thing they want you to be. I worry that if I'm not on their side, who else will be? In the courtroom, I try to be professional, but at the same time, I hope I seek justice without regard for whether or not I hurt someone's feelings."

From the beginning, St. James was prepared for the possibility that he and Saint-Veltri might quarrel in court. The Denver lawyer's reputation for slickness had put St. James on the alert to be ready for anything. As it turned out, these two men got along fine. St. James was pleasantly surprised by the professionalism and cooperative spirit of his legal counterpart. He respected basically everything Saint-Veltri did throughout the duration of the case and came away feeling that the attorney's manner evoked a long-forgotten era of the gentlemanly lawyer.

It was Davies and St. James who could not abide one another. They sniped and they sneered. At times, things between them turned caustic and they had to be separated by Judge Doucette. With words and looks, with body language and expressions of mutual disdain, the two men struggled at the preliminary hearing, at subsequent legal proceedings, and on almost every other occasion when they met in the courtroom. It was hard to say who was the more outraged by the other's behavior.

During the preliminary hearing, Saint-Veltri asked CBI agent Susan Kitchen about the immunity agreement that had recently been struck between Seth and Julie Coit and the Routt County D.A.'s office. The lawyer inquired if the young couple were granted immunity for everything potentially criminal in their past, or just for their involvement in this particular case.

Kitchen hesitated and said, "They were granted immunity on an insurance scam and immunity for this murder. They knew about this murder before it happened and told no one and were then silent for several months . . ."

"Will Seth and Julie," Saint-Veltri asked, "be in a better position for running and owning the bed and breakfast by coming forward with this information to the police?"

"I don't know," the agent replied. "They said they want to sell the bed and breakfast and leave Steamboat Springs."

"Would that be easier if Jill Coit were out of the picture?"

"They didn't say that."

When Saint-Veltri pointed out that there was no one anywhere to corroborate what Seth and Julie had told the authorities about Coit and Backus, the remark left the agent unfazed.

Davies asked Kitchen if she knew that Troy Giffin, whose memory she had largely relied on to bring charges against his client, had fallen out of a tree in the summer of 1993. Did she know that he'd landed on his head and was on serious medication when the agent had interviewed him? Did she know that Giffin had a criminal record?

She knew all that, Kitchen told the lawyer, but still found him to be a very credible source of information.

In his closing argument, Davies said that "the case is singularly circumstantial against Mr. Backus. There's no evidence that Mr. Backus was anywhere near Steamboat Springs at that time. And he had no motive to do this . . . you have to disregard the man's work history, his military history, and you have to stand logic on its head to infer that he was involved in this crime.

"That he's being held on five million dollars' bond—which is no bond at all—is unconscionable!"

In his summation, Kerry St. James told the judge that Jill had clearly informed her son of when she'd committed the crime—"between three-thirty and four P.M. on October 21, 1993. The motive here was simply money. The bed and breakfast was in dispute, and this was bringing up things uncomfortable to Ms. Coit. Bigamies in several states. Bigamy against

Gerry Boggs. And Ms. Coit was very concerned about the reopening of the Houston murder . . ."

While St. James was speaking, Harold Boggs leaned over and touched his shoulder against his wife's. The old man's head was shaking badly, and Sylvia had raised her hand to cover her mouth in an effort to stifle her tears, but she could not. Harold patted her arm and the elderly woman looked down at her lap.

"These two defendants," St. James was saying, "intended to stay in Mexico after they fled from Colorado. They sneaked back into the country, but were planning on taking off again . . . We ask the court to consider the shovel blow to Gerry Boggs . . . and that six days before the murder, Backus was in Steamboat Springs to 'take care of business,' as he told Seth, and that he had a clean, untraceable gun. This was a highly deliberated murder."

Without fanfare, the judge ruled that Coit and Backus would stand trial on August 29, more than six months away. The Boggs family greeted this declaration with smiles, but they were hesitant smiles, half-smiles, as if they realized that nothing had yet been accomplished and there was a very long way to go.

Thirty-eight

For a year, very little happened. In June of '94, Seth and his mother sold the bed and breakfast, after a Steamboat judge allowed Gerry Boggs's old lien to be removed from the property. The bed and breakfast brought $470,000 and Jill's lawyer was paid from these proceeds. Seth also received $100,000 from the sale (he and Julie made plans to move to Sandpoint, Idaho). Doug Boggs and some other locals were disappointed with this legal decision, but in the end there was nothing they could do about it.

In July of that year, the prosecution began its experiments on the anesthetized pig, and in August, Gerry's body was exhumed and reexamined for stun gun wounds. The trial, set to begin later that month, was postponed until early February of 1995. At the defense's request, it was also moved out of Steamboat, because of the bad publicity and ill feeling that Coit and Backus had generated in the Boggses' hometown.

When Saint-Veltri and Davies had asked Judge Doucette for a change of venue, they'd hoped to have the trial take place in a larger Colorado city, perhaps even Denver or its environs. Instead, the judge chose an even smaller town than Steamboat Springs. Hot Sulphur Springs, the county seat of Grand County, was seventy miles southeast of Steamboat and had a population of three hundred. If the defense attorneys were not pleased with the trial's location, they would become even more upset when they learned that Judge Doucette lived in Hot Sulphur and would be able to oversee the proceeding without leaving home. And the lawyers would become downright disturbed when they discovered, about halfway through the trial, that the office being used in Hot Sulphur by Routt County D.A. Paul McLimans was leased by Christine Doucette, the judge's wife.

The knowledge of a connection between Judge Doucette's wife and the prosecution caused Saint-Veltri and Davies to ask for a mistrial. It was hardly the first time they'd done this. The notion of a mistrial was one of the constant themes of the event. Every few days, a controversy would arise in the courtroom, the defense would seek a mistrial, Davies and Kerry St. James would argue heatedly in front of the bench—or with one another—and then Judge Doucette, after brief consideration, would decide that the trial was going forward.

After the defense uncovered the connection between Paul McLimans's office and Christine Doucette, a retired suburban Denver judge was called in to hear a motion on the matter. The judge ruled that because Christine Doucette leased the building from Grand County, and because neither she nor her husband had negotiated directly with McLimans, this was not a violation of the judicial code of ethics. Judge Doucette stayed and there was no mistrial.

* * *

In February of 1995, Hot Sulphur lacked everything when it came to excitement, but not when it came to scenery. At sunset the snow-topped peaks of the Continental Divide were visible in the distance, ragged and rosy with alpenglow. Elk bugled on the hillsides—a wild, high, echoing cry—and on one occasion Judge Doucette interrupted the trial to point out the window as a herd of the stately animals walked past the courtroom windows. Riding through a valley outside of Hot Sulphur, a driver could be utterly transfixed by the sight of mustangs running in a line through the snow, hooves churning and manes aloft.

Sometimes, in the early evening, while all this beauty was raging in the countryside, you could see Kerry St. James and Paul McLimans huddled together, working late in the A-frame building on Main Street, which the district attorney had rented for the duration of the trial. And sometimes, in the mornings, you could see St. James muttering to himself before he entered the courtroom; he was talking to Gerry Boggs and asking the man to be with him and to help him in whatever he could, so that the prosecution could win.

Hot Sulphur Springs was a terribly intimate place for a murder trial, and for six weeks everyone rubbed shoulders with everyone else, whether they wanted to or not. The lawyers clashed bitterly in the courtroom and an hour later walked past each other on Main Street. Or they ate dinner seated next to one another in the only café in town. The Boggs family, Cathy McCullough, and other townspeople who'd come in from Steamboat stared glumly at the defendants in court; but on the street, they could not avoid running into Jill's mother and father, who attended the trial every day, or into the parents of Michael Backus. No one could avoid an enemy or potential enemy, but everyone tried hard to be civil.

Judge Doucette and his minions were nothing short of paranoid. Every spectator entering the courtroom was asked to identify himself and his purpose to the bailiff—an unheard-of procedure anywhere else. Whispering was not allowed, and chuckling opened one up to the threat of punishment. The judge had banned TV cameras from the courtroom, and more than once he declared that if the observers didn't straighten themselves up right now, he was going to dismiss everyone and conduct this affair in private.

For the duration of the proceeding, the controversial O. J. Simpson double-murder trial was unfolding in California, and it cast its long shadow all the way to Hot Sulphur Springs. Not only was the Simpson case mentioned in several of the judge's most important rulings (he ultimately refused to allow in much of Jill Coit's past), he made it very clear that the circus atmosphere dominating the trial in Los Angeles was not at all welcome in his courtroom. Small town justice would be much swifter and much leaner. Those who preferred monkey business or wanted to argue the fine points of law endlessly would be shown the back of his hand.

Hot Sulphur Springs never had seen, and never would see, such a cast of characters again. Striding down the street wearing a long denim duster with leather lapels and a silver-buckled broad-brimmed hat, Leonard Davies looked for all the world like John

Wayne having just dismounted his steed. In striking contrast, Joe Saint-Veltri, dressed in well-tailored suits and polished, sophisticated shoes, looked like a bon vivant ready to go out on the town—even though there was no town to go out onto. And the media, after court had recessed for the day, consistently repaired to Ernie's Tavern, the only bar in town, for elbow-bending and amateur lawyering.

Inside the courtroom itself, the parade of witnesses was every bit as colorful as the attorneys. Jill Coit had not only affected numerous lives in various parts of America, she'd done this across a wide band of society. Mo Hanley marched up to the witness stand wearing a Western-cut shirt, Western-cut pants and boots, and a short, manly hairdo. A self-proclaimed lesbian, she was refreshingly pleased with who she was. If Saint-Veltri had attempted to intimidate some other prosecution witness with his big-city talk and sneering manner, he tried no such thing with Mo.

As she told the story of raising herself on the streets of Ottumwa, Iowa, amid rape and drugs and other forms of violence, Saint-Veltri seemed to listen to her with a deepening respect. Nothing about her looked or sounded like a victim. Here was a survivor who asked for no sympathy and apologized to no one for what she'd been through and who she'd become. She would not curb her appearance or her speech for anything, including the solemnity of a murder trial in a small town. By the time she'd finished testifying, she'd captured the imagination and admiration of everyone in the courtroom.

When Troy Giffin took the stand, he looked beyond nervous. He seemed almost ill. His voice repeatedly halted, and he fidgeted and squirmed, unable to glance over at Mike Backus. Giffin was present in the courtroom for only one reason, and that was to convict his buddy and co-worker at U.S. West for many years. Giffin had good reason to be queasy. Over the past fifteen months, he'd received some harsh treatment at the phone company, from close friends of the defendant's who felt that Troy was not merely betraying Backus, but taking away his life. The defense would later call some of these people, who told the jury that Giffin was not at all a reliable person and was given to making up fantasies. When Troy left the Hot Sulphur courtroom for the last time, he looked profoundly relieved.

Kathy Backus also testified against her ex-husband and the father of their young daughter, Erin. On the witness stand, she listened to a tape, recovered from Gerry Boggs's home, in which a man threatened to expose one of Gerry's homosexual relationships. Kathy told the court that the person who identified himself on the tape as Don Cole was in fact Michael Backus.

The testimony—and the things that former family members or friends were doing to one another at the trial—were occasionally almost too painful to absorb. For several moments, Vance Halvorson provided some much-needed relief and humor when he was asked by the prosecution what kind of birth-control Gerry and Jill had used during their marriage.

With a knowing smile, he turned to the jury and boomed out, "Condominiums!"

Seth, William, and Andrew Coit all testified against their mother. Each of them referred to her as Jill, and each avoided eye contact with the woman. She, on the contrary, grinned up at them and even waved. Her three sons stated that they were flat-out afraid of their mother, and in the courtroom they seemed frightened telling the jury what they knew about her. Their impact as witnesses came not just in what they said, but was also conveyed in their obvious discomfort at finding themselves in these circumstances.

Despite everything that Jill had done to them and to others, her sons appeared deeply hurt by what they were doing to her now. Out of necessity and social duty, they were being forced to violate not just one of the most mysterious and powerful of all human bonds—between mothers and their children—they were also violating something within themselves.

During his cross-examination by Saint-Veltri, Andrew became visibly upset, scolding the lawyer and saying that he [the attorney] could not possibly understand what a disrupted life the young man had led because of his mother. All of the brothers, he said, had been dragged around the United States since infancy, pulled into and out of schools, uprooted at their mother's whim. It had left him feeling torn and fragmented.

William seemed much cooler under fire than Andrew, but inside, he was also in turmoil. More than any of the brothers, he'd not only felt revenge toward Jill, he'd taken it. He'd made the calls that had put his mother in jail, but he, too, looked haunted by traces of ambivalence. While he was on the stand, the expression in his eyes said that if there'd just been a way to reach her, to change her, to convince her that she was damaging others, he would have done that, but . . .

Seth testified far longer than either William or Andrew. He had much more to answer for, and although he tried to tell a consistent and logical story, he often fumbled around and sounded utterly confused. He did a lot of yawning and tugging at his ears. Some people found him to be humorous; others thought he was a terrible phony who was only attempting to cover up his own involvement in the crime.

Several observers in the gallery again compared him to Forrest Gump, but one woman said that he reminded her of Jerry Lewis in *The Nutty Professor.* Outside the courtroom there was much debate about how intelligent Seth was—or how mentally disabled. The general consensus was that he was smart enough to remember what had happened in and around the bed and breakfast in October of 1993. By the time he'd left the witness stand, you weren't at all certain that he'd told you nothing but the truth, but you also leaned toward giving him the benefit of the doubt. No one could imagine what it was like to have Jill Coit for a mother.

Near the end of Seth's testimony, Leonard Davies rose from his chair and approached the young man closely. Davies accused him of having had the motive, the means, and the opportunity to kill Gerry Boggs.

Seth, Davies said, was responsible for the death of Boggs, wasn't he?

"No," he replied, and in this instance, he did not have to hesitate and grope for an answer.

After Backus had come to Steamboat Springs, Davies said, and after he'd failed to commit the murder on the weekend of October 15, Seth had been enlisted by his mother to kill the man, hadn't he?

"No," he said again, more forcefully this time. "Because of the conversations I had with Jill, I was involved, but . . ."

"But what?"

He held his silence, as if trying to think of the best thing to say.

"You had a stun gun, didn't you?" Davies said.

"Yes."

"And other guns?"

"Yes."

"You had a motive."

"No."

"You killed Gerry Boggs, didn't you?"

"Wrong!" Seth shook his head.

Davies came nearer, leaning forward and repeating the charge. "You killed him, didn't you?"

Seth looked straight at the lawyer and said something that may have resolved once and for all the debate about his intelligence.

"I wouldn't be that stupid," he said.

Thirty-nine

The jury was decidedly rural. The six men and six women on the panel ranged from their mid-twenties to their mid-seventies, and all were working folks from in or around Hot Sulphur Springs. They dressed casually, one fellow coming in every day in a T-shirt and colorful surfer pants. He drank continually from a styrofoam cup. The foreman, with gray hair and a weathered face, looked like the classic Western rancher, and another gentleman regularly wore red suspenders. The women favored jeans and sweaters. The jury was all-white and all-business. Only one person wore any emotion on her face, and this was a middle-aged woman who constantly nodded at the witnesses, as if she were really enjoying their testimony and wanted them to go on.

Jill was as animated as the jury was subdued. She smiled a lot and at humorous moments she laughed more loudly than anyone else. She constantly ate licorice bits or sucked on hard candy. She flirted with Saint-Veltri. She filled his water glass before it ever reached empty (her attorney seemed embarrassed by her attentiveness). One time, when she'd taken off her jacket and was obviously sticking out her breasts for others to admire, he quietly suggested that she put the jacket back on.

She wore a camel pantsuit with a cream-colored silk blouse and an orange kerchief tied jauntily around her neck. Or she wore a white wool blazer, a brown turtleneck, and a gold chain. Her appearance was critical to her. Sometimes, she used crutches and aggressively limped in front of the jury—a reminder of her 1993 surgery—but at other times, she walked on her own and seemed completely healed.

Her dark hair was now short and straight. She was more attractive in person than in newspaper photographs. She had a good figure and a fine complexion, and she usually looked harmless. Her rage was deeply settled into the back of her jaw and somewhere behind her eyes. These features were normally used to smile, but occasionally, while she was sitting at the defense table or glancing around the courtroom, some muscle slipped or some doorway opened and you were suddenly staring at a face that had no remorse and no self-control—just blind will. Then she would smile again and look friendly and warm. It was the easy and fluid way she moved in and out of these things that scared people.

When the crime scene photos were shown to the jury—and when Gerry's parents and other relatives began to weep at the sight of them—Jill got out of her chair and walked to where she had a better view of the images. She stared at them wide-eyed and fascinated, like a child taking in some drawings she had just completed. When Boggs's bloody clothes were brought into evidence, she acted the same way.

Michael Backus responded in exactly the opposite

manner. He could not look at the pictures or the clothing, he could not look at anyone in the courtroom. He seemed ashamed of himself for being here.

While the testimony slowly unfolded, Cathy McCullough, who drove to the trial every day over the wintry roads from Steamboat, worked on a cross-stitch of various fruits against a black background. Jan Boggs cross-stitched a baby bib for her granddaughter. Another Boggs relative played a silent game of electronic poker. The family was staying at a condo, which they'd rented in a nearby town, and they came to Hot Sulphur in full force and sat in the front row. Doug missed a few days because of a hip-replacement operation, but he showed up soon afterward, aided by a walker and committed to being present for the duration of the proceeding.

Jill's mother and father sat and watched the event in silence and with gloomy resignation; nothing was going well for their daughter in this trial. Once, when her father dropped a pen on the floor and a woman spectator bent down to retrieve it for him, he looked at the stranger and smiled a smile of overflowing gratitude, muttering his thanks. He hadn't expected to be treated so well in this courtroom, and he seemed taken aback. Moving along the streets of the small town, wrapped in their heavy coats and leaning into the cold wind, this elderly couple looked absolutely alone.

By early March, three weeks after the trial had begun and as the prosecution neared the end of its case, it seemed unlikely that the defendants would be found anything but guilty. The circumstantial evidence against them was strong, and the words of

Seth Coit and Troy Giffin had been especially damaging. If the Boggs family and the prosecutors were not feeling relieved yet, they had good reason to be confident. Then something happened that threw all of them into a panic.

During the week of March 6, when the defense was presenting its own witnesses, Leonard Davies announced to the press that he had a surprise witness who would "blow your socks off" and lead to an exoneration of his client—if not to the freeing of Jill Coit as well.

A few days earlier, Jan Bertrand, who was employed as a clerk at the Pilot Office Supply store in Steamboat Springs, had gone to Davies and told him about something that had occurred on October 21, 1993. She was working that Thursday afternoon when Gerry Boggs had come in and purchased a set of chair arms and some copy paper. She was certain that she'd sold him these items at just a few minutes before 4 P.M.

Through the newspapers, Bertrand had been closely following the murder trial in Hot Sulphur Springs. On February 20, when she read that the prosecution's case was based on the notion that Boggs had died between 1 and 3 P.M. on the twenty-first of October, she was convinced that this could not have been possible. He had to have been alive longer than that because she'd seen him as late as 4 P.M. If this was wrong, the question arose in her mind, what else had the prosecution said that was misleading? And was their theory of the murder nothing more than that? What if Boggs had died considerably later and these two people were not responsible for his death?

After reading about the time of death, Bertrand

called the district attorney's office in Steamboat. Her information was passed along from Rachel Dorr, a secretary in the office, to Tim Garner, the lead investigator for the D.A. Garner, when questioned about this later, said that he was under the impression that Bertrand had mixed up her days and had actually sold the items to Boggs on Wednesday, the twentieth. Because of this, he saw no reason to pursue the matter further.

When Bertrand realized that she was getting nowhere with the prosecution, she decided to contact the defense. On March 1, she called Leonard Davies, who was utterly delighted to speak with the woman. He well knew that if her information was accurate and if she could hold up under cross-examination, she could provide the kind of testimony that might throw reasonable doubt into many jurors' minds. For the first time since the case had begun, he felt hopeful.

When Kerry St. James and Paul McLimans, both of whom were prosecuting the case in Hot Sulphur, learned about Jan Bertrand, they were outraged and immediately declared that the defense was engaging in "trial by ambush." Doug and Jan Boggs were also stunned. They'd been silent about Jill Coit for nearly a year and a half since the murder, avoiding the media and doing everything they'd been told to do by the prosecutors, in order to ensure a conviction. Now, less than a week from the trial's completion, it looked as if everything might come undone.

The cross-stitching suddenly stopped. Jan and Cathy McCullough were too disturbed to stay with it.

Well before Jan Bertrand surfaced at the trial, the tension in the courtroom had reached the level of draining. The woman's appearance only made it worse. Davies and St. James now glowered at one another and whispered things under their breath. The lawyers had grown pale and frayed; courtroom civility was deteriorating. Judge Doucette, who had been impatient to start with, grew even more ill-tempered, and the spectators felt as if they were watching a drama that had to be resolved soon—or someone was going to snap.

The only person who did not seem much affected by all this was Jill herself, who looked on as if she found it diverting and amusing.

Davies asked the judge for an independent investigation of Bertrand's recollection of events, but his request was denied. Then the prosecution asked Doucette for more time to look into the woman's claims, but the judge was determined to move ahead without delay. As Bertrand took the stand on Friday, March 10, St. James and McLimans scrambled to come up with any evidence that would indicate she was mistaken.

The attorneys contacted the owner of the office supply business, Chuck Leckenby, who was a long-time acquaintance of the Boggs family. During Bertrand's direct examination by Davies and Saint-Veltri, rumors filled the courtroom about the witness's current relationship with her employer. People said that she was being harassed at work because she'd come forward with this information. They said she'd been known to use Prozac—and was therefore not a credible witness. They said she was going to lose her job. As the gossip flew and as the woman's testimony unfolded, Leckenby and his staff searched frantically for any record of the last transaction Gerry had ever had at the store.

By Friday evening, Bertrand was still on the stand and the trial recessed for the weekend. On Saturday and Sunday, Leckenby, aided by the prosecuting lawyers, kept looking in his files. He maintained a log that showed the exact time of sales, but only for the past thirty days. The one for October 21, 1993, had long since been thrown away. After exhaustive digging, he was able to come up with a receipt indicating that Gerry had in fact come into the store on October 21 and purchased chair arms and paper. But the location of the receipt indicated to Leckenby that Boggs had not come in at 3:45, as Bertrand now claimed, but between 12:30 and 1 P.M.

On Monday, March 13, St. James and McLimans, who'd worked nonstop throughout the weekend, began their rebuttal of the woman's testimony, using what they'd just learned from Leckenby. Bertrand, they contended, had simply confused the time of day in which she'd made the sale. While presenting his point of view, St. James let it be known to the court that he was furious with Davies for using this "surprise witness" tactic. He declared that there was no exculpatory evidence of any kind in what Bertrand was saying, and he was angry at Davies for spreading rumors that the witness's life could be at stake because of what she'd done. Davies vehemently denied saying anything of the sort.

During the heated proceedings on Monday, when the two prosecutors were bending over a table together and looking for an exhibit, their case hanging on their ability to disprove what Bertrand had claimed, St.

James grinned mischievously and whispered to McLimans, "I love it when things get like this."

The D.A. glanced over at the recreational race car driver working beside him and said, "I know that, Kerry. You're sick."

Many weeks later, Chuck Leckenby would say that Bertrand's testimony had been based purely upon her memory and her memory had been faulty. He would also say that while Bertrand stated that she'd turned over the final details of the transaction with Gerry that day to another clerk, the clerk she referred to had not even been working on that afternoon.

"We had pretty conclusive evidence," he said, "that what she remembered happening just could not have happened."

Bertrand was by far the strongest witness the defense presented, and once she'd left the stand, testimony ended and the jury began its deliberations. Not long after that, Jan Bertrand got another job.

First-degree murder cases, of course, are often the most difficult ones for jurors to render verdicts on. They frequently debate and argue nastily among themselves for days before deciding that someone is guilty or innocent—or that they cannot reach a decision. The prosecutors and the Boggs family were prepared for a long wait between the conclusion of the testimony and the end of the trial. With the fate of two defendants at stake in this case, the expectation was that the wait would be even longer, perhaps stretching to as much as a week. All of them would simply have to find something to do in Hot Sulphur Springs, while hoping that the time passed quickly.

On March 17, to the astonishment of everyone involved in the trial, the jury came back after only five hours of deliberation. There had been virtually no disagreement between any of them. Both defendants were guilty of murder and conspiracy. The citizens of Grand County, Colorado, had done their work and were ready to go home.

When the verdict was announced, the Boggs family rushed forward, weeping and hugging the prosecutors. Cathy McCullough sobbed, while Harold and Sylvia Boggs clung to one another, as if standing alone, each of them might fall down. Doug and Jan could not contain their relief, and Doug looked happy for the first time in seventeen months. He was finally ready to talk to the media.

When asked about the verdict by a TV reporter, he summed things up as succinctly as possible.

"This time," he said, "she picked the wrong town, the wrong family, and the wrong man. My brother died so that she would never do this to anyone again."

Saint-Veltri and Davies departed without a word to the press (Jill's parents were not present for the verdict, and neither were Backus's). In defeat, the telephone repairman remained silent, but Jill herself was not so quiet or passive. Earlier in the trial, when the judge had asked her if she wanted to testify or say anything on her own behalf, she declined the offer. Then she told Doucette that it had been impossible for her to get a fair trial with him sitting on the bench, because he knew the Boggs family and had even met Gerry and herself on one occasion.

Listening to these comments, Judge Doucette was

stonefaced. Then he said that he'd never met the woman before the trial had begun.

Following the verdict, as Jill was being led away from the courthouse by police officers, she looked into the assembled TV cameras and defiantly said that because of Judge Doucette, she could never have received justice in Hot Sulphur Springs.

Forty

After the trial was over and people had returned to
Steamboat Springs, Doug and Jan threw a party for
the members of the D.A.'s office and the law enforcement officials who had worked on the case during the
past year and a half. St. James appeared more relaxed
than at any time since the end of 1993. During the
party, some of those who had been the most involved
in prosecuting Coit and Backus began to speculate
about what they believed had happened in Gerry
Boggs's home on the afternoon of October 21, 1993.

The general conclusion was that the couple had
been in the man's house when he'd returned home
from eating at the Shack. Coit and Backus had let
themselves in through the back door (she had a key)
and were lying in wait with a shovel, a stun gun, a
plastic bag, and a .22-caliber pistol.

When Gerry entered the kitchen, the authorities had
decided, Backus slipped the bag over his head. Jill
applied the stun gun to his face, temporarily leaving
him helpless, Backus hit him in the head with the
shovel, and she shot him three times. The small size

of the firearm told the prosecutors that a woman had probably used it and done the actual killing.

Several weeks after this party, Jan and Doug Boggs invited two other visitors out to their spacious and attractive home in the countryside near Steamboat. The foursome ate dinner over a large bottle of wine and as the sun fell behind the mountains, Doug began to speak more openly about his brother than he had for a very long time.

He said that because Gerry had always made a point of stopping at lemonade stands in the summertime and buying a drink from the kids who were selling the refreshments, he now did the same thing. He said that he'd gotten to know his brother a lot better since the man's death; people in and beyond Steamboat Springs had told him so many things about Gerry's kindness and generosity that he himself had been unaware of. At one point, Doug looked across the table, with a loving expression directed toward his wife, and said that of the two brothers, he was always the lucky one, because he'd met just the right woman and Gerry never had.

Since Jill had been convicted, Doug had received many calls from people all across the United States who wanted to express their gratitude to him, to his family, and to those who had successfully prosecuted the woman. The callers had something in common with Doug and Jan, because they, too, had been hurt or scammed by Jill Coit—they'd lost money or a piece of their innocence or trustfulness through their dealings with her. They'd always been too frightened of Jill to attempt to get her into a courtroom or a prison cell, and they were now deeply grateful that at long last someone had done what was necessary to bring the woman's criminal career to an end.

Talking to these people on the phone, Doug was astonished at how many lives Jill had come into contact with and how shabbily she'd treated all of them.

As the night grew darker and the wine flowed, Doug was asked if it seemed strange to him that all the information on Jill's past that had once been gathered—by Judy Prier-Lewis, Vance Halvorson, Thane Gilliland, and Gerry himself—and then stored in five boxes—had not totally emerged during the course of the murder trial. Nearly two years earlier, it was supposed to have come out during the civil suit, but that had never happened. Most people had then expected it to surface in Judy Prier-Lewis's testimony in Hot Sulphur Springs, but after much thought and legal argument, Judge Doucette had finally decided that a sizable portion of Jill's history was not relevant to these proceedings. Prier-Lewis's time on the stand had been brief.

Doug took a sip of wine, lit a cigarette, and said, "Gerry wanted the whole story of what happened to him to be told. He always wanted that, even if some of it didn't make him look very good, and I have the feeling that he still does. He was the one who pushed everybody to get more information on her so he could expose her for what she was. He was the one who wanted people to know the truth about her. He didn't want anybody else to suffer the way he had."

Doug continued speaking about his brother, recalling anecdotes and adventures from the past, pouring out the love he'd felt for the man, and as he did this, a very odd thing occurred. It really wasn't an event as much as a feeling, and it was the kind of feeling that is difficult to put into words. Even if you do attempt to put it into language, it never quite fits within those boundaries. Yet when it happens, it seems un-questionably real.

Gerry, or the spirit of Gerry, was moving in and around the conversation, touching everyone present and reinforcing the notion that he did indeed want his story told about what had taken place in his home-town.

Epilogue

Forty-one

A great many folks had waited a very long time for Jill Coit and Michael Backus to be sentenced to life in prison. Their moment came on May 23, 1995, a little more than two months after the verdict. It would be the last time the defendants would ever appear together in public in Steamboat, the last time that the townspeople would be able to gather in one place and finish the ordeal of a long and complicated murder trial. On this occasion, Doug Boggs and other family members would be given the opportunity to stand up in the courtroom and say what they felt about either Coit or Backus. Ever since the verdict had come in, Doug had been preparing his speech.

By 8:45 on the morning of the twenty-third, the largest courtroom in the Routt County Courthouse was filled to capacity. The Boggses were all there, and their friends and acquaintances were also present. Bob and Cathy McCullough had arrived with their two children, Mark and Colleen, and Thane Gilliland had come up from Denver. The media was covering the sentencing en masse: the jury box was crammed with both law enforcement personnel and reporters. Before Judge Doucette entered the court-room, the spectators were smiling and joking. The tension that had permeated the trial in Hot Sulphur Springs was gone; Coit and Backus had been found guilty and virtually everyone looked delighted.

The convicted killers wore gray sweatshirts and bright orange pants and had shackles on their ankles. They also seemed in a much better humor since leaving Hot Sulphur behind. Jill sat alertly at the defense table, her eyes constantly moving, as if she were plotting a new scheme. Backus spoke playfully to her and to Leonard Davies. The former telephone repairman appeared considerably more at peace than he had during the trial.

When Judge Doucette commenced the hearing, the room held a charge of true expectation and excitement. It was highly unusual for a community to be given the chance to strike a blow for old-fashioned goodness and decency, but the local citizens had come out this morning for just that purpose. Jill had hustled them, in one form or another, for years. Now it was their turn to show her and tell her what they thought of her and her co-murderer. Some people in the gallery looked like they had a taste for blood.

The hearing began very slowly. Saint-Veltri had filed yet another motion asking that the judge disqualify himself at this late date because he'd known the Boggs family before the killing occurred and this gave his role at the trial "the appearance of impropriety." Tediously, the lawyer then went over a number of issues that had surfaced and resurfaced in Hot Sulphur Springs: the time of death; the semen found at the crime scene (which could have, Saint-Veltri implied, belonged not to Backus or Boggs, but to the real killer); and the general unfairness of the judge and prosecution toward his client.

Two hours passed and the mood in the courtroom fell sharply. People had grown bored with these arguments and discussions; they'd heard them too many times before. This was not at all what they'd wanted or expected to happen this morning. The Boggs family looked restless, and young Mark McCullough was leaning against his mother's shoulder, as if he were drifting toward sleep. He was not alone.

Davies stood and once again strongly declared that Backus should have had a separate trial. His client had been cheated and justice had not been served by lumping him together with Jill Coit.

Once Davies had concluded his remarks, the prosecutors asked the court to have the defense team pay for some of the expenses they'd incurred during the trial, including a $16 pizza. This produced an outburst of indignation from Saint-Veltri and Davies, and by now it was clear that the bad feelings that had been stirred in Hot Sulphur had not evaporated with the verdict. They were still alive and flowing through all of the attorneys.

By noon the lawyers were still arguing and people in the gallery were beginning to stand and slip out the door. It had become apparent that in a curious sort of way, Jill was going to have the last laugh on those who'd so eagerly come together to dump scorn on her and Michael Backus. While endlessly challenging the judge on legal issues Saint-Veltri had already lost many times before, her attorney was leaving people almost too weary to pay attention. By the time Kerry St. James finally stood and asked the judge to give the defendants the harshest possible sentence, even he seemed worn out by what had just taken place. Yet he tried to speak with fervor.

"The state of Colorado," he said, "has no interest in seeing either of these two individuals rehabilitated . . . We are asking you to give them life without parole plus forty-eight years for conspiracy plus a million-dollar fine for each of them, so that they can never profit by selling their story to the media . . . They committed this crime in a heinous, cruel, and depraved manner. They applied a stun gun to Gerald Boggs while he was still alive, as shown by tests on living flesh . . . Michael Backus agreed to this conspiracy for five long months. His character is nothing but evil . . . and it was money that enticed him to participate in this."

People had stopped snoozing and were listening closely to the prosecutor.

"As for defendant Coit," he said, "she attempted to enlist Mo Hanley to commit the murder. She also manipulated her own son, Seth, who could not free himself from his devious mother. Finally, she asked Michael Backus to kill for her . . . The exhumation of Gerry Boggs and further tests show that he was tortured before he died and that he fought back against his killer. His exhumation was, we believe, what he would have wanted and it was also a courageous thing for his family to allow us to do. We ask you to feel what a family must feel when they have to exhume a loved one almost a year after he's been laid to rest.

"Jill Coit would have lost between $100,000 and $200,000 in the civil suit. She'd already lost $100,000 in her divorce settlement with Carl Steely and she was broke. For $100,000 to $200,000 she was willing to commit a murder. This decision carried with it malice, a true ill will, and an evil intent . . .

"Her entire life has been one of criminal acts, scams, and manipulations of those she became involved with, including the men she married. To her it was a game, and she thought she could outsmart her victims, and many times she could. When people caught on to her, she moved away and took on a new identity. Over the years, she became bolder and bolder in her deceit. She could only succeed by preying on the kindness and trust of others . . .

"She never expected to run into such determination to stop her as she found in this small town. She wasn't expecting Gerry Boggs or his family. She wasn't expecting Detective Crotz or CBI agent Susan Kitchen. She didn't think these people would go to any length to bring her to justice, but she was wrong. Justice, which this community has waited for so patiently, should be carried out by imposing the maximum penalty on these two defendants."

St. James sat down and the judge asked Coit and Backus if either of them wanted to say anything. Backus declined.

Jill stood. In a sweet and shaky voice, she said, "I don't think I got a fair trial. I know that you knew Gerry Boggs. You met Gerry and joked with him for at least five minutes. You might not remember me. I'm not that special. You were polite and courteous and you laughed. If you went into Boggs Hardware, you knew Gerry and Doug Boggs. In my heart, I know you knew him, but I can't prove it."

"All I can say," the judge replied calmly, "is that you have me mixed up with someone else."

She took her seat, looking genuinely disappointed

and hurt by his comment. It was the most telling thing that had happened in all of her courtroom appearances.

Unlike in many other cases where someone has been convicted of first-degree murder, people in Steamboat Springs did not spend a lot of time psychoanalyzing Jill Coit. It was as if they understood that this wouldn't have accomplished much of anything. You weren't going to penetrate the woman with rational thought. In a courtroom full of people, most of whom hated her for killing one of their relatives or friends, she focused all of her attention on one thing and one thing only: her own feelings and memories, whether they were real or not.

It was as if what everyone else knew had happened in Steamboat had never happened for her. Other people's reality was not merely an inconvenience for Jill; it didn't exist. She was without empathy of any kind, and that was a horrible thing to contemplate. She couldn't feel what others were feeling, and she didn't give the impression that she was repressing her ability to do this. She was simply hollow or dead in places that are not visible. And no one knew why.

At 1 P.M., the judge asked Doug Boggs and his family members if they had anything to say. Harold declined the offer. Doug himself had been ready to address Michael Backus at length, but now, after listening to the impassioned words of Kerry St. James, he felt there was nothing more to add. He was also very tired of sitting in the courtroom and wanted to leave. Doug told the judge that he would pass.

Doucette imposed the heaviest sentence he could on both defendants: life without parole, plus forty-eight years for conspiracy, plus a million-dollar fine for each of them. They would be kept in the Steamboat jail a while longer, until they could be sent to Canon City or another Colorado state prison.

The Boggs family had not known that the $1 million fine was coming, and it filled all of them with a particularly gratifying joy. At the hearing's end, they cried once again and then quickly disappeared from the courthouse, wanting to be around no one but each other.

Some time later, after Jan and Doug had returned from a long-awaited vacation, Doug said, "That day at the sentencing, I was going to say that some people have seen Backus as just another one of Jill's victims and basically a good guy. I don't. I was gonna tell him that he didn't want his Vietnam buddy, Troy Giffin, to rat on him, but he didn't mind putting a plastic bag over my brother's head before he killed him. Gerry did two tours of duty in Vietnam and got the Bronze Star for his service to his country. I was gonna say that Backus had to cover Gerry's head so he couldn't see his eyes when my brother was begging for his life. But I didn't say that. It just wasn't worth it.

"It didn't bother Jill to get sentenced to life, but it really upset her to get that million-dollar fine on top of everything else. I talked to the people who drove her back to the jail that day and they said she bitched the whole way about that. Everything was a joke to her but the money."

A few weeks after Jill had been shipped out of Steamboat Springs, one of her jailers since November of 1993 said, "We were really glad to get rid of her. We've seen some bad ones in here, but she was the worst prisoner we've ever had. She complained all the time and she tried to manipulate everybody who works here. She tried to turn us against one another. The only reason that didn't happen is because we all despised her."

"When it was all over," Doug Boggs said, "I bought champagne for the police and for all of those people at the jail who've had to put up with her during the past year and a half. They've earned it. One woman guard told me that she was going to drink a whole bottle herself."

A Brief Summary
Of The Life
and Marriages
Of Jill Coit

1. As a sophomore in high school, she left New Orleans and moved in with her maternal grandmother in North Manchester, Indiana. Several years later, in 1961, she married Larry Ihnen in Indiana. She was about 18. The marriage lasted only a few months.

2. In 1965, she married a Louisiana college student, Steven Moore. She gave birth to her first child, Steven Seth Moore, in March of 1965. Two years later, she was divorced.

3. In November of 1965, while married to Moore, she met William Clark Coit II, an engineer for the Tenneco Corporation. She and Coit were married in Houston in January of 1966. This was Jill's first bigamy. She changed her son's name to Johnathan Seth Coit and had two more sons in this marriage. Andrew arrived in 1966 and William III in 1968. Her husband William Coit II was found murdered in their Houston home in March of 1972, a few weeks after he and Jill were separated.

4. In August of 1973, she was adopted by Bruce Johansen, a wealthy Californian in his nineties. He died the following year and left Jill several pieces of property.

5. In California in November of 1973, she married Donald Brodie, a major in the U.S. Marines. They had no children and were divorced in July of 1975.

6. Louis DiRosa, a lawyer in New Orleans, had helped Jill with the settlement of Johansen's estate. She and DiRosa were married in Mississippi in October of 1976. They were remarried again—although they were not divorced—in Louisiana in 1977. They were divorced in Haiti in November of 1978, and divorced again in the United States in August of 1985.

7. Jill also married Eldon Metzger, an auctioneer and real estate agent in Indiana, in 1978. There is no record of the couple getting a divorce.

8. In January of 1983, Jill and Carl Steely, a teacher and administrator at a boy's prep school in Culver, Indiana, were married in that state. In December of that year, they were divorced in Haiti. They returned to Indiana and were soon married again (they got married three or four more times in front of a minister, even though they didn't get a divorce in between these weddings; Jill just liked the ceremony). They were divorced for good in December of 1991.

9. In mid-1990, Jill met hardware store owner, Gerry Boggs, in Steamboat Springs, Colorado. They were married in April of 1991. In November of that year, the marriage was annulled, after Boggs learned that she was still married to Carl Steely. Jill claimed to have had a baby girl named Lara with Boggs. He disputed that claim and they each filed a lawsuit against the other one. A civil trial that would have settled the dispute was scheduled to begin in Steamboat on October 27, 1993. Five days before that, Boggs was found murdered in his home.

10. In February of 1992, Jill married Roy Carroll, who was in his late sixties and lived in Houston. There is no record of their divorce.

11. In 1993 she lived in Greeley, Colorado, with

telephone repairman, Michael Backus. They claimed to be married but no record of that union exists. On March 17, 1995, in Hot Sulphur Springs, Colorado, they were both convicted of murdering Gerry Boggs. In May of 1995, each received life sentences, plus 48 years for conspiracy, plus million-dollar fines.

The following are many of the names used by Jill Coit:

Jill Lonita Billiot
Jill Johansen Coit
Jill Steely
Jill Steeley
Jill Coit-Steely
Jill Boggs
Jill Johanson
Jill Carroll
Jill Theresa Kisla
Terrie Kisla
Jill Ihnen
Jill Brodie
Jill Metzger
Jill Moore
Jill DiRosa